"Are you...married, Thomas?" Abby asked abruptly.

"What?" he said, because the question caught him completely off guard.

"Guire wrote us you were engaged. Did you marry her?"

"No, I didn't marry her," he said, surprised that the letter he had written to Guire advising him of his matrimonial intent had actually reached him.

"Good," she said. "I wouldn't want to die...coveting someone else's husband."

He frowned, thinking that he had misunderstood, and she suddenly smiled. "Poor Thomas. I've scandalized you...haven't I? I know you always thought...I was a child. Do you...mind very much?"

"Mind?"

"That I...love you?"

"Abby—"

"Don't look so worried, Thomas. Nothing...is required of you. I'm only confessing because I'm dying...."

"You're not dying—so you'd better watch what you say."

She smiled slightly and whispered, "I don't mind...dying so much...now...."

Dear Reader,

This holiday season, we've selected books that are sure to warm your heart—all with heroes who redefine the phrase "the gift of giving." We are absolutely thrilled about *Harrigan's Bride,* the new Civil War romance from the immensely talented Cheryl Reavis. Cheryl has received the prestigious RITA Award, not once but *three* times, twice for her contemporary romances for Silhouette and once for her Harlequin Historical novel *The Prisoner.* In her latest, Thomas Harrigan returns from war and chivalrously marries the bedridden, abandoned daughter of his late godmother. Don't miss this heart-wrenching story!

Be sure to look for *A Warrior's Passion,* book nine of Margaret Moore's medieval WARRIOR SERIES. Here, a young woman is forced into an unwanted betrothal before the man she truly loves—and whose child she carries—can claim her as his wife. *Territorial Bride* by Linda Castle is the long-awaited sequel to *Fearless Hearts* in which a cowgirl and an Eastern rogue prove that opposites attract. Their love is tested when Missy is seriously injured....

Rounding out the month is *The Shielded Heart* by rising star Sharon Schulze. Set in eighteenth-century Europe, this is a gripping tale about a warrior who learns to accept his special psychic gift as he teaches an enamel artisan about life and love.

Whatever your tastes in reading, you'll be sure to find a romantic journey back to the past between the covers of a Harlequin Historical® novel.

Sincerely,
Tracy Farrell, Senior Editor

Please address questions and book requests to:
Harlequin Reader Service
U.S.: 3010 Walden Ave., P.O. Box 1325, Buffalo, NY 14269
Canadian: P.O. Box 609, Fort Erie, Ont. L2A 5X3

Cheryl Reavis
Harrigan's
Bride

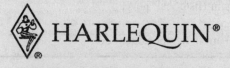

HARLEQUIN®

TORONTO • NEW YORK • LONDON
AMSTERDAM • PARIS • SYDNEY • HAMBURG
STOCKHOLM • ATHENS • TOKYO • MILAN • MADRID
PRAGUE • WARSAW • BUDAPEST • AUCKLAND

ISBN 0-373-29039-X

HARRIGAN'S BRIDE

CHERYL REAVIS,

award-winning short story author and romance novelist who also writes under the name of Cinda Richards, describes herself as a "late bloomer" who played in her first piano recital at the tender age of thirty. "We had to line up by height—I was the third smallest kid," she says. "After that, there was no stopping me. I immediately gave myself permission to attempt my *other* heart's desire—to write." Her Silhouette Special Edition novel *A Crime of the Heart* reached millions of readers in *Good Housekeeping* magazine. Both *A Crime of the Heart* and *Patrick Gallagher's Widow* won the Romance Writers of America's coveted RITA Award for Best Contemporary Series Romance the year they were published. *One of Our Own* received the Career Achievement Award for Best Innovative Series Romance from *Romantic Times Magazine*. A former public health nurse, Cheryl makes her home in North Carolina with her husband.

To Kelly Jamison, Juliette Leigh and Cait London.
Thank you, ladies. What would I do without you?

Chapter One

December 17, 1862

The front door stood ajar, and the wind blew dead leaves directly into the wide hallway. Apart from the open door, the Calder place looked very much as it always had. The bloody struggle for the town of Fredericksburg, and General Burnside's ass-over-teakettle retreat back across the Rappahannock hadn't disturbed anything here—on the surface at least. There was some comfort in that, but the fact remained that no one who had a choice would leave a door wide-open on a bitterly cold day like today.

Thomas Harrigan urged his mount slowly forward, still alert, advancing until he could walk the horse along the length of the front porch. He couldn't hear anything or see anyone inside the house. There was no smoke coming from the chimneys.

Perhaps the Calder women had gone to a safer place, he thought, then immediately dismissed the notion. He knew Guire Calder's mother and sister well. As Guire's classmate and friend, Thomas had been a guest here many times before the fall of Fort Sumter. He knew that neither Miss Emma nor Abiah would ever willingly leave this house, not as long as it was still standing. They loved the place, as he himself did. He had once been welcome here, regardless of his miscreant parent and regardless of his "Yankee" ways.

Now he had returned, this time uninvited and in the wrong uniform, and he doubted that Miss Emma and Abiah would be happy to see him, in spite of the fact that he had managed to get here at great risk. For all intents and purposes, if he was caught here, it would be assumed that he had willfully and wholeheartedly deserted his post. He supposed that it might be a mitigating circumstance that he had chosen to leave the ranks *after* the battle instead of during it.

Not that it mattered. Nothing much mattered to him anymore—except perhaps knowing how the Calders fared. His mind resolutely refused to consider anything else. Not the thousands of good soldiers who still lay dead and frozen on the field at Fredericksburg. Not the consequences of his blatant disregard for military discipline. Not even his grandfather's reaction to it.

Thomas realized suddenly that here was the only place he had ever considered his home. He had intended to bring Elizabeth Channing to this quiet valley to live after they were married. Beautiful Elizabeth, who had insisted that she wanted to be his wife and who had been so eager to give him *almost* everything before they even set a date for the ceremony. What a surprise then, when she had suddenly, inexplicably, broken their engagement. He had read her letter of polite dismissal over and over after it came, as if there was some part of it he might have misunderstood. He had gone to battle with it in his breast pocket, and very interesting reading it would have made for the scavengers, if he'd been killed.

He abruptly dismounted, stepping up onto the porch as he must have done scores of times. In his experience, the Calder house had always been filled with laughter—something he had never known growing up in Boston with his sad, gentle mother and a father who was never there. Even as a boy, Thomas had understood the humiliation his mother must have felt at having to beg his grandfather—her father—to let her come back home to Maryland after her husband had abandoned her. But Grandfather Winthrop was a charitable and forgiving man—and he never let Thomas or his mother forget it.

Except that Thomas had forgotten, here in the bosom of the Calder family. The memories, suddenly unleashed, swept into his mind. The summer evenings he'd spent sitting right here, holding his own in a gathering of arrogant and supposedly intellectual young men like himself, drinking brandy and smoking cigars, convinced that there was such a thing as a "just" war. He remembered the fireflies all across the meadow and Miss Emma playing the pianoforte in the parlor. He remembered a solitary moonlit walk and the smell of honeysuckle, and all the while he could hear Abiah somewhere in the house, singing a plaintive ballad in her sweet lilting voice....

He gave a sharp sigh and drew his revolver. The sudden longing he felt was akin to physical pain. How had he lost all of that and come to be here now with a gun in his hand?

He stepped inside the open doorway, but he didn't call out. He walked quietly down the hallway, pushing open the parlor door with his boot and peering inside.

Empty.

He moved across the hall to the dining room, leaving tracks in the frost that had accumulated on the bare wood floor. No one else could have walked here for a while.

He opened the next door, and he saw her immediately in the shaft of sunlight that came in through the window.

"Oh, Jesus," he whispered.

Emma Calder was lying on the great four-poster bed. Someone had wrapped her tightly in a quilt with only her face showing, someone who was perhaps still in the house. He edged closer, trying to keep an eye on the door because there was no other way out of the room.

She was dead—long dead. The layer of frost was on everything in here as well. And whoever had wrapped her like this had intended a burial. He looked down at the sweet face of the woman who had been more of a mother to him than his own, and he had to struggle hard for control.

Miss Emma.

He turned abruptly at a small sound, revolver leveled.

"Abiah!" he called loudly, no longer caring who else might be here. "Abby—!"

"It's me, Cap," someone said from the hallway. Sergeant La Broie stepped abruptly into the doorway.

"I could have shot you, man! What the hell are you doing here?"

"Well, sir, I'm thinking maybe that's something neither one of us ought to go inquiring into."

Thomas looked at him. La Broie was regular army, a man of undeniable military expertise, who had been dragged back—kicking and screaming most likely— from one of the cavalry outposts on the western frontier. He had then been plunked down horseless in a company of infantry in one of Burnside's Grand Divisions, thereby adding at least one person who knew what the hell he was doing—usually.

"I asked you a question, Sergeant," Thomas said.

"I am trying to make it look like you ain't deserted, sir," the man said patiently. "The major got to wondering where you was. I said the colonel sent you someplace, so he sent me to fetch you. You might say *I'm* the one here officially."

"How did you find me?"

"Weren't hard, Cap. You been asking the refugees out of Fredericksburg if they knew anything about the Calder family ever since we crossed the river. And then this very fine Reb cavalry mount surrendered itself to me—a prisoner of war, you might say—and somebody pointed me in this direction to get to the Calder farm. She dead?'' the man asked, jerking his head in the direction of the bed.

''Yes,'' Thomas said.

''Then we got a grave to dig, I reckon. I'll see what I can find to do it with—unless you want help checking the house.''

''No,'' Thomas said. ''There's a door to the cellar at the end of the hall. There should be a shovel down there.''

''Ground's froze hard, Cap. Going to take more than a shovel.''

La Broie walked away, and Thomas gave Miss Emma one last look before he followed him down the hall.

''Mind how you go, son,'' La Broie said as Thomas started up the stairs. Under less-pressing circumstances, they might have had yet another one of their discussions about familiarity and La Broie's penchant for always having the last word, but there was no time for that now. Thomas could say with certainty that La Broie was no hypocrite. He thought his duly elected captain was about as useful as a teat on a bull, and he took no pains to hide it.

Thomas made the search of the second floor quickly, room by room, trying to convince himself as he went that Abiah wasn't here, that she must have gone with the other women and children and the elderly who had had to flee the army's advance into the town by taking refuge in the surrounding woods. But he found her in the last room he looked. She was lying facedown on the floor, half in a patch of sunlight. She, too, was wrapped in a quilt.

"Abiah?" he said, kneeling down by her and expecting the worst. "Abby?" He gently turned her over.

Incredibly, she opened her eyes. They were bright with fever.

"Abby, it's me," he said, when she closed them again. "It's me—Thomas. Look at me. It's Thomas—"

"Thomas?" she said weakly, trying to lift her head. "Thomas, I...couldn't get...the fire to...burn...."

"I'll take care of it," he said, moving to grab another quilt off the bed and covering her.

She closed her eyes, and he moved her slightly so that she was in the warmth of sunlight again.

"Everybody's...gone, Thomas. Mother is...is..."

"I know, honey," he said.

"I got sick...first. Mother was...looking after...me. But then..." Tears ran out of the corners of her eyes and down her face.

"Don't talk. It's going to be all right."

He moved away from her to try to get a fire going in the fireplace. There were still some embers burning beneath the ashes, and it took him only a moment to coax them into flames. "Let's get you back to bed," he said.

"No, just leave me here. I hurt so..."

"Come on now," he said, rolling her to him so he could lift her. She made a small sound when he stood up.

"I'm sorry about Miss Emma," he said as he carried her to the bed. Abiah was so pale and thin. He had always thought her a pretty little thing, but now he hardly recognized her. And it wasn't just the illness. It had been nearly two years to the day since he'd seen her last. During that time she seemed to have made a remarkable transformation from a gangly girl to a young woman.

"You shouldn't be here, Thomas," she said as he laid her on the high feather bed, but she clutched the front of his coat when he tried to straighten up again. "You're...in the wrong army."

"Well, that's a matter of opinion," he said.

She tried to smile. "You'll have to...forgive me...if I don't care to discuss that right now."

He gently removed her hand from his coat front and covered it with the quilt.

"I could...hear the guns," she whispered. "It was a...terrible battle, wasn't it?"

"Yes," he said.

"Guire's dead," she said. "Did you...know that?"

"No. No, I didn't know. When—?" He stopped because he didn't trust his voice.

"It was at Malvern Hill. He..." She began to shiver. "I'm so...cold..."

He waited, but she didn't say anything else.

"Abby?" he said after a moment. He needed to get more wood. He needed to see if he could find something in the house to feed her. And then he needed to decide what he was going to do with her. He couldn't leave her here. She'd die here alone in the cold if he did.

"Are you...married, Thomas?" she asked abruptly.

"What?" he said, because the question caught him completely off guard.

"Guire wrote us you were engaged. Did you marry her?"

"No, I didn't marry her," he said, surprised that the letter he had written to Guire advising him of his matrimonial intent must have actually reached him.

"Good," she said. "I wouldn't want to die... coveting someone else's husband."

He frowned, thinking that he had misunderstood, and she suddenly smiled. "Poor Thomas. I've scandalized you...haven't I? I know you always thought...I was a child. Do you...mind very much?"

"Mind?"

"That I love you."

"Abby—"

"Don't look so worried, Thomas. Nothing...is required of you. I'm only confessing because I'm dying...."

"You're not dying, so you'd better watch what you say."

She smiled slightly. "I used to hide and listen to you and Guire discuss...philosophy. 'I think, therefore I am.' Isn't that the way it goes? Whoever said it is right, you know...." She said something else he didn't understand.

"What?" he said again. He sat down on the edge

of the bed, with no thought as to the propriety of such a gesture. She turned her head to look at him.

"I said, God is…good."

"I don't understand," he said, because he was sure now that she was delirious.

"I don't mind…dying so much…now."

"Abby—"

"It's a…gift, you see? It gives me such…joy…to see you one last…time. I—" She broke off and gave a sharp sigh. "I'm going to cry…and I don't want to. I don't want you to…think I'm sad." Her dark eyes searched his. "I wanted to marry you, Thomas, did you…know that? I told Guire. He said you were…too…wild for…me."

Wild? Thomas thought. If he remembered correctly, that word was synonymous with the name Guire.

"He told me about…those places…the two of you went to…in New Orleans. Those 'houses' with the red velvet…draperies and the crystal…chandeliers and those strangely colored birds in golden…cages all along the verandas. He said all the fancy women there…adored you."

"Now, why in God's name would he tell you something like that?" Thomas asked, more than a little annoyed at the direction this conversation had taken.

She smiled. "Did he…lie?"

Thomas didn't answer her.

"That's what I…thought," she said.

"Sometimes the truth is not required, Abiah."

"And sometimes it is. He said if I had my…heart set on you…then…I should know these things. I should know the real…man is not the same as a schoolgirl's…idea of him. But I didn't…care about the fancy women. Or about the trouble with your father and grandfather…or anything else. I only cared about you. I was going to trap you the next time you came here to visit…so you'd have to marry me. I was going to wait until everyone had gone to sleep…and I was going to…come into your bed—''

"Abiah!" he said, because he was indeed shocked now.

"You needed me, Thomas…even if you didn't know it. You were so…serious. I could have helped you with that," she said, completely undeterred. "So now you know. I was prepared to be shameless where you're concerned. Aren't you lucky the war came along to save you—''

"Cap," La Broie said from the doorway, and Thomas had no idea how long he'd been standing there. He held up his hand to keep La Broie from advancing. He didn't want Abiah any more distressed than she already was, and he didn't want La Broie to hear her confessions—if he hadn't already.

Thomas got up and walked to the door. "What?"

"There's a little garden on the south side of the house. The sun shines there most of the day, I reckon. The ground ain't froze. I'm about to put the lady under. Is *she* all right?" he asked, looking past him to where Abiah lay.

"No."

"We ain't got much time, Cap," La Broie said unnecessarily.

Thomas drew a quiet breath and looked back at Abiah. She was lying very still now, and he didn't want to disturb her. He didn't want her to be afraid if she woke up alone, either.

He walked to the bedside. "Abby?"

She opened her eyes.

"I'll be back."

She shook her head, the tears once again sliding out of the corners of her eyes. "No. Go from…here, Thomas—"

"I'll be back," he said again.

"Please! I want you to go—"

"Try to sleep."

"She understands how things are, Cap," La Broie said on the way downstairs, but Thomas made no reply.

He carried Miss Emma out of the house himself. La Broie had gotten the grave dug quickly, a skill Thomas supposed he had had to learn as a professional soldier. And it was La Broie who spoke over the grave.

"The souls of the righteous are in the hand of God," he said. "And there no torment shall find them. Amen."

Thomas stood looking at the raw mound of earth. "Amen," he said, earnestly hoping that that was the case for Miss Emma. And his mind was already working on the problem at hand. He had to get Abiah out of here—and he had no place to take her.

"You don't have to wait for me, Sergeant," he said.

"Yes, sir, Cap," La Broie answered, but he made no attempt to leave.

"I want you to go back and tell the major you couldn't find me."

"You want me to lie to Major Gibbons?" La Broie said, as if such a thing would never, ever have crossed his mind.

"I do," Thomas said. "And try to make it as good as the one you told him when you came out here."

"You're going to stay here with the lady upstairs, Cap?"

"No, I'm taking her with me," Thomas said, stepping around his sergeant to get back into the house.

"Moving her might kill her, Cap," La Broie said. "If she's in a bad way."

"What do you think leaving her here alone will do?"

"You planning on riding back to our lines with her, just like that, sir?" La Broie said. "That is, if you can get her back across the river."

"In lieu of a better plan, yes."

"Ain't there somebody you could get to stay with her?"

"Yes," Thomas said. "Only I don't know who it would be at the moment. I'll have to worry about that when I get to Falmouth."

"*If* you get to Falmouth," La Broie said. "Reb patrols are out, sir."

"There's a truce long enough to bury the dead. I'm going to have to rely on that. Well, go on, man. You have your orders."

"Begging your pardon, Cap," La Broie said, still following along. "But we ain't exactly on the battlefield at the moment, now are we? If we run into one of them Reb patrols, they're going to think we're ransacking the place and then there's going to be hell to pay. And besides that, I have put in a lot of hard work breaking you in, sir—if you don't mind me saying so—and I ain't a bit happy thinking I'm going to have to start over with another captain. Hard telling what kind of jackass they'd put in your place.''

''La Broie, do you know how close you are to insubordination?''

''No, sir. It's high praise I'm giving and not insubordination at all, sir. You have turned yourself into a good, sensible officer...'' The rest of the sentence hung in the air unsaid.

Until now.

''Thanks to you, you mean,'' Thomas said.

''It was my pleasure, sir,'' La Broie said, almost but not quite smiling.

''Get going,'' Thomas said. ''I mean it.''

He went back upstairs. Abiah seemed to be asleep. He opened the armoire and searched until he found her portmanteau, but then immediately disregarded it as too awkward to carry. He took a pillow slip instead and went from drawer to drawer, dumping in things he barely bothered to identify—stockings, undergarments, a frayed wool shawl, a hairbrush.

There was a sudden commotion downstairs. He swore and drew his revolver, trying to identify the source.

''Cap!'' La Broie yelled, and Thomas ran to the landing. The sergeant had ridden his mount into the front hall and he was leading Thomas's bay. Both horses were having trouble getting their footing and both were wild-eyed at the straight chairs and small tables crashing around them.

"Hand your lady down, sir!" La Broie yelled. "The sons of bitches are almost here!"

Thomas ran back to do just that. Abiah was trying to get out of bed. He gave her no explanation of any kind. He grabbed her and the pillow slip and a quilt, leaving everything else behind and carrying her bodily out of the room. Halfway down the stairs, he handed her roughly over the banister to La Broie and tossed the pillow slip after her. The sergeant's mount pranced and reared at the loose-flowing quilt, but La Broie held him in.

"Hurry, sir!"

Thomas mounted the bay with some difficulty, then took Abiah out of La Broie's arms. She was completely limp, and he could hardly hold on to her.

"I'm going to let them see me, Cap," La Broie said. "I'll meet up with you at the river—"

He gave Thomas no time to approve or disapprove the plan as he urged his captured horse back out the front door and leaped in a great arc off the porch.

Chapter Two

*W*hat's happening? Abiah kept thinking. She tried to follow the conversation around her, but it made no sense.

"Will you kindly shoot this man, Sergeant La Broie? My hands are full."

"My pleasure, Cap. Or if you want him skinned alive and roasted over a hot fire with a stick—"

Abiah winced at the specifics.

"—I can do that, too, sir."

"No. No, a ball between the eyes will do. You'll have to excuse the sergeant here. He's just come from the West. They handle things a bit differently out there. You and I are more apt to just kill a man outright when he irks us. But where the sergeant comes from, they like to savor the demise. Who was it you learned that from, Sergeant?"

"Apaches, sir. And, of course, the—"

"All right! I'll take you across," a third voice said. "You Yankees are damned attached to your whores, is all I got to say—"

There was scuffling then. Abiah cried out.

"Abby," Thomas's voice said close to her ear. She tried to answer him and couldn't. Then she lost his voice and the others in a wave of soft, white nothingness.

It was raining when she heard voices again. She could feel the raindrops beating down on her face.

"I've got no room here, Captain."

"Well, make room, damn it!"

"Where? We've got more wounded men than we can handle! You wouldn't want to leave her here, even if there was a place for her. Who would take care of her, sick as she is? Look, why don't you try one of the churches? Maybe there's somebody there who can take her in."

And then they were riding through the darkness again.

"I think you better let me take her, Cap," a man's voice said. "You go get Major Gibbons satisfied so he don't have you shot. I'll see to your lady."

She heard Thomas swear.

"Ain't no other way, Cap," the man said. "I got a notion about what we can do—where I can take her."

"We've been everywhere," Thomas said.

"I'm thinking Gertie would take care of her—but she'd have to have money to replace what she'd get otherwise. How much have you got?"

"Are you out of your mind? She's a camp follower. She is *not* somebody who goes around ministering to the sick with a basket on her arm."

"We ain't got much choice, Cap—and Gertie ain't

had much in the way of choices, neither. She's a good girl, Gertie is. You can't fault a woman for what's she's had to do to keep herself alive. I'm telling you, she'll take good care of Miss Abiah—if she's got money enough to do it with. Like you said, we've been everywhere. The only thing we ain't done is break down somebody's front door and hold a gun on them until they turn into the Good Samaritan. I say we quit going around Robin Hood's barn here and get Miss Abiah in out of the rain, sir—and I don't think she'd be very happy if she knew she was the cause of your court-martial.''

Abiah stirred at the last remark, trying to raise up. But she couldn't manage it, no matter how hard she tried.

''We ain't far from the Lacey house,'' the man said. ''You go on there and let Major Gibbons see you. Tell him, *if* he asks, that I was wrong. Say the colonel didn't send you no place, you been around here all the time. Say you been trying to account for the wounded and missing out of your company. I'll take care of Miss Abiah and then I'll find you.''

''La Broie—''

''Give me your money and your lady, sir.''

''Abby, can you hear me?'' Thomas said, his breath warm against her ear. ''Abby…?''

She strained toward the sound of his voice, but the harder she tried to hear it, the more it drifted away. The soft whiteness closed over her.

What's happening?

She tried to focus on her surroundings, but the light

was too poor. She could see a candle burning on a table to her right, and a fire burning in the fireplace. It was raining still—it always seemed to rain after a battle. She could distinctly hear the patter of raindrops against the window.

The window.

She wasn't outside then. She was warm and dry and in bed.

She wasn't alone in the room; she could hear someone moving around. She turned her head slightly.

"Is she awake?" a man's voice asked.

"No, I don't think so," a woman said. "Is the captain coming? She asks for him sometimes."

"He's confined to his quarters until somebody decides how bad he broke rank."

"How long will that be?"

"No time soon—not the way people are talking. I'll tell him she's been asking for him. No, maybe I won't. He's liable to come to see about her whether Gibbons says he can or not. You've got everything you need?"

"I've got more than I need."

"You don't mind the room being down here with the servants?"

"Now, why would *I* mind that? The kitchen is close. I can get her the things she needs to eat. And there's people I can talk to, so I'm not lonesome. But I'm wanting to know something, La Broie. How did you get Zachariah Wilson to give up a room in his house, even if it is below stairs?"

"He's being paid well for it, Gertie."

"He doesn't need the money."

"He's a greedy man, Gertie, darling. Greedy men always *need* the money."

"I'm thinking maybe you asked this greedy man in a way he couldn't refuse."

He laughed softly.

"Maybe."

"What did you do, Pete?"

"Nothing much. I only mentioned that I knew he'd been a...acquaintance of yours. And being such a pillar of the church and everything—well, now he had the opportunity to help you change your ways *and* give shelter to the sick."

"And why would you do that?"

"Why?"

"You heard me."

"Well, because I could see you didn't have the heart for the business you was in."

"Since when do men care what's in a woman's heart?"

"Some of us do, depending on the man—and the woman."

"And the rest of you are like Zachariah Wilson."

"You ain't had no trouble with Wilson, have you?"

"No. He's not here. He's gone off someplace on business. Nobody knows when he'll get back."

"If he bothers you, you let me know. I mean it. I wouldn't have put you here if I could've done better—"

"How long?" Abiah said abruptly.

"My God, she is awake," the man said.

"How long have I been here?" Abiah asked.

"Well, let's see," the woman said, coming closer to the bed. "It must be eight days now."

Eight? Abiah thought in alarm. She couldn't remember any of them—at all. How could she completely lose track of eight days?

"Who are you?" she asked the man.

"Sergeant Peter La Broie," he said.

"You're not in Lee's army."

"No, ma'am. I'm not." He pulled a ladder-back chair around and sat down where she could see him. "And this here is Gertie. Captain Thomas Harrigan and me—we brought you across the river on a raft. Do you remember that?"

"No," she said. But then she suddenly recalled something about Apaches. Whatever it was, however, slipped away. "I don't understand," she said after a moment. "Why are people talking?"

"Talking?"

"You said people were talking. Why? Tell me. I want to know."

"It's on account of you being a Reb girl and Cap being in the Union army and stealing you back across the river the way he did. Some think the captain ruined your reputation when he did that—maybe his, too, because he wasn't supposed to be over there in the first place, much less coming back with you on his saddle. But you'd be dead if he hadn't, and that's for damn sure."

Abiah closed her eyes. She was so tired. Too tired

to try to sort this out. She did know that she hadn't been stolen. She'd been…

She didn't know what she'd been. She opened her eyes again as one particular memory suddenly came to her.

"Oh…"

"What is it, Miss Abiah?" the man said kindly.

He knows my name, she thought. *He must have something to do with Thomas.* She gave a wavering sigh.

"What is it?" he asked again.

"Where is…my mother…?"

"The captain said I should tell you everything straightaway, if you asked, because you're not a person who likes the truth hid from them no matter how bad it is."

"She's dead…isn't she?"

"Yes, ma'am. Your mother—Miss Emma—died. You're remembering that now, I guess."

Abiah nodded, wiping furtively at the tears that ran down her face.

"We buried her in that little herb garden near the house—where the ground was soft enough. And words was said over her, so you don't have to fret yourself on that account. Cap says to tell you he did the best he could by her."

Abiah believed that without question, but the tears came anyway, tears and then finally the welcome refuge of sleep. She woke from time to time, wondering if the sergeant would be there. He never was, and she began to wonder if he'd actually sat in the chair by her bed or if she'd been dreaming. There was only Gertie, who seemed to know exactly what to do to make her more comfortable and who, more often than not, insisted that Abiah drink a hot, salty chicken broth and then take some bitter tasting medicine, after which she fell into yet another dream-ridden sleep. It was so hard to think clearly, to know what was real and what wasn't. But conversation took far too much effort, regardless of Abiah's growing curiosity.

"Miss Abiah, look who's here," Gertie said one afternoon, and Abiah opened her eyes to see another enemy soldier, who after a moment turned into a very awkward Thomas, standing at the foot of the bed. She stared at him, not at all sure if he really was here or not. There had always been a sadness in Thomas Harrigan; it was one of the things that had drawn her to him from the very first time Guire brought him home. But at this particular moment, he looked so lost.

"What's wrong?" she asked him, and he looked at Gertie instead of answering.

"Tell me," Abiah said. "What's wrong with you?"

"That is my question, I believe, Abby," he said, and she smiled.

"Oh, well, then. If that's the case, the answer is 'nothing'—if you don't count the fever…and being out of my head most of the time."

"So how is your head at the moment?"

"I don't know," she said truthfully. "Sometimes I think Gertie is Mother. Sometimes I think Guire's here—or you. You *are* here, aren't you, Thomas? I'm not talking to the bedpost, am I?"

"Most definitely I am here," he said.

"Say 'heart,' then. So I'll know."

"Heart?" he asked, clearly puzzled.

She immediately gave a soft laugh. "Yes, it's you. *H-a-t*—'heart.'"

He smiled in return. "You are so very bad for my masculine certitude, Abiah. You are the only female I know who always makes fun of me."

"I have to. You'd be insufferable if I didn't."

Gertie laughed in the background.

"I see you agree with her, Gertie," Thomas said.

"I can't help it, Captain," Gertie said.

"Well," he said, still forcing himself to be cheerful. This was a Thomas Abiah had never met before. "The doctor tells me you're doing better."

"Does he? He doesn't tell *me* anything."

"He says you mustn't get overly confident. You must continue to play the invalid even if you feel like dancing."

"Dancing? I'm having trouble knowing the day of the week."

He smiled again, but this smile quickly faded. He stood there with his hands behind his back, tall and handsome, once her brother's greatest friend and then his sworn enemy—and hers.

"I need to ask you something, Abiah," he said.

She waited while he looked around the room as if it were of great interest to him, and then just to her left—everywhere but at her.

"I was wondering if you would consider something," he said, now looking at the floor. He abruptly pulled around that same ladder-back chair and sat down. Then he cleared his throat and noisily slid the chair closer to the side of the bed. He brought the fresh smell of the cold outdoors with him. Damp wool and wood smoke. Soap and tobacco. Horse and leather. She longed to be closer to him still.

"If you intend to catch me...while I'm still lucid, I think you'll want to hurry this along, Thomas," she said.

"All right. Abiah, I was wondering if you would marry me."

He finally looked at her, met her eyes briefly and glanced away.

"Too late," she said, in spite of her astonishment. Even at her most mentally confused, even if she'd been in a room full of fever-spawned Thomases, she would not have expected that question.

"I beg your pardon?" he said.

She smiled slightly, because once again his Boston accent had determined that he leave out an *R*. As a Southerner, she had a bit of a problem with that letter of the alphabet herself—only *she* didn't leave it quite so blatantly out of the middle of words or add it onto the end where it didn't belong. The years he had lived in Maryland with his grandfather hadn't erased his accent at all. Knowing even so little of the relationship between the two men as she did, she wouldn't have been surprised if Judge Winthrop hadn't made an effort to weed out that particular reminder of his daughter's failed marriage, just as Abiah wouldn't have been surprised if that was a reason Thomas might have tenaciously retained it.

Guire had told her once that Thomas looked very much like his father—who being the only son of a wealthy shipowner, had enough inherited money and enough favors owed him to open at least some of the doors kept firmly closed to those with an Irish surname. But there the similarity ended. Unlike his father, Thomas Harrigan clearly didn't abandon a woman who needed him.

"I said 'too late,' Thomas."

"You mean your lucid moment is going?"

"No, I mean someone else…has already asked for…my hand in marriage."

He looked startled. "May I ask who?"

"John William Miller," she said.

"Johnny Miller wants to marry you?"

"Well, you needn't make it sound so…incredible, Thomas. I believe he has been of a mind to since I was fourteen."

"This is the same Johnny Miller who was at your mother's house practically every time I came to visit."

"Yes."

"I suppose he's in the *other* army?"

"Yes."

"He's an officer, no doubt?"

"Yes."

"And you're making plans to marry him?"

"No."

"No?"

"I didn't give him an answer."

"Why not?"

She looked into his eyes. "You know why not," she said.

He flushed slightly.

So, she thought. She *had* told him precisely where her heart lay. She was very much afraid that that particular memory was real.

"You don't have to do anything else for me, Thomas," she said. "I know you have saved me by bringing me here, and I shall try my very best to get well. But you don't have to save my reputation, too."

"You've got it the wrong way around, Abby. I was asking so you could save mine."

"I would think stealing me out of my mother's house and bringing me here would only enhance yours."

"Alas, no. The story has reached General Sumner's attention, and he doesn't approve of such audacious conduct in his officers. At all."

"I'm afraid I don't much care whether Yankee generals approve or not, Thomas."

He leaned forward so that he could look into her eyes. "The truth is a marriage to you would help my military career, Abby."

"I don't see how. I support the Confederacy in every way I can."

"If I can forgive you for that, then I'm sure General Sumner will. Will you marry me, Abby? For my sake. I know you have a kind heart."

"No," she whispered.

"Yes," he said, taking her hand. His fingers were

still cold from his ride here and he slid them in between hers.

"No," she said again. "I will not."

"I need you to let me me explain, at least. Let me try to tell you the way things are."

"Then tell me."

He took a deep breath. "The Union army didn't have a chance at Fredericksburg because there were serious tactical errors made. The general who made them—Burnside—knows he is in danger of being relieved of his command. He is an incredibly arrogant man. He's going to try to save face now, and he's going to sacrifice his Grand Divisions to do it. I will do my duty when the time comes, but I need…" He stopped, holding her hand in both of his for a moment. "Guire was my friend. You are all that is left of his family. I need to know that you'll be taken care of. Do you understand? I need to be sure. As my wife—or my widow—"

"Don't," she interrupted, trying not to cry. "Guire would never have expected you to do this."

"I want to do it, Abby. I haven't much time for persuasion. I can't make pretty speeches to convince you. I can only tell you the truth."

"Look at me, Thomas. What good am I to you like this? I'm an invalid. I may stay an invalid." She couldn't bring herself to speak the real truth—that she might not survive this illness, just as her mother hadn't survived.

"You are my sweet Abiah. You are all I have left of the one truly happy time in my life. I'm asking you to let me go into this folly of Burnside's with my mind at ease.''

She closed her eyes to keep from crying. She couldn't waste her strength on tears. She had to save it, so that she could do the right thing.

''Abby, answer me.''

She looked at him. Marrying Thomas Harrigan was all she had ever wanted, but her heart was breaking— and for his sake, not hers. She loved him too much to ever want to hurt him. In the naive and reckless plan she had once contemplated to trap him into becoming her husband, she would have at least been a healthy wife and not a sickly burden. It would be wrong for her to say yes to him now. She knew that, just as she knew that she hadn't the will to refuse him.

''We have some major political differences, Thomas,'' she said.

''I think they would make for very lively discussions at the dinner table,'' he countered easily.

She smiled slightly at the idea, even knowing that it was improbable that they would share a dinner table ever again.

''Won't your engagement get in the way?'' she asked.

''That arrangement no longer exists.''

''Does *she* know that?''

''She docs. And she has nothing to do with this.''

Abiah looked into his eyes, believing him because she wanted to. What did it matter that this was only a gallant gesture on his part? An attempt to give her her heart's desire, because he was fond of her and because he thought she wouldn't recover?

So be it, she thought. She would take the only chance for happiness she would ever have, however fleeting it might be.

"All right," she said. "You bring the minister— and I'll try to remember who you are."

Chapter Three

Of all the emotions he had anticipated when he went to ask Abiah to marry him, surprise wasn't one of them—at least not on his part. And he had certainly been surprised. First, when she told him she had another suitor, and then, when she had been so unwilling to even consider his own offer of matrimony. But most of all, when he realized how much he minded on both counts.

It had all seemed so clear to him beforehand. He was honor and duty bound to take care of the last member of the Calder family as best he could. It was something he simply had to do. Now, through no conscious effort of his own, he was afflicted with the added burden of *wanting* it.

Thanks to La Broie and his machinations, Thomas had gotten away to see Abiah long enough to make his proposal, but since then he could only sit in the drafty, abandoned brick building where he'd been banished until the generals decided what they were going to do with him. He had no idea what this place had once been. Nothing comfortable, in any event. The room he had taken at the end of the hall had a window big enough to let in some light and lessen the dungeon atmosphere, but many of the glass panes were broken. It took all his physical energy just to stay warm.

He still had to pen a number of letters of condolence to the families of the men who had been killed at Fredericksburg, but he was too distracted to accomplish very much. He realized immediately that it was not just the cold that caused him to be so unsettled. No, indeed. His mental turmoil had come about because, whether Abiah had agreed or not, he absolutely did *not* want her marrying John William Miller. It irked Thomas a great deal how much he didn't want it. He had no right and no reason whatsoever to object.

Johnny Miller was a traitor to the country, of course, but then, by her own admission, so was Abiah. Thomas had always thought Miller a decent enough sort. There was nothing about the man as far as Thomas knew that would keep him from being entirely suitable for Abiah. Besides all that, Thomas was supposed to be heartbroken over his failed engagement to Elizabeth. He had certainly felt heartbroken when her letter came. Now it seemed as if all that had happened to someone else.

It suddenly occurred to him that the only explanation was that he must have believed Abiah when she said she loved him, even if she had since taken great pains to behave as if she had no memory of having done so. Clearly, it was a decided character weakness on his part—to always believe women when they professed a fondness for him. He had believed Elizabeth. He still believed Abiah, in spite of her reluctance in agreeing to marry him. He kept thinking about that one particular moment when he'd asked her why she wasn't making plans for her wedding to Miller. Thomas could almost *feel* the way her dark eyes had stared into his.

You know why not.

He supposed that that was as close as Abiah would come to mentioning the embarrassing incident—embarrassing for her, not him. At least not since he'd recovered from the initial shock of learning how she had planned to "trap" him into matrimony. Assuming she had been serious, he wondered if she had any idea what coming into his bed like that might have precipitated. He would like to think that he would have behaved honorably, but if he had had one too many brandies on the porch, he might have forgotten that she was his best friend's little sister.

He gave a quiet sigh. Perhaps Abiah did know. If Guire had been so imprudent as to tell her about their adventures in a New Orleans bordello, there was no telling what else the rascal had taken upon himself to explain. In any event, this bold plan of Abiah's would certainly give Thomas something to contemplate during the long winter nights to come.

He picked up his pen and immediately put it down again. The ink in the bottle had frozen. His cigar had gone out and his fingers were numb with cold. An abrupt gust of wind caused the smoke from what he optimistically called a fireplace to billow back into the cavernous room. He gave up all pretense of working, the full import of the predicament both he and Abiah were in making a jarring return. He had no patience left. He had to get this marriage done.

"La Broie!"

"Sir!" the sergeant answered almost immediately, his voice echoing in the outer hallway. Thomas suspected that La Broie's staying so close at hand had less to do with efficiency and devotion and more to do with the fact that Major Gibbons had probably ordered him to do so—in case that wild Captain Harrigan went a-roving again.

"Have you heard anything yet?" Thomas asked when La Broie appeared in the doorway.

"Nothing, sir," La Broie answered, giving no indication that Thomas had already asked him that same question a dozen times.

"Why is this taking so damn long?" Thomas said, more to himself than to La Broie.

"You know by now how the army works, Cap. It takes as long as it takes."

Thomas gave La Broie a scathing look. He was *not* in the mood for any of the sergeant's military truisms, sage though they may be. He was trying to take care of Abiah. She was ill, and gravely so. The doctors gave him absolutely no encouragement as to her chances for recovery from an illness they couldn't even diagnose. Typhoid pneumonia, perhaps, they said. The problem was that Abiah had been examined well after the telltale "rose spot" stage indicative of the disease. She had a "continuous fever" to be sure, but no one would—or could—give it a name. The army hospitals were full of "continuous fevers," which were fatal more times than not.

The best Thomas could do was to make sure Abiah had good nursing care, preferably by someone who understood the dangers of these fever-ridden illnesses. He felt an occasional twinge of guilt that the only person even remotely knowledgeable about these things also happened to be a camp follower. But, like everything else in this situation, he had had no choice but to bow to La Broie's opinion of Gertie's willingness and competency, and to hire the girl. So far Thomas hadn't had cause to regret it—as far as he knew. Gertie seemed happy to have a paying job that didn't involve throwing her petticoats over her head.

But he had precious little time left before Burnside began his redemptive push toward Richmond, and whatever time Abiah had, Thomas intended it to be as respectable and comfortable as it was in his power to make it. He knew exactly what had to be done, yet not one damn superior officer would tell him anything. How hard could it be to let him leave his quarters long enough to get married?

"La Broie!"

"Sir!"

"I want you to go see how Miss Abiah is this afternoon."

"Sir—begging your pardon. Wouldn't it be better for me to see Miss Abiah when I got something to tell her? If I go now and she's awake, she's going to ask me things I ain't got the answers to. If I can't say for sure you're going to make it to the ceremony, it'll just worry her. And she ought not to be worried, sir, I'm thinking. Besides that, she might have gone and changed her mind about marrying you. Maybe you don't want to give her a chance to retreat before we even get on the field.''

Thomas had to agree, even if he was absolutely convinced now that La Broie had been given unofficial guard duty, and even at the risk of letting him have the last word yet another time. "You've got the chaplain ready?''

"Sir, I've got three chaplains ready. I've got a doctor ready if Gertie needs him—besides the one Miss Abiah's already got. And I *didn't* send off that telegram to your mother,'' he added significantly, because, surprisingly, he didn't approve of Thomas's having changed his mind about notifying his family. "There ain't nothing left to do but wait, sir, and that's the sad truth of it.''

"You're sure about the arrangements?'' Thomas said, looking at the morning muster roll again and trying to get some idea of who was fit for duty—just in case he ever got out of this building and back to soldiering.

"Yes, sir. I'm sure. Zachariah Wilson has been well paid for the room and board—even if he wasn't using the space nohow. He knows which lawyer will keep on paying him. So Gertie and Miss Abiah can stay right where they are while you and me and the army is gone on this here fool's errand. Oh, and I been turning people down."

"What people? For what?"

"People wanting to come to the wedding, sir. We got all manner of volunteers to stand witness for it—from both armies—plus a whole slew of bushwhackers and newspaper people and deserters. You know, it's kind of hard to tell which is which when you get them all in a bunch. And then there's some church folk from Falmouth and Fredericksburg trying to get invited. I'm thinking we might need a guard at the door. Miss Abiah ain't well enough to have a bunch of nosy strangers gawking at her—and you—on account of she's supposed to be ruined and not long for this world. I did tell all these hopeful guests they could send you and her a wedding present, though."

Thomas looked up at that impertinence, but La Broie wasn't in the least discomfited.

"Sir, I ain't never been one to let opportunity stand around knocking on a shut door," he said. "And while I'm at it, I reckon I need to be begging your pardon—"

The heavy outer door of the building slammed loudly interrupting whatever La Broie had been about to reveal.

"This is it, Cap," he said instead. "That's one of Sumner's aides coming. The one with all them little-girl curls."

"Now how the hell do you know that?" Thomas said, trying to at least appear as if he wasn't affected by the footsteps echoing briskly down the hall in their direction.

"It's them prissy little silver spurs he wears. He's the only one that jingles like that."

It was indeed the aide-de-camp in question, an overly serious lieutenant, who knocked loudly and who snapped a salute when he was given leave to enter. Thomas was notoriously serious himself—but he chose to leave out the jingling and the posturing.

"Sir!" the aide barked, presenting Thomas with a folded piece of paper and causing La Broie to almost but not quite roll his eyes.

It was a pass, granting one Captain Thomas Harrigan a three-hour furlough in Falmouth. He read it over—twice—and then exhaled quietly in relief.

"No message from General Sumner?" he asked, without looking up.

"No, sir."

"Then you are dismissed, Lieutenant."

There was no jingling.

Thomas looked up. "Is there something else?"

"Yes, sir," the aide said.

"Then what is it?"

"I'm not at liberty to say, sir."

"Well, I'm not in the mood to guess, I can promise you that—"

The outside door banged loudly again, only this time it sounded as if an entire company were advancing up the hall—singing.

"Sir!" the aide barked. "It is my duty to announce that your groomsmen have arrived!"

* * *

Abiah noted two things when she asked to speak to Thomas alone. That he had gone to a great deal of trouble to look presentable and that he wasn't entirely sober. She was familiar with the custom of fortifying the groom with whatever strong drink his friends could find prior to the actual ceremony. Hardly any of the weddings she'd ever attended in her whole life had seen the groom *not* tangle-footed. She just hadn't considered that this particular wedding would precipitate the ritual and the boisterous male revelry that accompanied it.

She had no illusions about why the marriage was taking place. How could she? Thomas had been nothing if not blunt about his motives. His military career. Her reputation. His obligation to, and his respect for, Guire and the Calder family. But regardless of the circumstances, here Thomas was, and he looked exactly the way a bridegroom was suppose to look. All spit and polish—except for the ink stains on his fingers. He was newly barbered and unsteady on his feet—and infinitely pleased with himself.

"You're looking lovely this afternoon, Abby," he assured her.

"You, sir, have had a lot more to drink than I first thought," she answered.

He smiled one of his rare smiles.

"Only a bit, Abby. To keep away the cold. The boys went to such a lot of trouble to get it. It would have been rude to decline."

"Is that the real reason?" she asked. "You don't want to be rude?"

"It is."

"Rude to them or rude to me?"

"To you?"

"Perhaps you need whiskey to get through this wedding, Thomas. Perhaps you've changed your mind but you're too honorable to say so."

He frowned. "I have not changed my mind. Have you?"

"Not as far as I can tell," she said.

He nearly smiled again and pulled the one straight chair close to the bedside and sat down. "So. You recognize me, then."

"Yes, but it wasn't easy. You look so much prettier today than when I last saw you."

He smiled genuinely this time. "I had a great deal of help, I can assure you. I'm especially partial to this very fine maroon-and-gold, nonregulation sash—I forget which of my groomsmen contributed it." He opened his coat so that she could see it better. "But it's not as fine as your ribbon," he said, leaning closer to inspect the pink ribbon Gertie had meticulously twined into Abiah's long braid and then tied in a dainty bow.

Abiah, too, had had a great deal of help getting ready for this event. Besides the ribbon, her plain muslin nightdress had been exchanged for a finely embroidered and tucked cambric *chemise de nuit*. It was quite beautiful, albeit too big for her. The sleeves kept falling over her hands. Of course, a pink ribbon and especially the *chemise de nuit* were hopeless gestures on Gertie's part, regardless of Thomas's compliment. Except for the sleeves, he wouldn't even see the night-dress. Abiah was covered up well past her bosom by a borrowed gray velvet quilt placed under a crocheted "wedding ring" coverlet—something someone in the household—or in the town or across the river—must have thought would be appropriate. Clearly, when the bride was too ill to be dressed, then one must dress the bed instead. Enough pillows had been found so that she could be propped almost to a sitting position. Her beribboned braid hung artfully over her right shoulder. She was even lucid, so much so that she had no delusions about the way she looked, just as she had no delusions about the way she felt.

"Don't," he said after a moment, and she looked at him.

"I see the second thoughts running rampant, Abby. I don't have any. I want you to put yours aside."

"I'm afraid, Thomas."

"Not of me, I hope."

She shook her head. "No, not of you. Of being…" She gave a quiet sigh. It was so difficult to put into words. If she were well, she wouldn't have all these misgivings. If she were well, she would have at least a fighting chance of keeping him from resenting her and a marriage he'd wanted no part of.

She sighed again. If she were well, there would be no marriage in the first place.

"I'm cursed with a conscience," she said finally.

"I wouldn't have you any other way, Abby."

She realized immediately that he was teasing her. "Thomas, you're not taking this seriously."

"Of course I am—"

Someone rapped sharply on the door. "Chaplain's here, sir!" a voice said on the other side of it.

"We're worrying La Broie," Thomas said. "Can we put him out of his misery?"

"He'll just have to bear up," she said. "I have a question."

"It's very improper for me to be in here, you know. Didn't you see your landlady's face when I came in here alone and shut the door?"

"My landlady will have to bear up as well."

"Abby, we have to have this ceremony right now."

"But we haven't discussed...anything."

"You're alone in the world and you're ill. And I'm going into God-knows-what with Burnside. We could discuss all manner of topics until kingdom come, but it would still come down to those two things. We have to concern ourselves with the present situation. Nothing else. We can't worry about what might come along later."

"Sir!" La Broie said, rapping at the door again. They both ignored him and the burst of rowdy laughter from Thomas's groomsmen.

"Have you sent word to *her?*" she asked Thomas quietly.

He didn't pretend not to know who she meant. "That wasn't necessary," he said after a moment.

"Not even to keep from being rude?"

"No."

She watched him closely, trying to decide if that was really the case.

Yes, she decided. It wasn't necessary for him to tell his former fiancée anything. And perhaps that was yet another reason why he wanted this marriage to take place.

"Your mother and grandfather? Do they know what you're doing?"

"No," he said again.

"Why not?"

"Because I anticipated *this.* Your uncertainty. It's better if they know later, after it's done."

"I see. They'd disapprove that much."

"I don't know if they would disapprove or not. The point is I don't have the time or the inclination to hear opinions, one way or the other."

"You and I have nothing in common," she said. "Besides the dire consequences of your bringing me across the river—and Guire."

"I wouldn't say that. Have you or have you not read Emerson?"

"Only because you insisted."

"That's not the point, either. You know his work. We've had some most interesting discussions about Emerson. And if I said George Tockner you'd know precisely who I meant."

She tried to interrupt. The fact that she could recognize the name of a hallowed Harvard professor signified nothing as far as she was concerned. "Thomas—"

"And William Cullen Bryant," he continued, undeterred. "You've read his work."

"I've read Walt Whitman, as well, but I doubt anyone would see that as a basis for a marriage."

That remark certainly got his attention. "You've read Walt Whitman," he repeated, as if he wanted to make absolutely certain he had this right.

"I have," she said.

"Leaves of Grass."

"That was the title, yes. Your Mr. Emerson approved of the work, I believe."

"Never mind that. How the devil did you get your hands on a copy of Walt Whitman?" he asked—demanded—and she tried not to smile. She found him entirely adorable when he was discomposed.

"Believe me, it wasn't easy. But that doesn't matter. What matters is the advisability of this marriage."

"What matters is that I can see right now it's going to take all my effort to keep you in hand. *Leaves of Grass,* indeed."

"Thomas—"

"My sergeant is going to perish at the door," he interrupted. "Can we not get on with this and save him—before it's too late?"

"Can you make me one promise?" she asked.

"What is it?"

"Can you promise not to forget that I gave you the opportunity to escape?"

"And may every other Rebel I meet from here on out do the same," he said elaborately.

She gave a sharp sigh. "And I was worried about *me* not being in my right mind."

He laughed and leaned closer.

"Now, Abby?" he whispered, teasing her again. "Will you give me leave to open the door?"

She didn't answer him.

"It's going to be all right," he said, serious suddenly. "I give you my word on that."

His word meant a great deal to her. "All right," she said finally. "Go open the door. Save La Broie and me both."

Thomas left her to fling the door open. A number of people stood gathered in the hallway and kitchen beyond, most of whom were straining to catch a glimpse inside the room. There would have been a great rush to gain admittance were it not for Sergeant La Broie. He allowed Gertie to enter, and then Mrs. Wilson, the dour lady of the house, who had clearly come out of duty rather than desire. It was the first time Abiah had seen her in person. Heretofore, the woman had only existed in the form of the verbal admonishments constantly repeated by Gertie and the household staff. Mrs. Wilson was full of don'ts. There was no doubt that she ran a tight ship; she was making an inspection even now to see if Abiah and Gertie had done any injury to her domain.

Not one but three army chaplains followed Mrs. Wilson into the room. All three came to stand around the bed. Abiah glanced at Thomas, who winked.

Ah, well, she thought. Given the apparent magnitude of the scandal precipitated by Thomas's rescue, they had best have the matrimonial knot firmly tied. The chaplains introduced themselves—Brothers, Hearst and Holmes. It was clear that they had already decided among themselves who exactly would do what when. The Reverend Brothers began the proceedings with a lengthy prayer. Abiah was grateful for the opportunity to close her eyes. She was very tired suddenly, and had to concentrate hard not to show it.

Someone knocked on the door. The Reverend Brothers prayed on. Finally, after the third knock, La Broie went to open it, and after a brief, whispered conference with whoever waited on the other side, he accepted an envelope of some sort and closed the door.

The prayer continued. Abiah opened her eyes enough to watch with interest as La Broie discreetly passed the envelope to Thomas, who glanced at it and put it into his pocket.

"If you would join hands, please," the second chaplain—Hearst—said as soon as the prayer ended. He opened the small leather book he carried and adjusted his spectacles, looking around sharply at another outburst of raucous laughter from out in the hall.

Thomas moved the chair closer to the bed and sat down, so that he could take Abiah's hand more easily. Hers was trembling, and he looked at her sharply when he realized it.

"I think they would both approve, Abiah," he said quietly.

"What?"

"Miss Emma," he said. "And Guire."

She looked at him a long moment, then nodded.

The Reverend Hearst cleared his throat. "May we continue?"

"Yes," Thomas said, without looking at him. His eyes still held Abiah's, and whatever indecision remained suddenly left her.

For better or worse till death do us part, she thought.

The ceremony began in earnest, but it was an obviously shortened version, to accommodate Thomas's lack of time and her illness. Because of their proximity to the kitchen, Abiah could smell bread baking. She wondered idly if many weddings took place with the aroma of baking bread wafting through. She glanced briefly at the people who stood witness. Gertie, who looked sad enough to cry, and La Broie, who stood ramrod straight next to Gertie and watched her intently. Hardened soldier or not, the man was clearly smitten.

Interesting, Abiah thought. La Broie so enamored, and Gertie so oblivious to it.

Abiah glanced at Mrs. Wilson, with her long-suffering countenance, and made a mental note. Should she and Thomas ever actually live together as man and wife, she would not go around looking like that. She wondered idly if Mr. Wilson was somewhere at hand, too. She hadn't met him, either, though Gertie had assured her when they first came to the house to stay that she wouldn't want to.

Abiah turned her attention to the second chaplain.

How determined he is, she thought.

He had offered no call to the ceremony, no "Dearly

Beloved…'' He had asked for no declaration of con-
sent, no ''Wilt thou have this woman…'' He had gone
straight to the marriage pledge.

Repeat after me.

''I, Thomas, take thee, Abiah…''

Thomas's voice was strong, unwavering. Whatever
happened in the future, she would always remember
that he'd said the words with a surety that belied the
true situation.

Then it was her turn, and she hesitated too long—
long enough to alarm Thomas and everyone else in
the room. She abruptly squeezed his hand.

''I, Abiah, take thee, Thomas…''

The last chaplain, Holmes, concluded the ritual with
a prayer, and suddenly it was over and done. Abiah
immediately looked at Thomas, searching for some indication as to whether or not he was now filled with
regret.

But he only smiled and shook everyone's hand.
Then he signed the marriage record and held the book
for her to do the same.

''Are you all right, Abby?''

''Tired,'' she said, trying to smile. She wanted to
say something to Mrs. Wilson, to thank her for her
charity and hospitality, but the woman had already
opened the door and stepped into the hall. Abiah's
attention was taken then by Sergeant La Broie, who
solemnly clasped her hand.

''I'm wishing you health and happiness, ma'am,''
he said.

"You'll watch over Thomas?" she whispered. "Keep him safe?"

"I'll do my best, Mrs. Harrigan, darling," he assured her. "I ask the same favor of you. You watch over our Gertie."

Abiah smiled. The man was completely smitten, she thought again, and she certainly had a profound empathy for anyone in that state. "I will," she said.

"Pete," Gertie said. "Don't let all those people come in here. Miss Abiah needs to rest now."

He immediately went to stop any uninvited wedding guests from pushing their way inside.

"I forgot, Mrs. Harrigan," he said, looking over his shoulder. "There's a wedding present out here for you."

"A wedding present?"

She looked at Thomas, who was reading the letter La Broie had given him earlier.

"It's from Johnny Miller," Thomas said.

La Broie was already bringing the gift in. She recognized it immediately. It was her own cedar hope chest, the one made for her fourteenth birthday by her grandfather Calder. Like most girls that age, she had immediately begun filling it with linens and quilts for that time in the seemingly distant future when she would marry. Seeing it again, when she'd thought everything in the abandoned house had likely been plundered by both armies, brought her close to crying.

"Johnny went to the house and got it," Thomas said. "Then he bribed a civilian from Fredericksburg to bring it across the river. Put it here, La Broie, where she can see it."

"How do you know that?" Abiah asked.

"It's in his letter," he said, holding up the envelope La Broie had given him. "The letter was for me. The chest, for you."

"What else does he say?"

"He…wishes us every happiness."

She smiled. "He was there—the day my grandfather gave the chest to me. And he and Guire teased me so about being an ugly old maid and not needing such a fine piece of furniture. And Mother was…" She stopped and took a quiet breath. She didn't want to reminisce about the past, even if the past was likely all she would ever have.

The sound of laughter and loud singing burst forth again from the direction of the kitchen.

"I guess more people knew about the wedding than I thought," she said after a moment.

"I dare say," he agreed. He was standing so awkwardly, as if he wanted to take his leave, but wasn't quite sure how to do it.

"I…have a gift for you, too," he said, and he reached into his pocket—for his watch. He opened it to check the time and then looked at the door.

"If you have to go now, it's—" she began.

"Sir!" La Broie said abruptly in the doorway, making her jump.

"You must overlook the sergeant, Abby," Thomas said, taking the bundle La Broie tossed to him. "Believe me, he all too often comes and goes like that."

He lay the bundle on her lap. "It isn't much. There aren't too many things here to buy."

She took the string off and unrolled enough of the muslin wrapping to reveal a green book. The title was printed diagonally across it in gold leaf: *The Scottish Chiefs*. It was beautiful.

"The story of William Wallace, by Miss Jane Porter. I always wanted to read this," she said. "There was only one copy at school. I never got the chance."

"I thought maybe you'd had enough of men writers and you'd like a woman's perspective for a change."

She smiled, running her fingers over the exquisitely tooled designs in the green leather cover—ivy and oak leaves and acorns, an exotic bird with long tail feathers that curved down across the banner with the title. She looked up at him. She loved books—almost as much as she loved him. "Thank you, Thomas."

"And the other thing…" He lifted a knitted white wool shawl with a delicate lace edge free of the muslin. "It's…well, it isn't much, but I hope you like it."

She leaned forward so that he could drape it around her shoulders. "It's beautiful. Thank you again. I wish I had something for you."

"Not necessary," he said, pulling the chair around and sitting down again. "There's one more thing here." He unfolded the muslin the rest of the way, and took out an envelope. "This is the name of my lawyer in Boston. And the one here in Falmouth who will take care of your expenses. I've included my mother's address in Maryland, if you should need to contact her. And there's a copy of my will." He was very careful not to look at her. "There's also a note with my proper address. I would like it very much if you would write to me if—when—you feel up to it."

"You're in the wrong army, Thomas. How...?"

"There's a chance that a letter will get to me as long as Falmouth remains in Union hands." He finally let his eyes meet hers.

So sad, she thought. *Still so sad.* She nodded, because she didn't trust her voice and because she was so tired.

"I've brought your toddy, Miss Abiah," Gertie said from the doorway, making a much less startling entrance than La Broie had. "And some very fine sipping whiskey for you, Captain Harrigan—from Mr. Zachariah Wilson, you might say. A little something to mark the occasion."

"Does Mr. Zachariah Wilson know how generous he's being, by any chance?"

Gertie laughed. "Well, sir, if you run into him on your way out, I wouldn't thank him for it, if I was you." She set the tray down on the table by the bed and quietly left.

"What is this, Abby?" he asked, handing her the flowered teacup.

"Hot milk, honey—and brandy. Every three hours, just like clockwork. I've been promoted from chicken broth."

"Well," he said, lifting his glass to her. "It could be worse."

They both drank. She was more used to her beverage than he was to his.

"I'm going to have to have help getting on my horse," he said.

"I guess that's what groomsmen are for."

"Well, not these groomsmen. If I have to depend on them, I'll surely have to walk."

She smiled, feeling the awkwardness between them growing by leaps and bounds.

My husband, she thought. Then, *Thomas, what have you done?*

He didn't say anything else, and neither did she. The silence between them lengthened as the revelry in the kitchen grew louder. Laughter. Singing. The smell of bread. She was glad someone found this a merry occasion. She and Thomas might as well be the chief mourners at a wake.

A log fell in the fireplace. The clock ticked quietly on the mantel.

"Thomas—"

"No more talking," he said, taking her cup away. "Rest. Go to sleep, if you can. I'll sit here by you until I have to go."

"Thomas—" she began again.

"No more talking," he insisted. "This wedding was supposed to be for your good. I don't want it to make you worse."

"I'd like to see inside the cedar chest. Could you open it?"

"There's no key."

"Force the lock, then."

He sat for a moment, then did as she asked, first

trying to open it with his bare hands and then the edge
of the shovel from the fireplace.

"This is going to ruin it, Abiah," he said after a
moment.

"Please, Thomas. Open it."

The lock finally gave, with a minimal amount of the
wood splintering. She raised up on one elbow to look
inside. Everything appeared to be there, even the gray
uniform jacket and the saber she'd packed away on
top. She realized that Thomas was looking at them.

"Guire's things," she said, and he nodded. She lay
back against the pillows suddenly and closed her eyes,
more exhausted than she realized. Thomas closed the
chest.

When she opened her eyes, he was once again sitting by the bed.

"Abby," he said, when he realized she was looking
at him. "If you should hear from my grandfather,
don't let him bully you."

"I don't think there's anything for your grandfather
to bully me about, Thomas—except perhaps my pol-
itics."

"Oh, the judge would find something, believe me."

"Then I promise I'll be every bit as obstinate as
you would be."

He looked at her a moment, then abruptly smiled.

"Go to sleep, Abiah," he said again, the smile still
lingering at the corners of his mouth.

"No," she said. "I'll have plenty of time to sleep
later. Talk to me."

"Are you warm enough? Shall I put more wood on the fire?"

"Don't do that. Don't remind me that I'm an invalid. Talk to me the way you used to when you came home with Guire."

"Shall I take the book away?" he asked, still intent on being solicitous.

"Thomas!" she said in exasperation. "Tell me about…about your family." It wasn't what she meant to ask at all. She had meant to ask about the woman he had really wanted to marry, but at the last moment, she lost her nerve.

He gave a resigned sigh. "What do you want to know?"

"Anything. Everything."

"I don't know 'everything.' The Winthrops aren't like the Calders. There's no openness, no…"

"What?" she asked, when he didn't go on.

"I was going to say affection. But I supposed there is some. We're just very careful to keep it hidden— as if caring for someone was some kind of weakness in our character. The judge does care for my mother— at least I think he does, in his way, or he wouldn't have let her come back home."

"But he doesn't care for you?"

"No. Never for me."

"Why not?"

"I did the unforgivable."

"And what was that?" she asked, determined to get whatever information from him she could.

"I was born. I am my father's son. That alone is sin enough."

She looked at him, and she made no token protests. It would be presumptuous of her to try to talk him out of his conclusions about the judge. Thomas understood the situation far better than she did. She had only to look into his sad eyes to know that. She wondered if he ever heard from the father who had abandoned him—but she didn't ask about that, either.

"What is the house like? The one in Maryland," she asked instead, turning to at least some of the things she'd always wanted to know.

"Big. Ostentatious, actually. Very much in keeping with the judge's idea of his status in society. It's always full of luminaries of one kind or another. The judge is very fond of holding salons. Everyone who is anyone strives to be invited, I believe—which is understandable. He is much more agreeable to the strangers who come to his house than he is to his family." Thomas was looking away from her when he said it, seeing again, she thought, that big—and lonely—house in Maryland.

"I'm sorry," she said.

He looked at her. "Don't be. My family is what made me appreciate yours so. Miss Emma and Guire. I will miss them all the rest of my life." He suddenly reached out and took her hand. "Go to sleep," he said pointedly. "I can see how tired you are."

"I'm not," she insisted. "Truly…"

But she must have been. When she opened her eyes again, the room was dark except for the glow from the embers in the fireplace. The chair where Thomas had been sitting was empty. The room had grown cold. There was no smell of burning wax. The candle had been out for a long time.

She struggled to sit up in bed, trying hard not to cry. She had wanted to be awake when Thomas left. She had wanted to tell him…

No. Perhaps it was better this way. No awkward goodbyes. No…anything.

She was still wearing the shawl he had given her, and she hugged it closer to her and lay back against the pillows. What if she never saw him again? What if—

She turned her head sharply at a sound on the other side of the door—a heavy thump, as if something or someone had fallen against it. She raised up on her elbow, listening intently, and just when she was about to lie down again, she heard a voice.

"Please!"

A woman's voice. Gertie's voice.

There were more scuffling noises—and a man speaking in muffled and angry tones. Abiah could hear him, but she couldn't understand the words.

"Gertie?" she called, growing more alarmed now.

She jumped at another loud thump against the door. The doorknob rattled.

"Gertie!" Abiah yelled. She shoved back the heavy quilt and slid her legs over the edge of the bed. The room swam around her. She had to sit there until the dizziness subsided.

And all the while the struggle outside the door continued.

Abiah slid to the floor and went directly for the cedar chest, flinging it open and tearing through the starched linens and dresser scarves inside.

"Where is it?" she whispered, throwing piece after piece onto the floor. "Where is it!"

If it was gone, she'd take Guire's saber—if she could lift it. She'd have to.

Abiah abruptly stopped looking. Gertie was crying. She could hear her plainly.

Dear God, what's happening!

Abiah was frantic now, running her hands among the remaining sheets. Her fingers finally touched cold metal. She dragged Guire's Colt revolver out, carrying it with both hands to the fireplace—the only source of light—so she could see. She had hated the thing, hated when Guire insisted that she learn to shoot it because he was away at school and she and their mother were isolated and alone.

She felt so weak suddenly, and she went down on both knees on the hearth, breathing heavily. The revolver slid out of her hands. She stayed where she was, her head bent low until she could pick up the gun again. Then took a deep breath and held it closer to the firelight, where she could see. It was still loaded.

She forced herself to her feet again, holding on to the furniture and then to the wall to get to the door. She didn't hesitate—she could hear Gertie sobbing still. Abiah opened the door wide and stepped unsteadily into the hall. The too-long sleeve of her nightgown kept sliding down and covering the Colt.

There was no one in the hallway now.

She heard Gertie give a muffled cry somewhere to her left. Something fell and broke. Abiah went in that direction, holding the revolver with one hand and leaning heavily against the wall with the other. She had to keep stopping to rest, but she was determined to go on.

The man had Gertie down on the kitchen floor, and he was so intent on what he was doing that he didn't hear Abiah. She brought the revolver up and pulled back the hammer. It was that noise that got his attention. He abruptly looked around. Only one lamp had been lit, and she couldn't see his face distinctly.

"Move away from him, Gertie," Abiah said, stepping closer to the end of the kitchen table so she could lean against it.

Gertie tried to stop crying, tried to cover herself. She made an attempt to scramble aside, but the man caught her wrist and struck her hard.

"Stop it!" Abiah cried.

He didn't stop. Gertie was struggling, he hit her again.

"Stop it! I mean it!"

When he raised his hand the third time, Abiah pulled the trigger. The revolver misfired. She gave a soft cry of alarm and fumbled to pull back the hammer. Her sleeves were in the way. Her hands were shaking, but she held on.

The revolver misfired again.

"I never knew whores stuck together," the man said, still holding Gertie down.

But then he was getting slowly to his feet. Abiah didn't dare take her eyes off him.

"What are you going to do now, whore?"

"I've got…four more chances…to send you to hell," Abiah said. Her entire body trembled from the physical strain. "If you don't get out of here, I intend to use them…all."

"She owes me, damn you!" the man said. "Come to think of it, so do you." He lunged suddenly in Abiah's direction, taking her completely by surprise, but not before she pulled the trigger again. There was a loud roar this time, and the man reeled away from her and fell heavily on the floor. Gertie screamed, and Abiah collapsed against the rough kitchen table and slid to her knees. The heavy revolver tumbled out of her hand. She had to cling to the edge of the table to keep from falling on her face.

"Oh, Miss Abiah! What have you done?"

Abiah found Gertie's question entirely beyond her comprehenion. She still held on to the edge of the table, trying hard to stay upright, trying to stop trembling.

It was raining again. She could hear it.

How strange, she thought, that she should take note of that.

Happy is the bride the sun shines on today.

And she suddenly thought she heard Guire's voice.

"What?" she whispered.

I mean it, Abby. Don't you ever aim this gun at anything if you don't mean to kill it.

"What?" she whispered again. "What did you say?"

"Miss Abiah, stand up! We have to get out of here!"

"No, I can't, Gertie—"

"You have to! Get up! Now!"

Abiah tried to do what Gertie wanted. She pulled hard on the edge of the table in an effort to get to her feet. The man was no longer lying on the floor where she had seen him fall. She closed her eyes for a moment, trying to understand. She didn't know what was real anymore. And at this point, she had no idea which would be worse—to be out of her head again and to have imagined it all—perhaps even her marriage to Thomas—or to have killed a man.

She looked up at Gertie. One eye was bruised and swollen nearly shut.

Not a dream then.

"Is he…dead?" Abiah asked, her voice trembling.

"Carl says not," Gertie said.

"Carl?"

"He's the hired man. He came when the gun went off."

"I…really shot someone?"

"Close enough."

"Where—where is he?"

"I don't know. Come on, Miss Abiah. We have to get out of here."

"No, we have to let somebody know what happened. Mr. Wilson, or his wife. Somebody needs to know about that man.''

Gertie gave a sharp sigh and stopped pulling on her arm. "Miss Abiah," she said in exasperation, "Zachariah Wilson *is* that man."

"What?" Abiah said, no longer trying to get up.

"You shot our landlord, Miss Abiah. Not that anybody is going to believe that even if you tell them— not with the likes of me standing right here beside you."

"But—"

"Miss Abiah, there ain't no use talking about it. We have to get out of this house. We don't wait until the rain stops. We don't even wait until the sun comes up. We go. Understand?"

Chapter Four

"**M**ind what you do with your face, Cap."

Thomas gave the sergeant a look in spite of the admonishment. The effects of his groomsmen's brandy had long since worn off, and the last thing he needed was to be instructed on his demeanor.

"The boys are ready to drop where they stand, sir," La Broie persisted. "You got to show them it ain't as bad as they think it is."

"Oh, it's nowhere near as bad as they think it is," Thomas said. "It's goddamn worse."

He had his own struggle to keep from dropping, and perhaps the only deterrent was the fact that he was standing in mud—and who knew what else—nearly to his knees. The roads had become completely impassible. He had long since given up trying to ride his exhausted mount; a horse mired in mud to its belly was completely useless. He walked like the rest of them, and every muscle in his body ached. He was shivering with the cold. He was hungry. And the rain. God, the *rain*.

The beginning of their little jaunt to surround the Confederates and utterly vanquish them began auspiciously enough, but by the first evening, the weather turned foul and stayed that way. By now they had been standing in a downpour for what seemed like hours, waiting for somebody up the line to decide what this dog-wet and mud-caked excuse for an army was going to do, and all the while it was common knowledge that they were giving Lee and his crowd the biggest laugh of their military careers.

There was a loud commotion up ahead, shouts and the neighing of distressed horses—another overturned baggage wagon. Thomas took a moment to indulge himself in a colorful assessment of General Burnside's family tree.

"He is that, sir," La Broie said appreciatively. "Indeed he is."

"Let's go, La Broie. And you can keep your remarks to yourself," Thomas said, forcing himself to begin a pass along the line to hand out words of encouragement he didn't begin to feel.

"Sir—" La Broie said.

"I know, La Broie! Mind my face."

Thomas had an admirably disciplined company, now—something he could only accredit to La Broie's reputation as an Indian fighter and his consummate ability to put the fear of God into a man with hardly more than a look. Unlike some of the other, more demoralized companies, this one was all present and accounted for. And it was safe to say that La Broie was the reason the men still had their "gum blankets" as well, that all-purpose piece of equipment that could be worn to keep the rain off or slept upon as a barrier to the wet ground.

Regardless of the fact that no one had been paid in recent memory, not a single man had dared give in to his craving for tobacco or whiskey by selling or bartering his blanket. So here they all stood, correctly outfitted for the weather, exactly by the book. Even so, it struck Thomas as he began his inspection that there was something entirely ludicrous about grown men standing out in the rain, apparently for no other reason than to make a great show of ignoring it.

"Rathbone," he said, stopping in front of one of the privates who had been so recently wounded at Fredericksburg and who had refused to be left behind. "How is the hand?"

"It's doing the best it can, sir," Rathbone assured him.

"So are we all, Private," Thomas said, drawing a few polite chuckles among those within earshot. "Anything you need?"

"Just my dear mother's apple pie, sir."

Thomas smiled and moved on, the remark immediately drawing his thoughts to a winter afternoon at the Calder house. Abiah and the apple pie she'd made and baked and finally cut for him in Miss Emma's kitchen. He tried to imagine Elizabeth in that same situation—wearing an apron, laughing and completely unmindful of the flour on her nose.

Elizabeth. What was *she* doing now? he wondered. Did she still attend the judge's salons? Probably so.

She dearly loved the attention her presence always garnered, and there was no reason why she shouldn't don yet another new satin frock and go. No one there would know she had broken her engagement to the judge's grandson. No one there even knew there had been an engagement. At her insistence, he hadn't mentioned it to anyone—except in his last impulsive letter to Guire Calder.

Thomas still didn't know what had happened to cause her abrupt change of heart, but as far as he was concerned, Elizabeth was safe from any further revelations on his part. Somehow it didn't matter anymore, and the fact that he'd been a consummate fool where she was concerned was something he would just as soon keep to himself.

He realized suddenly that one of the company—a myopic and freckle-faced lad named Bender—had spoken to him.

"Pardon? Private Bender, is it?"

"Yes, sir. We want to give you our compliments, sir," the boy said.

"Compliments," Thomas repeated, not quite understanding.

"On account of you getting married, sir," the boy said. "We wish you a happy marriage."

"Yes. Thank you," Thomas said, clearing his throat to cover his embarrassment. Of course the men would know all about his recent adventure across the river, and they would know about the subsequent hurried nuptials to rectify the damage he'd done. But knowing about it was one thing. Discussing it in formation was something else again.

"This ain't much of a way to spend a honeymoon, Cap," one of the older men standing nearby said, because Bender had thrown the door wide-open.

"No, Corporal, it's not," Thomas said, moving on. He glanced at La Broie.

"It was the only way I could explain your face, sir," the sergeant said quietly. "Better they think you're missing your bride than you're expecting Burnside to march us right square into hell. There's enough deserting going on in this army as it is."

Thomas couldn't argue with that, and if the truth be told, perhaps his absence from Abiah did explain, to a certain degree, his apparently downcast visage. He thought about her all the time. Ill or not, she had been quite pretty with that pink ribbon in her hair. For a long time that afternoon he had watched her sleeping still clutching the book he'd given her. And he had deliberately waited until after he left her to finish reading the letter Miller had written.

Thomas hadn't quite told Abiah the truth when he said that Johnny Miller wished them well. The man apparently wished Abiah well, as evidenced by the effort he'd put into getting her hope chest to her. But he was of an entirely different mind when it came to Thomas.

"Be advised, Harrigan," the letter concluded, "that I consider you a blackguard and a scoundrel in your behavior toward Miss Abiah Calder. You have ruined her good reputation. Thanks to you, she has become the talk of two armies. Should we meet again, on the battlefield or off, it will be my great pleasure to kill you, you son of a bitch. You can believe me when I tell you I will do what Guire can't.''

It occurred to Thomas suddenly that perhaps Miller hadn't known that Thomas and Abiah were about to marry, that perhaps he'd sent the chest simply because he knew how much Abiah treasured it and how much she might need something from her mother's house to comfort her. Not that it mattered. From the tone of the letter, Thomas wasn't going to be given the time or the opportunity to explain that the blemish he'd placed upon Abiah's reputation had been eradicated. Somewhat. He still didn't regret his admittedly impetuous actions. If he'd left Abiah alone in that deserted house, then and only then would he have deserved Miller's threats.

But he couldn't worry about any of that now. He had other, more pressing matters—like pretending that the Grand Divisions weren't permanently stationed under a dark cloud of misfortune, and that General Burnside knew exactly what he was doing. Given the current weather situation, Thomas would have to concede the two days of hard rain. He continued along the line, speaking to a man here and there, modeling himself after Private Rathbone's injured hand and doing the best he could.

''Now what is it, La Broie?'' Thomas asked as they walked—struggled—back to the head of the line. It amazed him, even as he asked, how sensitive he'd become to the man's moods.

"I reckon I'm going to be glad to get back to Falmouth, sir."

God, yes, Thomas thought, but he didn't say it. La Broie in particular was privy to entirely too much of his personal life as it was. Thomas had been married three days, and emotionally, nothing was going the way he'd planned. He had *planned* to have some peace of mind knowing that Abiah would be taken care of, regardless of what happened to him. What he hadn't taken into account was how much he would want to take care of her himself.

The rain beat down on him. He stopped abruptly and stood there, the fatigue threatening once again to overwhelm him. He wanted a cigar. He wanted hot coffee heavily laced with whiskey—any kind would do. He wanted a warm, dry bed and he wanted a woman in it.

No. He wanted Abiah.

Abby—

"Cap!" La Broie called to him. "Something's happening."

Thomas looked around, expecting to see another overturned wagon. But something was indeed happening. Richmond, for the time being, was safe. Unlike Caesar's legions, this army, which had not even seen the enemy, much less conquered him, was now in a massive, unwieldly retreat.

Unfortunately, moving backward was no more easy than moving forward had been, and the return to Falmouth was anything but triumphant. Thomas completely lost track of time in the effort it took just to keep order. Tempers flared as only the tempers of men publicly humiliated, not once but twice, could. Bad food, *no* food, too many dead comrades and too many tactical mistakes made the need for vindication run high. And their only available targets were each other.

There was no question of Thomas getting away long enough to see about Abiah—not without getting shot. The piney woods were full of deserters. Entire units were threatening to leave the ranks, and subsequently the upper echelons were in an even greater stir about Burnside's fitness to lead. Thomas had hoped, as a lesser officer, to be able to quietly stand back and let the palace intrigue unfold as it would, but with higher-ranking officers forever conferring, there was no opportunity for him to do anything but take up the slack in the business of settling the army back into winter quarters—where it should have stayed in the first damn place.

"La Broie," he said at one point. "I want to see Bender."

And if La Broie wanted to know why, given the testy mood of everyone in general and Thomas in particular, he had the good sense not to make inquiries. The boy came promptly, obviously expecting at least a court-martial and a subsequent execution. It was comforting for Thomas to know that *he* was not the only one about who needed to "mind his face."

"Private Bender, I want you to take a message into town."

"Sir?" the boy said, clearly alarmed at the prospect of such a thing.

"Don't worry," Thomas said. "You'll have a pass, so I don't expect the pickets will shoot you."

"Yes, sir," Bender said, but he was not necessarily reassured.

"I want you to take this letter to a Mr. Zachariah Wilson's house. It's for my...wife," Thomas said, pausing long enough for Abiah's new designation to register—with them both. "I don't want you to give it to anyone but her. If she's absolutely not available, then give it to Gertie."

"*Our* Gertie, sir?" the boy exclaimed. And he couldn't have been more incredulous.

"How many Gerties do you know, Private?" Thomas asked, and he did *not* mean in the biblical sense—he hoped.

"Just the one, sir. And she—"

"Never mind that. Take the letter and do what I tell you. Mr. Wilson's residence is beyond General Sumner's headquarters at the Lacey house. If anybody stops you on the way, I want you to say you're going *by* there—which is the truth. If you get asked anything else, say you're just the message runner and you don't know. Period. Do *not* say you're carrying a letter to Ab—Mrs. Harrigan, understood? And report to me immediately when you get back."

"Yes, sir."

"Are you sure you've got all that?"

"Yes, sir. I'm sure."

"Then tell me."

"Well, sir, you don't want nobody to know you're

thinking about your lady when you should be thinking about the army's business.''

Thomas looked at him. That was pretty much the entire matter in a nutshell. Now if the boy understood the actual logistics of the thing half as well, Thomas could rest easy.

''When you get back, don't you go letting La Broie send you off someplace. You wait until you've seen me. And if Mrs. Harrigan wants to send a return letter with you, wait for that. While you're at it, you make sure she isn't in need of anything. You understand me?''

''Yes, sir. I wait and I make sure she don't require nothing.''

''Any questions?''

''No, sir.'' He wiped his nose on his uniform sleeve.

''Very good. Dismissed,'' Thomas said.

Bender was gone a long time—longer than Thomas initially realized, because he was intensely occupied with the logistics of getting some decent provisions for the company. He had enough of his own money put aside to buy raisins or some kind of dried fruit for the men—if he could find a sutler who had any. He had long since given up on getting the regular government issue of salt pork and desiccated vegetables, regardless of how eloquently he challenged the quartermaster's legitimate birth. He tried to keep watch for Bender's return, but without much success. The rain had finally stopped, and the weak winter sun appeared briefly in the late afternoon. A brisk wind rose, clearing the sky enough for a brilliant sunset.

Evening mess, such as it was, came and went. Finally, when Thomas had all but decided he was going to have to go look for the boy himself, Bender appeared outside Thomas's drafty tent-and-pine-bough quarters. The boy was completely out of breath when he came in, as if he had run all the way. The knee on one trouser leg was ripped.

But Thomas had no patience whatsoever to wait until he recovered enough to make a report.

"Bender, did you get the letter delivered or didn't you?"

The boy shook his head, still unable to speak. He reached inside his tunic and handed the letter back.

Thomas took it and stared briefly at his own handwriting. "You better not tell me you got lost—"

"Cap...no, sir! I found...Mr. Zachariah Wilson's...house. That weren't the trouble. Your lady...she wasn't there—"

"What do mean, she wasn't there?"

"She wasn't there, Cap. Gertie, neither. Weren't nobody...around inside...or out. The place was shut up tight. Weren't no lamps lit or nothing. I knocked at all the doors...and I looked in the windows—"

"Bender, she has to be there."

"No, sir, Cap. I waited at the house. I waited a *long* time. Nobody ever came back. I never heard one sound come from the inside."

"My wife is very ill! She has to be there!" Thomas said, realizing the implication of what Bender was telling him. Surely to God nothing had happened to Abiah while he was gone. Somebody would have come here to tell him, would have sent word if she...

"You didn't ask anyone?" he asked abruptly, knowing he should try not to scare the boy any more than he already had. Bender had been gone a long time—long enough to make any superior officer uneasy, given the number of desertions since the "mud march." It would have taken a considerable amount of nerve for Bender to come back at all, much less report that he hadn't carried out his orders.

"Cap, weren't nobody to ask. I waited and waited—"

"La Broie!" Thomas yelled, making the boy jump.

"Sir!" the sergeant answered immediately.

"Find out if anybody's seen Gertie."

"Gertie, sir? Ain't no civilians allowed into camp, sir—"

"Now, damn it!"

"Yes, sir," La Broie said, trotting away.

Thomas knew with certainty that Abiah wasn't well enough to go anywhere. He wasn't going to just assume that Gertie was still with her, still taking care of her—but whether she was or wasn't, he still had no idea where Abiah could be. He glanced at Bender. For a moment he thought the boy was going to cry. He was enough of a child still to want to make some kind of excuse for his failure, and enough of a soldier to know that that was not appropriate.

"Captain Harrigan," someone called from outside the hut.

"What, damn it?" Thomas said, with little thought to who it might be.

A soldier immediately came inside, regardless of the tone of Thomas's response.

"Major Gibbons's compliments, sir. You are to report to the Lacey house immediately."

"Do you know what for?" Thomas asked, more than a little worried now. He was too far down the pecking order to be sent for without good—serious—reason.

"No, sir. I'm thinking he wants you to hurry it along, though."

"Get my mount," Thomas said to Bender.

"Yes, sir!" the boy said, clearly relieved to be given something to do. He brought the horse around quickly.

"Go tell one of the cooks I said to feed you," Thomas said as he took the reins.

"Yes, sir."

"And tell Sergeant La Broie where I've gone."

"Yes, sir," the boy said again.

Thomas mounted and wheeled the horse sharply. There was no way he could delay whatever this might be. There was no way he could pretend that there was some urgent military matter that required his invaluable expertise. Even so, he set off at a gallop into the cold night, leaving the message runner who had come to summon him to headquarters trailing far behind.

But his head start did him no good, and it wasn't until the pickets refused to let him pass that he realized that, given half the chance, he would have gone "by"

the Lacey house in just the manner he'd instructed
Bender to do. He would have gone to see about Abiah
himself, and Major Gibbons be damned.

Where are you, Abby?

The night was starry and sharply cold. He had to
wait until the message runner caught up and could
vouch for him before the pickets would let him pro-
ceed. He made the rest of the ride more sedately, following the lanterns, lit and hung on cedar posts along
the way, until he reached Sumner's headquarters. But
even in the dark, the place would have been easily
recognizable.

The house was an incredible hodgepodge of archi-
tectural designs. Huge one-story wings had been added
to either end of the original two-story structure, and
then yet another wing added to those. Nothing was to
scale. None of the rooflines matched. The place looked
as if it had been the work of someone who had the
money to buy the building supplies, but not the blue-
prints. At this point, nothing could have improved the
look of it save burning it to the ground and starting
over.

Thomas was passed through quickly and sent upstairs. He stood in the wide hallway while the messenger approached Major Gibbons, who manned a
small table near the turn in the stairs. It appeared to
take the major a moment to remember what he had
wanted with Thomas, but whatever it was, it didn't
require his personal attention.

"You are to go down there, sir," the messenger told

him. "Down to the last room on the left at the end of the hall."

Thomas felt the wind go out of him. This was it then. Something had happened to Abiah and they were going to tell him in private.

He stood there for a moment, then nodded. He had to force himself to go in the direction the messenger indicated, stepping over sleeping soldiers and unattended weapons and haversacks along the way.

He took a deep breath and reached to open the door. The room was dimly lit and smelled of cigar smoke. He didn't see the other man immediately, not until he spoke.

"All right. What have you got to say for yourself?"

Thomas looked around sharply. His grandfather stood near the window. It took Thomas a moment to recover, to remember that he was a grown man now and beyond the judge's intimidation. He had long since resigned himself to the fact that he could never please the old man, and the pain that had caused him as a boy had now translated into a kind of muted sadness at the loss to them both. Thomas still wanted to believe—did believe—that, had he not had to play the scapegoat for his father's wrongdoing, he and the old man could have at least maintained a mutual and satisfying respect. But it was too late now.

"Not much," he said lightly. "Why?"

"My God! You think this is cause for humor?"

"Well, hardly, sir, since I don't even know what 'this' is."

"Your behavior is an abomination," the old man said.

"And what behavior is that? I can assure you the recent misadventures of the Army of the Potomac are *not* my fault."

"You have no regard for this family whatsoever. You are your father's son. There is no doubt about that!"

"So you've told me many times, Grandfather. Did you miss your favorite sport so much you had to come all this way to say it again?"

The judge ignored the remark.

"You have hurt your mother deeply. I trust you realize that."

"Sir, I don't know what—"

"A Harrigan will not drag the Winthrop name through the mud again. I will not have it!" the old man interrupted, his voice rising, likely to the appreciation of everyone on the second floor. Thomas could hear movement outside the door, either the curious or the concerned trying to ascertain exactly what was transpiring in here. But he wasn't about to acknowledge any wrongdoing until he specifically knew the charge. He had no interest in this repeat of an all-too-familiar scene from his boyhood. He had to find out what had happened to Abiah.

"Exactly what is it you think I've done?"

"You've proved to me beyond a shadow of a doubt that I've been right about you all along. And now you have proved it to your mother, as well. *She* heard about your entanglement on the steps of the church after the Sunday service. Did you honestly think you could carry on as you have with this rebel harlot of yours and the scandal wouldn't reach our ears?''

"Sir—"

"Have you gotten this girl with child? If you have, you needn't think a bastard of yours will ever lay claim to a Winthrop inheritance. And you needn't think that I won't speak to your commanding officer—"

"And have him do what? Put me in the front lines? I'm there often enough without your help."

"I can assure you there will be consequences!"

Thomas stared at him. He was so weary of this, too weary to even attempt to explain. "You know, I do wonder how you've stayed a respected jurist when you are always so anxious to rush to judgment."

"Rush to judgment? No, indeed. I simply have no interest in hearing your excuses!"

"Good. I have no interest in making any. If that's all, then I'll take my leave. I have more pressing matters to attend to than this."

"I am not finished here! Did you honestly think you could flaunt your whoredom and no one would dare challenge you?"

"Sir! You don't know what you're talking about!"

"I know enough! Have you nothing to say about this?"

"No. I don't."

"Then you leave me no alternative but to tell your mother you are completely unrepentant."

"While you're at it, tell her I send her my fondest regards. Safe journey home, Grandfather."

Thomas headed for the door, but someone knocked just before he reached it. When he opened it, the same message runner who had fetched him here waited in the hall.

"Sir, you have somebody asking after your whereabouts," he said.

"Who is it?"

"Well, sir, I, ah…" He lowered his voice. "The person won't say."

Thomas frowned. "What am I supposed to do? Guess?"

"There's a bit of a fuss, sir—about the money."

"What money?"

"She says you owe her, sir."

"She?"

"It's one of the, ah, women, sir. You know."

Thomas didn't know at all—at least not precisely. He could feel his grandfather's attentiveness behind him.

"We aren't sure how she got in here, sir. There have been strict orders ever since we got back—absolutely no civilians in camp, much less strolling right into headquarters. Half of Falmouth has been trying to get up here to see a general so they can make some kind of complaint, but the pickets aren't supposed to let anyone pass—unless they come in like your grandfather, with enough passes to get into Jeff Davis's front parlor."

"Where is she?"

"Lieutenant Noah had her detained where—where…"

"Where what!" Thomas said impatiently.

"Where she's not apt to run into anybody in authority, sir. The lieutenant says to tell you it's a belated wedding present."

"Show me," Thomas said, and he left without saying anything more to his grandfather. The old man would think the worst no matter what, and this latest development, whatever it was, couldn't help the situation.

The woman had been forcefully invited to wait in a room at the very end of the last addition to the lengthy house. There were a few soldiers about, but most of them were sitting around the walls, asleep. Thomas had been half hoping it would be Gertie, though he couldn't think of any reason why she wouldn't give her name. This stranger was much older than Gertie, and had the hard look of someone who had been in her line of work for a very long while. Everything about her seemed to be in disarray. She was sitting on a washstand near the outside door, ignoring pointed remarks from the soldiers still awake, while she intently inspected her fingernails.

"My compliments, ma'am," Thomas said, and she looked at him sharply, he supposed for some veiled sarcasm on his part.

"You took one of my best girls," she said after a moment. "You—" she added, pointing a finger at his chest "—cost me a lot of money."

"I don't see how," Thomas said easily. "This army never gets paid."

She continued to stare at him, then abruptly laughed.

"Now that's the God's truth—but you better have a dollar or two on you now, deary."

"Why?"

"Why? Because I got me a grievance and you got to settle it."

"I think not, ma'am," Thomas said, turning to go.

"I know what's become of the Reb girl," she called after him loudly.

Thomas looked at her. She smiled.

"It's going to cost you," she assured him.

"You couldn't possibly know anything about that."

"Couldn't I? Try me, deary."

"You tell me what you know, then we'll see."

She laughed. "I get the money up-front, Captain Harrigan. I *always* get the money up-front."

"Not this time," Thomas said. Once again he turned to go. "Send her back wherever she came from," he said to the message runner. "And tell Noah I appreciate his...consideration."

"I talked to Gertie," the woman said, still bargaining. "Yesterday," she added as a selling point.

And a very fine selling point it was.

"All right," Thomas said, capitulating. "Where is she?"

"Gertie?"

"No, damn it!"

"Oh, you mean the Reb girl."

Thomas took a step in her direction and she hopped off the washstand.

"The money, Captain," she said, holding out her hand.

He reached into his uniform pocket and brought out a coin—a silver dollar he could ill afford to part with—and tossed it to her without even looking at it. She caught it easily and made a great show of trying to decide if it was genuine. Then she dropped it down her cleavage.

"Now," he said. "Where is she? And keep in mind that there is a whole roomful of men here who would be delighted to do whatever it takes to get me my money back."

The woman hesitated, possibly calculating whether or not she could escape out the door.

She apparently decided against it and smiled. "She's gone home to Mama."

"Her mother is dead," Thomas said.

"Not *her* mama, Captain. *Yours.*"

Chapter Five

"**D**id you find her?" Thomas asked, trying to get as close to the fire as he could without setting his blanket ablaze. It had been raining again, heavily enough to seep through the pine-bough-and-canvas roof and drip onto his head. He was half-sick with what the surgeon loftily called "catarrh." Thomas's head ached. He couldn't breathe through his nose. He couldn't hear. And he was in no mood to be thwarted.

"Yes and no," La Broie said.

"What the hell does that mean?"

"Sir, it means Gertie is still here someplace in Falmouth, but I can't find her. I reckon she's hiding."

"Why would she be hiding, for heaven's sake?"

"Don't know, Cap, but I think she is. Somebody may know where she got to, but they ain't saying."

"Well, keep looking. I want to know how the hell Abiah ended up in Maryland."

"We ain't sure she is there, are we, sir?"

Thomas didn't answer. That was true enough. All

he had was the word of a camp follower, and he'd had to pay a bribe for that.

If Abiah was somehow at the Maryland homestead, the judge certainly didn't know it. Thomas didn't even want to think about what it would be like in that house when his grandfather returned and found he had a new houseguest.

"You reckon she's all right, don't you, Cap?"

"How the hell should I know?"

"You think she ain't?"

"I think she wasn't in any condition to make that kind of trip. Damn it all! Did you find out what happened to Zachariah Wilson, at least?"

"He took his wife off to her relatives—on account of she can't stand no more battles going on around her—but don't nobody know where that is exactly. Cap, I'm thinking maybe this is my fault."

Thomas looked at the sergent. For the first time since Thomas had known him, the man fidgeted under his gaze.

"Go on," Thomas said.

"Well, Cap, see—Zachariah Wilson—he sort of knew Gertie."

"You mean he was one of her customers," Thomas said bluntly.

"Yes, sir. I figured he wouldn't want nobody knowing what he'd been doing with his spare time, so when I suggested he give Gertie and Miss Abiah a place to stay—"

Thomas held up his hand. Some things he was better off not knowing.

"No, this is *my* fault," he said. "For thinking I could leave Abiah with a camp follower and there wouldn't be any consequences."

"I told you, Cap. Gertie is a good girl."

"La Broie—"

"Sir, I'm thinking the money you was paying Wilson just wasn't enough to hold him that's all. We was desperate for someplace where we could get Miss Abiah in out of the rain that night. There weren't no other place. You know that, sir—"

"All right! The plan was just fine given the circumstances—except now my wife may be in absolutely the last place on this earth I would want her to be, and who knows where the hell Gertie is."

"I reckon she'll hear I'm looking for her, sooner or later."

"It had better be sooner."

"Yes, sir, Cap."

"The mail come in?"

"No, sir. No mail. No furloughs, either."

"You sure about that?"

"That's what I hear, Cap. Ain't nobody leaving winter quarters to go home. Too many desertions since the 'mud march.' And I hear we're getting a new general."

"Who?"

"My guess is Hooker, sir. He's been working hard to get the job—tattling back and forth to Washington like a crazy man. He's got friends in high places, they say. 'Course, the way Burnside keeps shooting himself in the foot, Hooker don't need no outside help. Hell, sir, the way things is been going lately, even *I* got a chance at it.''

Any other time, Thomas would have appreciated his sergeant's droll wit. But not today. Once again he was caught. He was desperate to know what had happened to Abiah, and there was nothing he could do about it. He couldn't leave camp—to do so would be pointless when he had no idea what to do or where to go. And even if Gertie was still in Falmouth and wanted to find La Broie, she couldn't get past the pickets—unless she had the same kind of leverage the other woman had had.

I want my wife, damn it!

He wanted Abiah here, safe, but even as the thought came to him, he realized how absurd it was to think a town that had essentially been a battlefield was preferable over the Winthrop house. But it wasn't just the matter of her safety. It was a matter of his pride. He simply didn't want Abiah knowing firsthand how little his grandfather thought of him, and he didn't want her suffering on his account—which she would. His mother wouldn't—couldn't—stand up to the old man on Abiah's behalf.

''Haul the boys out,'' he said abruptly to La Broie.

''Sir?''

''Haul them out, La Broie. You know what Napoleon says.''

''Ah, no, sir, I can't say that I do.''

''He didn't believe winter quarters were good for his army, La Broie. He said the idleness promoted disease. We might as well drill, don't you think?''

"Sir, ain't he the one that got most of his army froze to death in Russia—"

"Haul them out!"

The doors were scarlet—all three of them. Abiah lay in the high bed, fully awake now and carefully inspecting her surroundings. She had once thought that the doors in that "house" in New Orleans where Guire and Thomas had gone might be red, but there was nothing inappropriate about this room, even with the rather startling portals. It was large and airy and quite beautiful, the white walls and mantel contrasting sharply with the red doors.

A fire popped and hissed in the marble fireplace. Every now and then she could smell wood smoke. Two brass candlesticks sat on the mantel at the end of a row of small, blue-and-white porcelain dogs. A framed painting of some kind hung just above them— perhaps storm clouds over a shoreline and tall cliffs; she couldn't quite tell. A small rocker sat in front of the fire with a pedestal table next to it. She looked upward at the crocheted bed canopy above her, and then to her left, but she couldn't quite see the window. *What a wonderful bed,* she thought, savoring the lavender scent of the sheets.

It was a bright, sunny day outside—she could tell that much, and she could tell that it must be windy and cold. She could hear the wind moaning around the corners of the house. She moved to sit up, surprised at how much her head ached in protest.

"Ah," someone said. "Awake at last."

She looked around sharply, and the pain in her head escalated. A woman sat in a nearby window seat. She had a knitted red afghan around her shoulders and her embroidery in her lap.

"Where is Gertie?" Abiah asked.

"I'm sorry," the woman said kindly. "I don't know who you mean."

"She was with me—Thomas hired her. She has to be here."

The woman gave a small shrug. "No, I'm sorry. She isn't. Are you feeling better, my dear? You've had a long sleep. I trust it has helped."

"I—yes," Abiah said, completely bewildered. One moment she was out on the street in the rain, and the next moment...

She gave a sharp sigh. What had happened to Gertie?

"Are you all right?" the woman asked, coming closer. "Should I send for the doctor?"

"No," Abiah said. "No, I just..." She sighed again. "I seem to keep waking up in strange places. It's very...unsettling."

"I dare say," the woman said. "But it's not surprising you don't remember the trip here. The doctor ordered that you be given quite a lot of laudanum, I believe. You've only just now really awakened."

"Laudanum?"

"He thought moving you would be less injurious to the present state of your health if you were given something to make you drowsy."

"I see," Abiah said, not seeing at all. "Gertie didn't come with me?"

"No, my dear, I don't believe she did. Perhaps there was some trouble about that. A lawyer and his spinster sister accompanied you here. A Mr. and Miss Staunton. They had no instructions about anyone else, you see. It may be that they didn't think they should allow this Gertie, is it?...to come with them."

"She wasn't to blame."

"Blame?"

"It was me. I did it...." Abiah closed her eyes. She felt so...bereft suddenly. The emotion was a now-familiar aspect of her illness. Profound despair and being completely incapacitated seemed to go hand in hand, somehow. And, of course, there was the fact that Thomas had gone marching off with that inept general and she might never see him again.

"You mustn't let yourself get upset, my dear. Try to rest now."

"I don't want to rest. I want to know what's happened. What about Thomas? Is he safe? That general, Burnside—"

"Every effort has been made to send Thomas word of your whereabouts," the woman said—which didn't quite answer the question.

"And where exactly is this? Who *are* you?"

The woman laughed. "Did no one tell you what was taking place?"

"I have no idea," Abiah said truthfully.

"Well, then, we'll just have to remedy that. I am Clarissa Harrigan."

Abiah stared at her. "Thomas's…mother?"

"Yes."

"You've come all the way to Falmouth?" Abiah asked, thinking the woman must really object to Thomas's marriage to have made such a trip.

"No, my dear. *You've* come all the way to Maryland."

"Maryland! But I…how? How can that be?"

"The lawyer in Falmouth, Staunton, sent me a telegram telling me that you were very ill and had no place to go—because the recent battle had left everything in such turmoil. Aside from that, I knew your brother, Guire, you see. We must have spoken at length every time I went to Boston to visit Thomas when he was at Harvard. Certainly I could not leave you homeless. It's a very unpleasant situation to be in. Believe me, I—" She abruptly stopped and smiled again.

"What about Zachariah Wilson?" Abiah forced herself to ask. "The man who owned the house where I was staying."

Mrs. Harrigan frowned. "Oh, I assume he and his wife arrived at their destination safely. Poor woman! I can only imagine what she—and you—must have endured having two armies do battle on your very doorstep like that. But I trust she will recover fully now that she's away from all that and safe in the bosom of her family—as you will, my dear. Luckily, Lawyer Staunton is a very resourceful man. He got you here very quickly, considering the railway situation these days."

"I don't want Gertie to suffer on my account."

Mrs. Harrigan gave her a quizzical look, but she didn't ask Abiah to elaborate. "The doctor should have come up to see you by now," she said. "I'll go find out what's keeping him. Is there anything you need? Anything at all?"

Abiah needed Thomas, but she didn't say so. "Nothing, thank you," she said quietly. It would have been appropriate for her to thank Mrs. Harrigan for bringing her here, but for the time being, even in the wake of having shot Zachariah Wilson, she would reserve judgment about that.

Someone rapped sharply on the door, and Mrs. Harrigan hurriedly answered it.

"The judge is back, ma am," the maid whispered urgently, and the effect the announcement had on Thomas's mother was nothing if not profound. Clearly, this was not good news.

"What kind of mood is he in, Bonnie?" Mrs. Harrigan asked lowering her voice so that Abiah wouldn't hear. Fortunately, hearing was about the only function Abiah had that hadn't been affected by her illness.

"I don't like to say, ma am," the girl answered.

"All right. Tell him I'm coming, but don't say where I am."

"Yes, ma am."

"Hurry now."

"Yes, ma am—"

"Clarissa!" a man's voice bellowed from somewhere down the hall.

"I'll be back to see you shortly, my dear," Mrs.

Harrigan said brightly to Abiah. Then she slipped out the door and firmly closed it behind her.

Abiah moved to the edge of the bed and sat up. If she could summon the wherewithal to shoot a man, she could surely find the strength to eavesdrop. She cringed inwardly at the memory of that last night in Zachariah Wilson's house. He wasn't dead, thank God, if he'd taken his wife someplace away from Falmouth.

She was about to put her legs over the side of the bed, but she got no chance to do any spying. The door burst open, and an elderly man strode in, with Thomas's mother following anxiously on his heels.

"Father!" She protested. "Father, please—"

"So this is the girl," the man said.

And this must be the judge, Abiah thought, but she could see no family resemblance to Thomas at all. Yes, she did. They were both tall and lean, but there the resemblance ended. Ever since she was a girl, she had noted the kindness in Thomas Harrigan's eyes. She saw no such thing in this man. He felt himself the victim in this situation, and he was not about to be kind.

"I fear, young woman, you will rue the day you put your trust in a Harrigan," he said. "I think you should know I spoke to Thomas the day before yesterday evening, and he made no mention of *you* whatsoever. None. How do you explain that?"

Abiah had to dig deep to keep her promise to Thomas and not let herself be intimidated.

"He doesn't like you," she said simply, and the man immediately grew red in the face.

"There, you see?" he said to Thomas's mother. "You see how your son maligns me—"

"No, he doesn't," Abiah interrupted. "You have asked me a question, sir. I have answered it according to my own opinion. Thomas was a guest many times in my mother's house. I don't think I have ever heard him even speak your name. In fact, he rarely mentioned his family at all." She immediately regretted her last remark, because she glanced at Mrs. Harrigan in time to see a fleeting expression of pain cross her features.

"But you still insult me to my face and then expect shelter in my house," the judge said.

"No, indeed, sir. From you, I expect absolutely nothing."

"My dear, please, don't upset yourself," Mrs. Harrigan said, still trying to intervene. "You need your rest—"

"Be quiet, Clarissa!" the old man snapped. "Who else have you told about this so-called marriage to my grandson?"

"I haven't told anyone. Who is it exactly you want kept ignorant?"

"You are a very impertinent young woman!"

"I am merely trying to find my way, sir. I don't know how I got here. I didn't even know where *here* was until a few minutes ago."

"Your family approves of this...fortuitous...alliance

with my grandson, I take it," he said sarcastically.

"I have no family now," Abiah answered.

"No? With no experienced hand to guide you, I must say I'm hard-pressed to see how this matrimonial arrangement—if, indeed, there is one—could have possibly come about."

"Thomas came to see about us—my mother and me—as soon after the battle at Fredericksburg as he could. He found her dead in the house and me too ill to do anything for either of us. He and his sergeant buried her in the kitchen herb garden—and then they brought me back across the river and into the Union lines. He did so to save my life. It was indeed a very fortuitous alliance, sir. I would be dead if not for Thomas Harrigan. And when he realized the damage done to my reputation by his very brave and kind act, he tried to save that, as well. Yes, I do believe my mother would very much approve. She held him in high regard—"

"You mean she held his supposed inheritance in high regard!"

"I *mean* that he didn't ride on the coattails of your family name or your reputation to earn her respect. He was always welcome at our house and I—I..." She was still sitting upright near the edge of the bed. She swayed for a moment, then fell back heavily onto the pillows.

Mrs. Harrigan gave a small cry. Abiah was very sorry to have alarmed her, but there was nothing she could do about it. She could hear Mrs. Harrigan's voice, but it came from very far away.

"Bonnie, fetch the doctor! Abiah!"

The room whirled around and around, and a rolling blackness crept into her field of vision.

"Clarissa, I refuse to be dragged into this! What proof do you have she is Thomas's wife?"

"The lawyer who brought her, Father—"

"Whom you had to pay handsomely for the wonderful news, no doubt. You are painfully ignorant of the ways of this world, Clarissa!"

"Hardly *my* fault, Father," Mrs. Harrigan said.

"Judge, what have you done to my patient?" a different voice demanded.

"*I?*" the judge demanded in return.

Abiah turned her face away. She was too tired to listen to any further discord.

"Yes, you! She wasn't in this state before you started your cross-examination, now was she? This is a sickroom, not a courtroom. And you," the man whispered to Abiah. "What have *you* done to the judge?" He picked up her wrist and held it between his thumb and fingers.

"I kept my…promise," she said.

"Which was?"

"Not to let Judge Winthrop…bully me."

The man laughed out loud. "And a fine job you've done, too—but at some cost." He let her wrist go. "Clarissa, we need to be very diligent about feeding her. Very soft foods—boiled potatoes, soups, broths. I want her to have a small feeding of some such thing now and then every two hours during the day and as desired during the night, all right?''

''Yes, certainly,'' Mrs. Harrigan said.

''Unless, of course, the judge has decided to throw her out into the street. What about it, Judge Winthrop? Your only grandson's new bride? This lovely refugee from the very battlefield in Virginia? What an interesting story for the front page of the *Baltimore American*—not to mention the *Washington Star*—don't you think?''

''I don't find you particularly amusing, Nethen.''

''Nor I you, Judge. But be that as it may. Is she staying here with her husband's family or shall I cart her away to the poorhouse?''

The judge made a sound of annoyance and strode out of the room.

''Dr. Nethen,'' Mrs. Harrigan said. ''Perhaps you shouldn't be so hard on him. My father is finding this all very…difficult.''

The doctor chuckled. ''My dear Clarissa,'' he said, shaking his head. ''That is obvious. I thought the plan was that he would be 'prepared' for his new houseguest.''

''I never got the chance. Elizabeth Channing was here when Abiah arrived. I fear she met the judge at the gate with the news.''

''Ah, well,'' he said. ''You and I shall just have to take it as it comes. And you, too,'' he said to Abiah. ''Young Mrs. Captain Harrigan, I order you to rest easy. We are not any of us out of the woods yet.''

Abiah managed a smile, knowing she should probably worry more about being out of the house than out of the woods. The judge had made it very clear that she wasn't welcome here—not an unexpected response, since he thought she had either lied about being Thomas's wife or had tricked him into marriage.

She gave a quiet sigh. Perhaps the latter wasn't all that far from the truth. Even if she hadn't precisely tricked him, she had certainly taken advantage of his sense of duty and obligation. But if she'd been capable of making any kind of protest at all, she would *not* have come here.

She closed her eyes. For the moment, she had no choice but to remain here, at least until she was carted off to the poorhouse. She had no one in this world to call upon for sanctuary—except perhaps Miss Gwen. Gwendolyn Pembroke was a distant cousin on Abiah's mother's side of the family, a quaint old dear who seemed to have been left over from the last century. Abiah had only met her once, when she came to visit—with a pair of beagle hounds—the summer before Fort Sumter.

Miss Gwen lived in New Bern, a town on the North Carolina coast. It had only recently fallen into federal hands. Burnside had been there, too, and if one could believe the rumors that followed the battle, he had allowed the town to be set upon and looted before he officially took control. Poor Miss Gwen. Living in a town occupied by an enemy army wouldn't suit her at all—any more than living near occupied Falmouth had suited Abiah and her mother. Abiah needed to write to Miss Gwen and tell her what had happened to her relatives.

But not now. Now she could only lie here and worry. She wondered where Thomas might be at this moment. He'd followed Burnside at Fredericksburg and later marched with him out of Falmouth to who knew where. He could very well be participating in more of the same sort of havoc that had fallen upon New Bern. Abiah supposed that he would do whatever he had to do. He was a soldier—and an enemy soldier at that.

She sighed again. Fort Sumter had become a kind of giant landmark in her consciousness. Everything in her life seemed to be divided into two categories— before Fort Sumter and after. Or perhaps now it would be before and after she married Thomas Harrigan. She loved Thomas, but she didn't want to stay in his grandfather's house. She wanted so desperately to go home, but as long as she remained ill, not to mention penniless, she would have no choice but to remain here. When she was well again, she would somehow take herself home to Virginia. The Calder house was the only thing she had left. If she were waiting there, in the one place Thomas had thought of as home, then perhaps he would come to her—if he could. She had no expectation at all that he would come here.

She heard music suddenly—someone elaborately playing the piano downstairs.

The salon, she thought. Thomas had told her about them, about the eclectic gatherings of the very prominent, and apparently the musically talented, in his grandfather's drawing room.

"My dear," Clarissa Harrigan said, and Abiah looked at her. They were alone in the room now. Abiah hadn't even noticed the doctor going.

"Guire, too?" Mrs. Harrigan asked quietly.

Abiah nodded, afraid suddenly that she would cry.

"I'm so very sorry. He was a fine young man. I was always happy that he and Thomas were friends. This terrible war—" She broke off. "Well, I'll go see about getting you something to eat now. Doctor's orders, you know," she added with a slight smile. "And Abiah," she said when she reached the door. "You mustn't worry. Our dear Elizabeth Channing knows you're here—which means so does half of Easton and probably all of St. Michaels. She's seen to it that the people who are downstairs at this very moment have heard. The judge can't put you out in light of all that interest—no matter how much he may want to."

Chapter Six

"Do you feel up to having a visitor?" the doctor asked when he'd finished counting her pulse.

Abiah looked at him warily.

"No, it's not the judge," he said. "Someone closer to your own age."

She had to work hard not to show her relief. She appreciated that Dr. Nethen understood her reluctance to see Thomas's grandfather again. Their last encounter could hardly be described as amicable. It had begun as before, with the judge assuring her that she would rue the day she'd put her trust in a Harrigan. It had ended with Abiah quoting the eighteenth chapter of Ezekiel. She could tell by the way the door slammed after him that biblical arguments were not acceptable in this particular court—particularly when the Good Book went contrary to the judge's own opinion.

"A change in routine would be good for you. You need to have your senses provoked," the doctor persisted.

It was Abiah's opinion that her senses had been pro-

voked quite enough of late. *He* should try dueling with
Judge Winthrop or waking up hundreds of miles from
where he believed himself to be. But the real truth of
the matter was that she was tired. She knew that she
must be improving physically—it had been days since
she'd suffered a noticeable fever—but her state of
mind was something else again. And it wasn't caused
by worrying about Gertie and Zachariah Wilson, or
even whether or not Thomas was safe. She just felt so
ill at ease here. And having to be on her guard all the
time so as not to do something that would reflect badly
on Thomas was absolutely exhausting.

"The young lady who inquires is Miss Elizabeth
Channing. She wishes to call upon you if you're feeling up to it. I can find no reason for you not to receive
her for a brief visit, if you so desire."

Abiah drew a quiet breath. She supposed this was
the price she must pay for having come here so precipitously. Naturally, people would be curious, and
naturally, the first one to seek her out would be the
person who had apparently taken it upon herself to
make Abiah's presence known among the locals and
the salon guests alike.

Abiah knew what this was all about—and it had
nothing to do with one's Christian duty to make a
visitation upon the sick. This was an expedition of
sorts to capture *the* topic for the next salon, so that
this Miss Channing could present, in a dramatic reci-
tation, perhaps, a lengthy description of Thomas Harrigan's new bride. Abiah had no wish to participate in
that, not when even she didn't think of herself in that

way. A "bride" was someone desired and longed for—not a millstone whose only incontestable attribute was…

Actually, there was no incontestable attribute, as far as Abiah could tell.

"I don't so desire," she said, and Dr. Nethen looked at her.

"Are my physician's skills not so finely honed, after all?" he asked. "Are you not as improved as I thought?"

"I have no wish to be put on display," she said bluntly.

"Display? But you wouldn't…oh, yes, I see," Dr. Nethen answered abruptly. "I suppose there would be a certain aspect of parading the enemy captive through the streets in chains, wouldn't there? Very well. I'll tell Miss Channing that she may *not* call on you just yet. Perhaps at a later time…"

He seemed to wait for her approval of that statement. Abiah didn't say anything.

"If you have no complaints you wish me to hear, then I'll be on my way."

"No complaints," she said, at least none she wished to share with him.

He smiled. "I wish my other patients were so inclined. It's quite refreshing. Have you still not had news of Thomas?" he asked.

Still.

The way he said the word let her know that her not having received even one letter from Thomas since she arrived had been the topic of discussion somewhere.

She had written to him when she was barely strong enough to hold the pen, and every few days since, but so far, there had been no reply. And she needed one. She had arrived here with nothing but the clothes on her back. The book, the shawl, the letter Thomas had given her containing the legal papers hadn't made the trip. She had no proof, save her word and the lawyer's communication with Mrs. Harrigan, that she and Thomas had ever married. It was no wonder that a man as skeptical as the judge would have his doubts. She herself sometimes found it hard to believe.

"No," she said. "I have not."

"Well, the army is in winter quarters now. I do know that much. Surely we won't have to worry about his going into battle again for a while. I expect you'll hear from him soon—the mails do go awry."

"Yes," she said. But any reason she could invent as to why he hadn't answered her letters only led to more worry.

"Is Miss Channing a Winthrop relative?" she abruptly asked.

"No, why?"

"I seem to hear her name a lot. You and Mrs. Harrigan have mentioned her. And when I ask about the mail, sometimes Bonnie says, 'Miss Channing hasn't fetched it yet.' I thought perhaps she was someone's kin and staying here."

He frowned slightly. "I didn't realize Elizabeth fancied herself a letter courier. Still, these are trying times and we must all do our part. She lives in that rather formidable granite house on the adjoining property.

You can just see it if you look out that window—
through the trees on the far side of the bowling green.
Her father and the judge have from time to time been
business partners, I understand. I always thought Mr.
Channing strongly favored an alliance—'' He stopped
abruptly. ''Well, I suppose even Elizabeth wishes to
be helpful.'' He looked at his pocket watch and compared it to the clock on the mantel. ''Your gears are
meshing nicely, but you're running a bit on the slow
side,'' he advised her, and she smiled, used to his wit
now.

''I must go make my report to your host—unless
you want to do it,'' he said, still teasing.

''I think not,'' Abiah assured him.

''Very wise,'' he said. ''Very wise, indeed. And
don't give yourself a moment's concern about the
other thing.''

''What other thing?''

''Saying no to Miss Elizabeth Channing.'' He rolled
his eyes to make her laugh. ''My dear, it is simply *not*
done.''

Abiah had no intention of concerning herself about
Elizabeth Channing. She had to concentrate on getting
well, and subsequently on getting home. What extra
energy she could muster went into letting the days fall
into whatever routine suited the household. She tried
not to be an inconvenience, and her growing loneliness
was alleviated only by the music from the salons that
always seemed to be going on. It was the only thing
she had to look forward to. Even listening from a distance she could understand why invitations here were

so prized. Thus far, she'd eavesdropped upon a pianist, a harpist, several violinists and a very strong voiced soprano. And she had enjoyed them all.

She felt that she must surely be better, because enough of her vanity had resurrected itself for her now to take some pains with the braiding of her hair. And, with Bonnie's help, every afternoon she moved unsteadily to the horsehair fainting couch brought in to give her some respite from having to lie abed all the time. The days stretched long, and the nights even longer. She remembered a remark old Miss Gwen once made the time she came to visit.

Sick people are afraid of the night.

Perhaps so, Abiah thought. But it wasn't fear, exactly, that kept her awake. It was the isolation, the profound knowledge that she did *not* belong here.

Today she sat looking out the tall, second-story window. A steady rain had been falling since dawn and showed no sign of abating. The rain and the bleak winter landscape only added to the aching nostalgia that oppressed her. She continued to write to Thomas—an ongoing missive that she added to every day, until it was finally substantial enough to mail. She said very little about her situation. Mostly, she reminisced about the past, selecting one stellar incident for each letter—stellar for her, at least—and writing it down for him in vivid detail.

In the latest one, she described a winter dance that he probably didn't even remember. It was the one when she had finally been allowed to put up her hair. The house had smelled of spice cake, red cedar boughs and coffee. The fiddler had played a waltz, and Thomas had come looking for her, because he had promised most sincerely to escort Guire's little sister onto the dance floor at her first grown-up dance.

"Sweet Miss Abiah," he'd said when he found her. "I believe you are promised to me for this one."

Abiah could still remember his hand in hers, warm and strong, as he led her to the middle of the room. It was the only time she had ever been in his arms, except when he had stolen her across the Rappahannock. She barely remembered that, but she remembered the waltz. It was something sad and haunting, in the key of A minor. Thomas had smiled at her slightly in that way he had, and his eyes—oh, his beautiful dark eyes! She had been lost in them. She was still lost in them. How could he not have known how she felt about him? She remembered enough of her deathbed declarations to know that he hadn't.

Thomas—

She looked around sharply, because the red door to the hallway suddenly opened. A young woman wearing a hooded cloak swept into the room with a basket over her arm. The woman's cloak was dark brown, but Abiah was still reminded of Red Riding Hood. She had no idea who the stranger was, and they stared at each other.

"Abiah?" the young woman finally said. "May I call you Abiah? It's such a beautiful name—is it biblical? Can you ever forgive me for not waiting for Clarissa to introduce us? It seems there's some crisis in the kitchen." She paused long enough to smile, but not long enough for Abiah to answer any of her questions.

"I am your neighbor, Elizabeth Channing. I've heard so very much about you. I said to everyone that I simply had to come and see if there was anything at all I could do for Thomas's poor wife. You see?" she said, lifting her basket higher. "I've come bearing gifts. May I join you for just a bit?" She plopped the basket down on the bare floor.

"This rain is such a burden. I do believe I am ruined," she continued, regardless of the fact that she bore no evidence of it. "You should be glad you don't have to venture out into it. I suppose we need it, but…" She gave a heavy sigh, and Abiah tried not to smile. Elizabeth Channing was exquisite in looks and dress, and well she knew it. Her honey gold hair was perfect in spite of the inclement weather—although Abiah suspected a hairpiece or two in the cascade of curls. Miss Channing wore a blue-and-brown-plaid taffeta dress over a huge crinoline. Abiah had all but forgotten about crinolines. She had donated hers to the war effort early on, and she supposed that they must now be part of some Confederate cannon somewhere. All the women she knew had done the same. She had grown accustomed to seeing herself and everybody else shaped more like sticks than bells, and she had completely forgotten how much floor space a crinoline demanded.

Miss Channing's very wide skirts rustled and swayed as she came closer. The dress was adorned with a single blue bow at the lace collar—specifically to accent her eyes, Abiah guessed. And regardless of her declarations about being "ruined," she had prepared herself very well for her outing by covering her expensive frock with that equally expensive, full-length sealskin cloak, which she took off carefully so that Abiah might have enough time to appreciate it. Abiah tried not to sigh. Her sense that she was somehow trapped in a topsy-turvy Red Riding Hood story was growing by the minute. Unfortunately, *she* was the poor old grandmother about to be eaten by the big bad wolf.

"You are very kind," Abiah said, determined to get a word in somewhere. Thus far, conversation with this person was very much like conversation with the judge. They both were interested only in what *they* had to say. "Please sit down. Did you walk over?"

"Walk? Oh, heavens no. I never *walk*. Do you?" Miss Channing asked earnestly, as if this were a piece of information she particularly required.

"I do. Or I did, when I was well. I'm a country girl. We country girls always walk places."

"Oh, I see. But really—you look absolutely lovely. One would hardly recognize that you've been ill. And did...Thomas walk, as well?"

"He did," Abiah said, admiring the speed with which Miss Channing got to what she really wanted to discuss.

"You've known him...long?" Elizabeth Channing persisted.

"About six years."

"Six! Well, I am surprised. I don't think I ever heard Thomas mention—" She abruptly smiled.

Abiah smiled in return. She was surprised herself—primarily that Dr. Nethen had so blatantly ignored her wish to be left alone. But the doctor had been right. She did need her senses provoked. And here she was, about to let herself be dragged into an overtly polite but thinly disguised, duel-to-the-death exchange of barbed remarks—which she was going to enjoy immensely.

"You're from Virginia, is that right?" Miss Channing asked next.

"Yes. Near Fredericksburg."

"I suppose Thomas went there often. Before the war, I mean."

"Actually," Abiah said, "when a visitor once asked my mother if Thomas and my brother, Guire, were her sons, she answered, 'Well, one of them is—but I forget which one.'"

"Oh, she had difficulty with her memory. How sad. I had an aunt like that."

Touché, Abiah thought, never for a moment believing this person had missed the point.

"Tell me, is Thomas better now?" Miss Channing asked.

"Better?"

"His bad cough. Is it better?"

Abiah stared at her, knowing she was caught uninformed. This king-of-the-hill game they had been playing suddenly wasn't much fun anymore.

"I believe it began just after that awful 'mud march'

or whatever the papers call it," Miss Channing said, pressing her advantage. "I understand it was quite severe. What does he tell you?"

"I—"

"Excuse me, Abiah," Mrs. Harrigan said from the doorway. " I thought I heard your voice, Elizabeth. I believe Thomas may not have mentioned his cough to Abiah because he didn't feel it advisable to worry her."

Elizabeth Channing actually blushed. And whatever was causing Thomas's lack of correspondence, clearly his mother considered it none of this young woman's business.

"Oh...dear me. Yes, of course, that must be it. I shouldn't have mentioned it, should I?" Elizabeth Channing said.

"I'm very surprised to find you here," Mrs. Harrigan continued, her voice quiet, but firm enough to unsettle what Abiah was beginning to suspect was the household's *other* uninvited guest. Perhaps the doctor had indeed told Elizabeth Channing no.

"Oh, I'm not visiting, I'm only making a delivery." Elizabeth smiled sweetly and swept herself and her big skirts toward the basket. "Abiah, I've brought you a few things—to enliven your long days, I hope. It must be so lonely here without Thomas. Will he come home to see you, do you think?"

"I'm sure he will," Mrs. Harrigan said for Abiah. "After all, he has good reason to get here as soon as he can."

Elizabeth Channing's smile faded. She handed

Abiah the basket. There was a nosegay of herbs and dried baby's breath, a tin of cocoa and a jar of what Abiah took to be blackberry jam—and an actual copy of *The Woman In White*.

"Thank you for all of this," Abiah said genuinely. "I've heard about the book. I understand people in London even miss their theater engagements because they can't put it down."

"Oh, it's all the rage. One of the judge's friends— a British sea captain, actually—brought a number of copies the last time he made the crossing. He's often here for the salons. Anyway, perhaps it will help you pass the time."

"I'm sure it will. You're very kind."

"Well, we must do our best to take good care of you and keep you safe—just as Thomas meant you to be. We don't want his sacrifice to have been for naught. We can do no less than follow his selfless example." She paused, and Abiah understood the innuendo perfectly. Somehow Elizabeth Channing had heard the circumstances of the marriage, and Thomas Harrigan's friends would consider his wife a pitiful charity case—just as he himself obviously did.

"And please, Abiah, do let me know if there is anything—anything at all—I can do for you in the—"

"Abiah is very tired," Mrs Harrigan interrupted. "I'll walk downstairs with you, Elizabeth."

Given no option but to leave, Elizabeth nevertheless tarried long enough to put her cloak on. Abiah leaned against the back of the fainting couch, and she couldn't help but watch—as she was meant to do. It was clear to her that Elizabeth Channing appreciated her own beauty only when it was reflected in the envy of others. And Abiah was admittedly envious. She couldn't begin to understand the kind of life Miss Channing must lead. Or Thomas, either, for that matter.

I have to get away from here, she thought—before she lost her own good sense and became the jealous creature she very much suspected the lovely Miss Channing intended her to be. She managed one last smile as Mrs. Harrigan hurried Elizabeth out the door, but the token smile quickly faded. How could Elizabeth Channing know that Thomas had been sick? Mrs. Harrigan had said many times that she hadn't received any word from him—so to which of them had she been lying?

No. It wasn't quite a lie. Clarissa had merely suggested a reason for Abiah's not having been told anything. She'd never said *she* had been notified of his illness.

Abiah closed her eyes for a moment. Trying to find her way through all this intrigue was exhausting. First the judge, now Elizabeth Channing. She wondered if it was like this all the time here. If so, no wonder Thomas had preferred the Calder house.

She was still holding the basket. She removed the book and set the basket on the floor. *The Woman In White.* It was an exceptional gift, regardless of the innuendos she'd had to endure to get it. She opened the cover and read the pronouncement in the first line— this was supposed to be the story of what a woman's patience could endure. Surely Abiah could find inspiration in that. She began to turn the pages, continuing to spot read here and there.

The sheets of paper were in the middle of the book. A letter, without the envelope. Abiah had no intention of reading it—at first—but one phrase caught her eye: "...the cough is much better...."

She hesitated, then picked up the pages and began to read. She didn't recognize the handwriting—but then why would she? She didn't recognize it, yet she was already afraid of what this must be.

...You have asked me again about my health. Please let's not dwell on that. Ask me instead how much I love you, and tell me that you love me, too. Tell me what it will be like when we are finally married. That is what I truly long to hear.

But since you have asked, suffice it to say that the cough is much better, my improvement, no doubt, coming about because of your faithfulness. Your writing to me means more than I can ever say. My sergeant tells me a letter from my "sweetheart" is the best of medicines.

It is so desolate here. I am so weary of the company of men. I long to be with you, my Elizabeth. I want to see you, even if it has to be from across the room. You are the one thing in my life that has given me joy. I wish I could offer you some words of comfort, but I have no idea how long it will take before I am finally free of my obligation. Yes, you are right in saying I am imprisoned by my duty. I am fully aware that it was done entirely by my own hand. Don't believe the things you hear at the Winthrop house. I promise you, I will be free again. I will be free, and wherever you are, I will come to you.

Thomas

Abiah put the pages back into the book carefully and with some difficulty. Her hands were trembling. She sat there, staring at nothing. She needed to sort out what all this meant, but her mind simply would not cooperate. She could hear her heart pounding in her ears. The book slid from her hands and landed with a thud on the bare wood floor.

Chapter Seven

Not again, Abiah kept thinking. *Please.*

But she had been through this enough times to recognize what was happening to her. She had a fever again. Her head pounded with it. She couldn't concentrate. Strange, disjointed thoughts came from nowhere and stayed.

The truth shall set you free.

No—the truth shall set Thomas free. The truth... It's not as if you didn't know the way of things, my dear Abiah. He thought you were dying—and you didn't cooperate.

"Abiah, listen to me," Dr. Nethen insisted.

No, thank you, she thought, perhaps said. She didn't want to listen. She never listened. She had made it her life's calling *not* to listen. All these days since the wedding she'd passed the time daring to imagine what a life with Thomas might be like. And now she knew. It was one thing to fear that he would one day despise her because of the circumstances of their marriage, and quite another to know that by surviving, she had kept him from Elizabeth Channing.

She made an anguished sound as she tried not to remember the things he had written in his letter.

"What happened after I left?" the doctor said. "She hasn't had another set-to with the judge, has she?"

"No, sir," a different voice said.

Bonnie. Bonnie had come to put her back to bed.

"Judge Winthrop's in Washington until Saturday, sir."

"Has anyone been feeding her the wrong things?"

"No, sir! Nothing but what you wrote down for Cook."

"She hasn't been overly exerting herself or been upset by anything? She didn't get bad news about Thomas, did she?"

"No, sir. Everything is just the same as it's been— except Miss Elizabeth came to call, but she weren't here long. Mrs. Harrigan seen to that."

"I see. Where is Mrs. Harrigan?"

"Gone into St. Michaels herself to fetch some things for the dinner party tonight, sir. I don't know when she will get back here."

"All right, we're going to have to—"

There was some commotion and the door to the hallway suddenly opened.

"Who the hell are you?" Dr. Nethen demanded.

"Who wants to know?" Gertie asked calmly.

"Gertie?" Abiah said. She tried to sit up and couldn't. She tried to turn her head to see, but it hurt too much. "Gertie...?"

"It's me, Miss Abiah," Gertie said, her voice closer now. "It took me a while, but I got here—what have you people done to her?" A cool hand suddenly touched the side of Abiah's face. "This is not how she was when she left Falmouth."

"Young woman, I suggest you take yourself downstairs right now—"

"Look!" Gertie said. "I was hired by Captain Harrigan to take care of Miss Abiah, and I ain't been told no different. I reckon I'm here to stay. What are you people wasting time for? She needs sponging to get that fever down—anybody can see that. Show me where I can find some water and some cloths—"

"Gertie, don't go!" Abiah cried in alarm.

"It's all right, Miss Abiah. You rest easy. I'll be right back. Well, girl—whoever you are—did you hear what I said?"

"Yes, ma am," Bonnie answered. "But Dr. Nethen didn't—"

"Go get what she needs, Bonnie," Dr. Nethen said. "You say you looked after Abiah in Falmouth?"

"I did. I was with her from the night Captain Harrigan stole her across the Rappahannock—until that lawyer took her off without me. But I'm here now and I intend to stay."

"You've talked to Captain Harrigan?"

"No. He's in camp and civilians can't go in there. And him nor none of the rest of the soldiers can come out. But I told you. He hired me, and as far as I'm concerned, I'm still hired until I hear different—from *him*."

"Oh, I have no objections. It's Abiah here who has the last word."

Abiah tried to sit up again. "Zachariah Wilson—he didn't—"

"Now we aren't going to go worrying about him, Miss Abiah. You hear? That's all water under the bridge."

"You're not to blame—"

"Right you are, Miss Abiah—but we're *not* talking about it now and I mean it. We're going to work on getting you feeling better. So, Dr. whatever-your-name-is—"

"Nethen," the doctor said.

"Dr. Nethen—are you thinking it's the sickness come back new, or is it just that fever people get sometimes when they're just about well and they get too big for their britches?"

"Ah, the latter, I believe," the doctor said. "I believe it's a recrudescence, not a true relapse."

"Well, good. Let's hope you know what you're talking about. A couple days will tell the tale, I reckon. Do you think I could get something to eat around here? It's been a while since I had the chance to feed my face, I can tell you."

"I'll have Bonnie bring up a tray."

"You can do that? Just wave your hand and somebody brings a tray?"

"I can," he assured her. "I can have this room cleared, too, if I think it's necessary."

"Well, it ain't. Miss Abiah is going to be getting better with me here."

But "Miss Abiah" didn't want to get better—and said so.

"Well, I can see right now it's a good thing I came," Gertie said. "Feeling sorry for ourselves, are we?" She took the basin of water Bonnie brought in and immediately set to work, ignoring Abiah's wants about that, too.

"Are you sure you understand what needs to be done?" the doctor asked, and Gertie gave a sharp sigh.

"Her skin is hot. I am going to give it a brisk rub with this wet cloth. Then I'm going to wait. The skin'll feel cool after a bit and then it'll get hot again. When it does, I'm going to start all over. Unless you got a better plan, Dr. Nethen."

"No, I believe that will work nicely. I'll leave you to it, then. If you need me, tell Bonnie here. She knows how to find me."

"Now what is the matter with you?" Gertie said as soon as everyone had gone. "And I don't mean the fever."

"I shouldn't have gotten married," Abiah said listlessly. The cool cloth on her face and arms was both a relief and a nuisance.

"Oh, is that all." Gertie flapped the wet cloth in the air to make it even colder.

"It's enough."

"Enough for what? For you to go belly-up and let all my hard work go for nothing? I'm beginning to know how Pete felt. He said your Thomas was about the worst excuse for an officer he ever seen—at first. Pete said it was hard work bringing him along, but it was worth it, and he wasn't about to let anything happen to him if he could help it. I reckon that's about the way I feel about you. I owe you, Miss Abiah. Ain't nobody ever done for me what you did, and I ain't letting anything happen to you. You understand me?''

"No," Abiah said stubbornly.

"Shame on you, Miss Abiah. Tell a *lie*…''

Gertie sounded so aggrieved that Abiah couldn't help but smile.

"There now," Gertie said. "You see? It ain't all that bad if you can laugh about it. Now what did our darling Captain Harrigan do?''

"Nothing.''

"Then what did he *not* do?''

"Gertie, I don't want to talk about this—''

"Well, that's too bad. How am I going to know what needs doing if I ain't got the particulars?''

"There's nothing to be done.''

"That ain't so. There's always *something* to be done. Like right now. We're going to get you better—get you up and about. Your mind gets to telling you all kinds of silly things when your body can't go no place.''

Gertie didn't say anything else, and neither did Abiah. She gave herself up to Gertie's ablutions instead. She was far too unhappy to do anything else.

"She's so beautiful," Abiah murmured after a time.

"Who?''

"Elizabeth Channing.''

"Is she the reason you're acting like this?''

"She's beautiful," Abiah insisted.

"So what? I'm beautiful, too," Gertie said. "So are you. But I don't see nobody up and leaving this world on account of it. And just because this Elizabeth Channing's beautiful self wants Thomas ain't no reason for you to let her have him."

"It's not what *she* wants. It's what Thomas wants—if that happened to be the problem—which it is not."

"Well, for the sake of curiosity, how do you know what Thomas wants?"

"I read it in his letter—to her."

"How in the world did you get a hold of that, you being the shut-in invalid and everything?"

"I found it in my book."

"Uh-huh. Ain't that kind of a strange place for him to keep letters to another woman? In *your* book?"

"Elizabeth Channing gave the book to me. *The Woman In White*. It's all the rage in London."

"Uh-*huh*. And this book that's all the rage just happened to have the captain's letter in it. And you just happened to find it. Then you read this letter, I guess, and now you just happen to be all undone about it and giving yourself a fever. You been bushwhacked, Miss Abiah. That Channing girl is good, I'll give her that. Or bad, depending on how you look at it. And you—you need a hickory stick taken to your backside if you let her get away with it. Just look at you. It's bad enough you've made yourself sick. Now you're wanting to cry about it, too. I don't know why I'm even bothering—"

"Gertie, I don't know what to do!"

"What you *do* is get better. Fast. You get yourself

up out of that bed and you start taking some pride in who you are. Thomas married you, didn't he? Can't nobody deny you was in need of marrying, but you didn't exactly make it easy for him. He didn't give up on the notion just because you told him no, did he? You gave him the chance to get out of it. I reckon he knew what he wanted, and if he's a little confused about it now, well, you just have to get him straightened out, that's all. It's up to you to show everybody around here *he's* the one that ought to be thanking his lucky stars he's got you—not the other way around. How's he going to know you're worth having if you don't act like it?"

"What if I do that and he still doesn't know it?"

"Well, then, I'll find you another revolver and you can shoot him in the earlobe like you did Zachariah Wilson."

This time Abiah laughed out loud, in spite of her misery. She was so glad, suddenly, that Gertie was here.

"Lord almighty, what is *that?*" Gertie asked of the singing that suddenly started up in the music room downstairs.

"That's the soprano warming up for the party this evening."

"Lord almighty," Gertie said again. "You reckon she sounds like that on purpose?"

Abiah's letters abruptly stopped coming. Thomas didn't worry at first, because the mail was unpredictable. He kept dismissing the delay as yet another war-

time inefficiency, because the expected weekly letter
from his mother hadn't arrived, either. But he was convinced now that something was wrong, something he
perhaps should have seen coming.

He took great pains to reread everything Abiah had
written to him, looking for some indication
of…something. He didn't quite know what. A wors-
ening of her condition, he supposed. There had been
a slight shakiness in her handwriting in the beginning,
but that had completely disappeared. She had been
perfectly coherent at all times. In fact, her letters were
wonderful. In each one she took him back to a place
and a time they both missed and cherished. And in
each one she made him recognize something he hadn't
really noticed before.

Abiah Calder.

No. He must have noticed in order to remember the
details about her so acutely now. He definitely remembered the waltz. He remembered dancing her around
and around the candlelit parlor. All of the furniture
had been pushed back to make room, and he'd kept
staring at her soft, slightly parted lips and wondering
whether or not she had ever been kissed.

Thomas smiled slightly to himself. *He* had been
wondering about kissing, while *she*—Lord knows
what she had been wondering. And the possibilities
had taken over his daytime and his nighttime fantasies.
He couldn't think about anything but her. La Broie
had caught him more than once supposedly "wool-
gathering," and neither he nor anyone else in the com-

pany believed for a moment that Captain Harrigan's mind had been on anything even remotely military.

But *something* was wrong and perhaps had been wrong the whole time. For one thing, Abiah never mentioned anything in her letters that he had written to her previously. All his questions were blatantly ignored. At first he put it down to some peculiarity of her illness. He had thought that perhaps she didn't want to address his ramblings about the painful and unsettled present. Perhaps she only wanted the quietude of the past.

His mother had reported in the last letter he'd received from her that Abiah was definitely progressing—that she was able to be out of bed for longer and longer every day, that she was following the doctor's orders carefully. The judge, on the other hand, was "himself," she wrote. Unfortunately, Thomas knew exactly what that meant.

But he couldn't get home to see about any of it. There had been yet another change in command, and with it, all the resultant "new" ways of doing things. Joseph Hooker had managed to get control of the Army of the Potomac, after all. Thus far, Thomas was guardedly hopeful. If nothing else, Fighting Joe had gotten the stockpile of provisions out of the commissaries and into the ranks. The sutlers were back, and he'd even lifted the ban on civilian "laundresses." And unless Thomas was seriously mistaken, the current quota underfoot far exceeded the regulation four.

A soldier could now get a halfway decent meal, a drink of whiskey or a warm body most anytime he wanted it. What he couldn't get was a furlough, especially if he happened to be a recalcitrant Massachusetts captain of infantry who was already on the wrong side of the powers that be. Thomas tried to keep his mind on the job at hand. There was a lot to be done. Warm weather was coming and Hooker clearly had his eyes on Richmond. Once again, Thomas didn't have much time left to see Abiah before he went marching off to war, and once again his commanding officers were completely unsympathetic.

"Maybe you could ask your grandfather to pull some strings for you, Cap," La Broie suggested one afternoon when Thomas was feeling particularly morose.

"Maybe you could mind your own damn business," Thomas advised him. How La Broie knew that going with his hat in his hand to the judge was a possible solution to his problem was beyond him.

"Yes, sir," La Broie said.

The sergeant also added a comment Thomas didn't hear clearly, but he chose to ignore it. "How much time do you think we've got until Hooker marches us out?" he asked abruptly.

"From what I'm hearing, I'd say maybe a month, sir. Maybe less if Massa Robert opens the ball first."

"I've got to get to Maryland."

"Yes, sir, Cap. But you ain't going to wear down Major Gibbons. He ain't going to let you do it officially and you can't go any other way. Not without getting court-martialed, not to mention shot or hanged for it. And I ain't wanting to give Miss Abiah that kind of news, am I?''

Thomas didn't answer. He could ask the judge to pull some strings. He *could,* but he wouldn't.

"Mail's here, Cap," La Broie announced, and Thomas nodded. He could already see the rider coming in their direction—and taking his own sweet time about it, because he was stopping to talk to everybody he knew along the way. Everybody female.

"Hurry that dandy along, La Broie," Thomas said after a moment.

"Yes, sir, Cap. My pleasure."

The exchange between the sergeant and the less-than-speedy letter carrier was noisy and something to behold. La Broie really did have a fine repertoire of colorful metaphors. He was back with the bulging leather pouch almost immediately.

"Summon the boys," Thomas said, unnecessarily. The company had heard the exchange and was already forming. He stood aside to let La Broie give the letters out, waiting to hear his own name called like the rest of them. There was no reason whatsoever why he couldn't, as an officer, take his own mail out first and let everyone else wait while he did it, but he chose not to. It was a precedent he had set early on, because he'd thought it would help establish some kind of loyalty, however minimal, for his men to see their captain not taking a privilege at their expense. He hadn't minded waiting before; now it was agony.

He smoked a cigar. He helped La Broie decipher

some poorly addressed envelopes from time to time. He waited.

"Captain Harrigan," La Broie said finally, handing him a letter.

Thomas took it without looking at it, knowing everybody was all too aware that he hadn't heard from his wife. He stuck it into his pocket. Even after the men had dispersed and gone, he took the time to finish his cigar.

Then he went inside his shelter. A spider had already strung its web in a place just right for Thomas to walk into. It was too dark to see, and he lit a candle stub.

The letter was from his mother.

"My dear son," it began.

"…I really am surprised at you. You wife simply will not write to you again, no matter how much I try to prevail upon her to do so, and I can't say I blame her. Couldn't you make some effort to correspond with at least one of us? Are you kept so busy that you are unable to pen even one line…?

"What?" he said out loud, knowing La Broie was probably somewhere close enough to hear him.

He went back to reading.

…Abiah is very much improved since Gertie arrived…

"What?" he said again, and this time there was a definite rustling outside the door. He ignored it.

...Abiah is well enough to sometimes sit in the gallery to hear the music played during the salons. All the convalescent soldiers who attend the performances make much of having her there, even if she doesn't actually socialize. She is a great favorite among them, and they watch eagerly to see if she will make an appearance. Sarah Mayron's son, Charlie, who is still home recuperating from the terrible wounds he received at New Bern, is very smitten. This Saturday past he managed to get some forsythia from somewhere and place it, with the help of his comrades, at the foot of the gallery stairway for Abiah. He is very young, but it was still a gallant gesture on his part, one meant to compliment her but not to intrude upon her delicate health or her loyalty to the Confederacy and Virginia. It was also a gesture many another soldier wished he had thought of himself. I'm afraid all the other young ladies present were very envious indeed. In their eyes, Charlie is the poor wounded, languishing knight of yore, offering with his last breath to champion a beautiful lady...

"The hell he is," Thomas said.

"Cap'?" La Broie said from outside.

"What!"

"Messenger coming."

Thomas skimmed the rest of the letter and put it back into his pocket. Thank God there were no more startling announcements. Now if he could just understand the thing. Abiah was apparently all right—or better, at least—but she wouldn't—*wouldn't*—write to him. And Charlie Mayron had damn well better be keeping his forsythia to himself.

The messenger arrived with a good deal more swiftness and purpose than the letter carrier had.

"Captain Harrigan, sir," he said. "This was left for you at headquarters. I believe it may be urgent."

Thomas took the envelope; his name and company were written on the front. He didn't recognize the handwriting. He removed the single sheet of paper inside. The message was succinct and to the point.

"Your lady is waiting in Falmouth."

Chapter Eight

"Bender's asking to see you, sir," La Broie said.

Thomas ignored him.

"I think you should talk to the boy, Cap."

Thomas continued to sit at the upturned barrel that passed for his camp table. He had enough problems of his own. He didn't want to have to deal with anyone else's. He needed to think. He had to figure out some way—

"He's been waiting outside a long time, sir."

Thomas gave a sharp sigh. "Well, get him in here, damn it!"

Bender rushed in before La Broie could give him leave, and for once he didn't look scared to death. In fact, he looked exactly like what he probably was—a mischievous boy with a tale to tell.

"What is it, Bender?"

"Sir, I think I know how to do it."

"Do what?"

"Get you into Falmouth without the pickets knowing it."

"How the devil did you know about…" Thomas glanced at La Broie. "Never mind. Tell me."

"There's a path that cuts across the railroad tracks—see, there's high banks on both sides for a ways. The path runs behind the banks. The pickets can't see you either way, except when you cross the railroad. You just got to keep an eye open and hotfoot it to the other side the minute you get the chance."

"I take it you've been hotfooting it on a fairly frequent basis."

"Well, uh, sir…" He glanced at La Broie. "You see, Cap, I got me a awful sweet tooth. I been that way ever since I was a kid. And I been sort of going into town to the confectionery. The store there—they don't charge me a arm and a leg like the sutlers do, even if I am in the wrong army. I didn't figure it would hurt nothing, Cap. It don't take me long. I always get back pretty quick. Nobody knowed about it or nothing—except Sergeant La Broie, I reckon. Somehow he knowed."

"It's his business to know, Bender," Thomas said.

"Yes, sir. Now that I think about it, I reckon it is."

"So you think you can get me into town."

"Yes, sir, Cap. The way I figure it, I'll go first when we cross the railroad tracks—"

"No, I think one deserter at a time is enough. You just tell me how to go."

"I can't tell it, sir. Alls I can do is *do* it."

"You can draw me a map."

"I could do that, sir, but you wouldn't be able to tell hide nor hair from it. There ain't no landmarks and I ain't no map drawer. Everybody that knows me knows that. All I can do is go and show you. And I'm thinking, Cap, maybe you won't want to waste the time making me draw you a map anyway, because you're going to see right off you can't use it. If we skip all that, it'll save you yelling at me and everything. Seems to me like we ought to just go, before the moon comes up—sir,'' he added, apparently in case he'd been too impertinent.

"I'm going alone. I'll stick out like a sore thumb as it is—''

"No, sir, Cap. We wouldn't be the only soldiers in town. There's lots of them around for one reason or another. Most of them is message runners and the like, and they got leave to be there. Ain't nobody going to know we ain't one of them, if we just mind our own business. I reckon them town people is used to seeing me, anyway.''

"How many times have you been into Falmouth, Bender?''

"I don't like to say, sir,'' he said, looking at the short tree limbs that had been cut and trimmed and put down to ''corduroy'' the mud floor.

Thomas drew a quiet breath. *This is insane,* he thought. But he was going to do it. Or at least try. He wasn't even sure where Abiah was, but he was sure she was in Falmouth. He had to go. "La Broie, I want you to stay here and mind the store—''

"Sir—''

"Don't interrupt me, damn it! I want you to cover our flank if anybody comes looking for me. You're the best liar I've got if Gibbons decides he needs me for something—"

"Sir—"

"I'm expecting a replacement officer to arrive tonight," Thomas continued. "A lieutenant, and it's going to take your expertise to explain why I'm not here—"

"Sir—"

"Damn it all, what?"

La Broie looked at him a moment, then sighed. "What exactly do you want done with him, Cap?"

"I'm sure you'll think of something. If this plan goes awry, I guess you can tell him he's the company's new commanding officer."

Thomas removed his saber and hung it on a nail in one of the pine pole supports. Then he checked his revolver to make sure all the chambers were full. "All right, Bender, lead the way."

"Yes, sir!"

Thomas glanced at La Broie. He had on his "mind how you go" face, but for once he didn't say it.

The evening was cold enough, but not unbearable. They crossed to the perimeter of the camp quickly and headed directly into the pine woods, breaking into a run the minute they were out of sight. Bender was hell to keep up with in the waning light, but Thomas wasn't about to tell him to slow down. The boy certainly appeared to know where he was going. In no time at all they reached the railroad cut.

But Thomas hadn't expected the pickets to be so close to the place where they would have to cross. He could hear them talking, could smell the wood smoke from their fire.

He caught Bender by the sleeve to keep him from blundering into them, but the boy held his fingers to his lips. Bender scrambled up to the top of the embankment for a moment, then slid back down again.

"Our luck's holding, Cap. Somebody's just bribed them with a bottle," he whispered.

"Bender, do you mean to tell me we're sneaking around like this when we could have bribed our way into Falmouth with a bottle of whiskey?"

"No, sir! Those men are from a Maine regiment. They ain't about to take a bottle from no Boston, Massachusetts captain. They'd think you was just trying to catch them at something so's you could send them to the stockade. We have to do it this way."

"We're too close to them here—"

"No, sir. It's the only place we can get through. There's vines and thickets all up and down the bank in both directions. We'd get all hung up and they'd hear us for sure. This is how you do it, sir. You make sure you see the bottle going around—they're all interested in getting their turn at that. Then you go. Step on the cross ties, not on the gravel and not on the rails. It'll make too much racket if you do, understand?"

Thomas understood. Instead of La Broie, he was now taking orders from a boy private. And it must be a treasonable offense to be this happy that Union army sentries were getting drunk on duty.

"Now, sir," Bender said. "I'm going. If I don't make it, you come out and say you was chasing me because I belong to you and I was skeedaddling—and if you don't make it, you say the same thing. The path picks up again on the other side of that bank over there, and I'm going to go pretty far down it before I stop. I'll catch you when you go by.''

Thomas nodded. *If I go by,* he thought.

Bender immediately scrambled up the embankment again, hesitating only a moment before he disappeared. Thomas followed. He lay on his belly on the cold ground at the top, watching the pickets through the branches of scrub pine, trying to think of something in his experience that this was even remotely like. There wasn't anything.

The men were talking now. And talking. They had a fire built off to the side of the tracks and the smoke was blowing in Thomas's direction. He could see almost immediately that Bender had been correct in his appraisal of the situation. There was a bottle, and there was somebody in charge of the bottle. And he wasn't being particularly generous.

Somebody protested. Somebody else protested louder. And when the bottle began to move again, so did Thomas, trying not to slide too fast or too noisily down to the rail bed, then running like hell when he reached the tracks. He expected every second to hear rifle fire behind him, and he didn't stop until he was well into the woods on the other side. He wasn't really sure whether he was still on the path or not. He kept going; he didn't dare call out.

"Cap! This way, Cap," Bender whispered fiercely behind him, and Thomas whirled around. "You did good, Cap,'' Bender took the time to add before he ran off toward the town.

Thomas could see already see the lights of the houses in Falmouth.

''Bender!'' he called as loudly as he dared. ''Bender!''

''Cap?'' the boy said, backtracking immediately.

''Is there a hotel?''

''There's this big old place they call a hotel, but I don't think it was one until we got here, sir. I think it might a been a boarding school or something like that. The dining room's got a blackboard on the wall.''

''Where is it?''

''It's on the main street, Cap. You can find it easy. You think your lady's there?''

''I don't know where the hell she is.''

''Well, sir, if she ain't at the hotel, I can help you look other places. We'll find her.''

Thomas smiled slightly at Bender's earnest optimism. But he didn't say anything. He didn't want to invite any more interest in his personal life than he could help. He wondered idly what the penalty for involving a boy private in his second flagrant disregard for military discipline might be.

They reached the outskirts of town, where they slowed to a more sedate and hopefully less conspicuous walk. Very few citizens seemed to be out and about in the immediate vicinity. The sun was gone completely now, and the air had turned colder.

''Hospital, sir,'' Bender said unnecessarily as they passed a particular two-story house with a low iron fence around it. Every window was shut tight against the winter evening, but occasionally the cries of the men inside still drifted out to the street. Thomas already knew about this place. It was one of many where he'd gone begging shelter for Abiah that rainy night when he'd brought her back across the river.

They turned a corner onto the main street.

"That's the hotel down there, Cap," Bender said, pointing to a two-story brick building with a big front porch held up by iron columns.

"Where's the confectionery?"

"On a ways past the hotel—on this side of the street."

"Here," Thomas said, reaching into his pocket and giving him two nickel cent pieces. "Wait for me there—or is it closed now?"

"Mary Ann—she'll open it up for me. She lives over the store—her pa owns it. She'll open it for me if she sees me."

"Mary Ann, is it?"

"Yes, sir, Cap. But you don't have to give me no money. I reckon she'll let me in without it."

"Bender," Thomas said, trying not to smile. "I'm beginning to see the reason for all this derring-do of yours. Take the money. You'll want to help Mary Ann's family all you can if she's worth this much trouble."

"Yes, sir, Cap," he said, embarrassed—but not embarrassed enough to deny the logic of the argument. He suddenly grinned. "I thought you was going to tease me, Cap. You know—'Bender's got a sweet-heart.' Something like that.''

"No, Bender. I'm not much for teasing."

"Yes, sir, and I'm glad of it, I can tell you. Some of the boys—they're good boys, most of them, but they really know how to make a fellow's life miserable over this sweetheart business."

"I can imagine," Thomas said, thinking that re-gardless of the hard time, Bender remained undeterred. He still, at significant personal risk, came into town to see the confectioner's daughter.

Bender sighed. "She's got two brothers and a cousin with Old Stonewall Jackson. I reckon you know how *that* is. Cap, what will you do if your lady ain't at the hotel?''

"Then I'll have to reconnoiter. See if you can find out from Mary Ann where Zachariah Wilson is while you're waiting."

"I'll do that, Cap."

Thomas left Bender and crossed the muddy street. There was much more activity in this part of town. The military was very much in evidence, as Bender had reported. Thomas made a point of nodding to the ladies he encountered along the way in the hope that it would make him look less guilty.

The hotel was bigger than he first thought, and he decided that Bender was correct about it once having been some kind of school. It certainly looked like a school. He supposed that the war had dried up the student enrollment, and some enterprising soul had seen the wisdom of taking up innkeeping in an area that seemed to be permanently occupied by two armies.

The inside of the hotel smelled of cooked cabbage. Thomas could see a few scattered pieces of furniture and a battered piano in what passed for the lobby. There seemed to be a host of people on the ground floor, either coming or going or simply standing around. He finally spotted a large woman who seemed to be the person in charge. She was seated at a desk in the wide front hallway.

"Excuse me," Thomas said, to make her look up. "Is Mrs. Harrigan—"

"Captain Harrigan!" she exclaimed, causing any number of heads to turn. "You are he, are you not?"

"Ah…yes, I am."

"At last! We—all of us ladies—thought you couldn't leave camp!"

"Well, I…only just got the message that my wife is here," Thomas said, lowering his voice in the hopes that she would take the hint.

She didn't. "Oh, but she's not here," she boomed.

"What do you mean, she's not here? Where is she?"

"Oh, dear. I said it wrong. I meant to say she's not here *now*. She's been invited to supper at the home of one of the local ladies. I'm afraid I don't know where exactly—but she should return any time now."

"She's well enough to go out?" he asked, his mind busy worrying the fact that in all these years he hadn't realized that his mother was given to such understatement. Somehow he hadn't equated Abiah's being recovered enough to sit in the gallery and listen to music with her actually being able to accept someone's invitation to supper.

"Yes, of course," the woman said. "She seems perfectly fine, Captain. Will you wait in the room for her or…" She was clearly open to suggestions, but he had none. He just wanted to get away from all the curious attention he could feel boring into his back.

"I…yes," Thomas answered. "Yes," he said again, wondering why she was smiling so.

"It's a *very* fine room. Mrs. Morse and Mrs. January have doubled up so that you and Mrs. Harrigan could have some privacy—oh, it's just so exciting. Torn apart by this terrible war the moment you were married—and to think *my* hotel shall play a part in the honeymoon!"

"Yes, well," Thomas said, clearing his throat and trying not to look as abashed as he was. This penchant complete strangers had to keep commenting on the circumstances of his marriage never ceased to amaze him. "If you'll direct me, then?"

The woman launched herself from behind the desk, still beaming. "Just follow me, Captain Harrigan. Follow me!"

Thomas mentally stepped over the ashes of his hopes to remain anonymous and followed the hotel woman and her torch upstairs. His visit to Falmouth would probably be in the town's newspaper tomorrow—or there would be a notation on the dining room blackboard at the very least.

"I understand you are a Maryland boy," the woman said as they climbed the stairs.

"I...yes," he said, deciding to agree. Regardless of Abiah's teasing, the proprietress hadn't noted his Boston accent or that he was in a Massachusetts regiment—and he certainly didn't want to have to explain it.

"I have relatives on the Eastern Shore myself—well, actually they are my late husband's kin. A beautiful place, don't you think?"

"Indeed," he said.

The place smelled like a school, with chalk and india ink all mixed in with the cabbage, he decided as he walked with her down the second-floor hallway. The room vacated by the matrons Morse and January was at the end of the hall. The woman knocked lightly—in case Abiah had returned and had somehow sneaked by her, Thomas supposed. After a moment she unlocked the door and led the way inside, lighting a lamp on the rickety dresser with a great flourish. Thomas only half heard what she said—something about the room being her best.

"Yes, it will do very nicely indeed," he responded—appropriately, he hoped.

The woman smiled broadly. "I'll be on my way then, Captain."

"Excuse me, Mrs..."

"Post," she said, still smiling.

"Mrs. Post, if anyone comes looking for me, would you be able in good conscience to say you haven't seen me?"

"Oh, *that* goes without saying, Captain," she assured him. "I shall keep your presence here very dark indeed. While I'm at it, shall I let you surprise dear Mrs. Harrigan with your arrival?"

"Ah…yes," he decided.

Happy now, the woman finally left him in peace. He stood in the middle of the room, wondering what to do. He couldn't stay here long. If Abiah didn't come soon, he'd have to leave without seeing her—that is, if Mrs. Post would let him.

The room was cold. There was a fireplace with a coal grate, but no coal. He doubted if there was any coal in the entire town.

The lamp began to smoke, and he adjusted the wick. Then he wandered aimlessly around the room, sidestepping the one straight chair. It, too, had seen better days. The upholstery on the seat was faded and threadbare. There were no brushes or personal items on the dresser. In fact, the room might as well have been unoccupied for all the evidence he could see of Abiah's having been here.

He gave a quiet sigh. As he recalled, Abiah didn't have very many personal items now to display, and it occurred to him that, as her husband, he needed to do something about that.

He looked around the shabby room again. He still didn't understand her being here. The only thing he was certain about was how much he wanted to see her.

He took a deep breath. He was used to living in what amounted to the out-of-doors, and in spite of the coldness of the room, he was feeling closed in. He was about to try to open the window when he heard someone outside in the hall. The doorknob rattled briefly, and the door opened.

"Abby?" he said, crossing the room to meet her. "Abby, I—" He stopped dead, completely disbelieving. "My God, what are you doing here?"

Elizabeth Channing smiled her very best smile. "Obviously, Thomas, I'm here to see you."

"Where is Abiah? Did she come with you?"

"Of course she didn't come with me, silly."

"Elizabeth, where is Abiah?"

"How should I know?"

"The woman downstairs told me that my wife was here."

Elizabeth smiled the smile he had once thought relentlessly appealing, the coy, mischievous one that so often preceded one of her carefully doled out favors. A kiss. A hand on her basque or her knee.

"You have actually told people here that *you* are Mrs. Harrigan?" he asked, still incredulous and still trying to understand.

"What if I did? I had to protect my reputation."

He didn't say anything and her smile abruptly faded.

"How could you do it, Thomas? How could you marry someone else?"

"How? Elizabeth, you sent me a letter. You broke the engagement."

"Oh, for heaven's sake, Thomas! I didn't expect you to *believe* it. Cordelia Major's fiancé certainly didn't believe her when she wrote the same to him. *He* came immediately to her side just to change her mind—''

''Elizabeth, this country is at war! You do remember that?''

''Cordelia's fiancé didn't find the war a particular obstacle.''

''Cordelia's fiancé is an errand boy for some Washington political appointee at the War Department. He's not on the front lines. Believe me, the generals out here take a dim view of men leaving the ranks to go court some woman—particularly when a battle is about to start. Now tell me. Where is Abiah?''

''Thomas, you are very tiresome—and I am not *some* woman.''

''Is she all right? I haven't heard anything.''

''Have you not? You'd think she'd make more of an effort to write to *you,* after all. She finds the time to write to a Major John Miller, I believe. And you, of course, have been such a faithful correspondent.''

Once again, words completely failed him.

''You look so perplexed, Thomas. It's all very simple. I love you.''

He laughed, in spite of his growing bewilderment. ''My dear Elizabeth, if you loved me so much, you would never, *ever* have written a letter like that.''

''I didn't think you would misunderstand!''

He could only look at her, amazed that she was entirely serious. And he finally voiced the thing he had known all along. ''If you had loved me, you would

never have insisted that we keep the engagement secret.''

"That was my father's doing. *He* is the one who
insisted."

"Why?"

"Because he didn't know if you were..."

"Were what?" he persisted.

She gave a sharp sigh. "Financially able to support
me in the way I am accustomed to living."

"You already knew I couldn't. You *said* you didn't
mind."

"My father minded—and he thought some attempt
should be made to convince the judge that you should
receive your inheritance."

"I would love to have been a fly on the wall for
that. Did he ask you to break it off?"

She came closer and laid her hand on his arm. "No,
Thomas."

He didn't believe her, and he immediately pulled
away.

"Thomas, there's no reason why we couldn't live
in my father's house."

"No reason?" he asked incredulously.

"Do you think I would be here if I didn't love
you?"

"It's a little late in the day, don't you think?"

She was taking off her jacket. She laid it over the
back of the chair and began unbuttoning her basque.

"Elizabeth—"

"I love you, Thomas. I'll do whatever it takes to
prove it."

She held the basque aside. She was more beautiful than he remembered. His eyes went to the soft swell of her breasts above her chemise. He could just see her nipples through the eyelet lace.

She stepped closer. "I'm not wearing corsets, Thomas—"

"Elizabeth, I am married," he said with his last ounce of control.

"It's not a *real* marriage. Everybody says that."

"Do they?"

"Yes! You thought she was dying and you are an honorable man. You wanted her to think her reputation was saved. I understand what you did, Thomas, and I forgive you."

"I have no wish to be forgiven."

She reached for him. "Thomas, my father can help you."

"I don't need help, Elizabeth." He meant to take her by the shoulders so that he could step away from her, but she saw it as a capitulation, and she was clinging to him then, her arms sliding around his neck, her mouth pressing fervent little kisses against his cheek, his chin.

"Elizabeth, for God's sake—"

He couldn't do this—*wouldn't* do this.

"Elizabeth, don't..." he said, still trying to loosen her grip on him. But he didn't mean it and she knew it. The scent of her, the feel of her ripped through him. His mouth came down hard on hers and his hand slid to her breast.

"Cap," someone said from the doorway.

He stiffened and thrust Elizabeth away from him. She gave a soft cry and grabbed up her jacket and held it in front of her. The door had been left ajar, and La Broie stood there. La Broie and Bender.

Thomas didn't say anything. He didn't owe either of them an explanation. The only person he would have to explain this to was Abiah.

Abiah.

"We got to go, Cap," his sergeant said finally, carefully ignoring Elizabeth, who stood huddled with her back to him. "The provost marshal and a detail of his men are out, sir. They're going door-to-door, checking passes. We ain't got much time."

"Very well," he said, trying to calm his breathing. "Wait for me downstairs."

La Broie hesitated. He glanced at Elizabeth, but he didn't say anything. Bender kept shifting self-consciously from one foot to the other.

"Downstairs, Sergeant," Thomas said again. Regardless of how it looked, he didn't need a chaperon.

Elizabeth reached for him the minute the door closed. "Thomas—"

"What have you told Abiah?" he asked, thrusting her hands aside. Abiah's sudden refusal to write to him made sense suddenly.

"Nothing—"

"You're a liar, Elizabeth. I just got a letter from my mother chastising me for not writing to her or Abiah. Yet *you* just called me a 'faithful correspondent.' How is it you know I'm sending letters home and my mother doesn't?"

She looked at him, but she didn't say anything.

"Does Abiah know about us?"

"Thomas—"

"Answer me, damn it!"

"Well, what if she does! It seems very strange to me that you hadn't even told her who I am."

"Abiah knows I was engaged. And she knows the engagement was broken. Beyond that—"

"Beyond that, I think you still have your hopes of marrying *me*. And I think she understands you only did it because you expected her to die."

He gave a quiet sigh and shook his head. Perhaps Abiah did believe that. Perhaps it had even been true—at first. But he hadn't been pining for Elizabeth Channing.

"Where does your father think you are?" he asked abruptly.

"In Washington—with Cordelia."

"Then I suggest you get yourself there as fast as you can."

"No, Thomas, I can wait here for you. I'll stay right here until you can come back—"

"No!" he said. "I have no intention of coming here again."

"Thomas, please! What will people say?"

"What people, Elizabeth? No one knew we were engaged…oh, I see. They did know. Then it must be very awkward for you now—having Cordelia and her friends think I forgot about you so easily and married somebody else. But that problem is yours, not mine. Whether it was with Cordelia cheering you on or not, you wrote the letter. *You.* My marriage may not be real to you, but I can assure you, it is real to me.''

He left her still clutching her jacket, and he heard her call him once after he'd stepped into the hall. La Broie and Bender stood waiting at the foot of the stairs, neither of them quite meeting his eye.

''Captain Harrigan! Oh, Captain Harrigan!'' Mrs. Post called, leaning across her desk as he walked briskly by. ''Did I say I should be going to Maryland soon...?''

He didn't stop, and his mind was in such turmoil, he barely remembered the trek back through the woods to the railroad cut. The pickets were on the alert now, and it took a long while for an opportunity to slip back into camp to present itself. La Broie finally had to move to a position above them and create a diversion in order for Thomas and Bender to get across.

Even so, La Broie arrived in camp only minutes after Thomas did. The sergeant busied himself immediately, his silence every bit as eloquent as when he'd chastised the indifferent mail carrier for dallying with the laundresses. Thomas took it as long as he could.

''La Broie,'' he said finally. ''If you've got something to say, damn you, say it.''

''I am sorry to be so wrong about a man,'' he replied without hesitation. ''And that's the God's truth. Sir,'' he added, the reproach heavy in his voice.

''This is none of your damn business.''

''No, sir. It ain't. Is that all, sir? I got that new lieutenant wandering around here someplace.''

"Fine. Dismissed," Thomas said—but he didn't quite catch whatever else La Broie felt he needed to add.

"Sergeant La Broie! What did you say?"

La Broie turned to look at him, his face unreadable. "I said, *sir,* better you had left that little girl sick to death in that freezing house."

Chapter Nine

Abiah walked carefully past the marble-topped table in the foyer. The mail had arrived, each letter carefully placed on a silver tray for the judge's perusal. She could read the addresses clearly. None of them was in Thomas's handwriting. None of them was for her.

Given the chance, she had no doubt that she would recognize anything written in his hand quite easily now. She was ashamed of how many times she had reread his letter to Elizabeth Channing. She couldn't seem to help herself, and she couldn't seem to part with it—when she should have shredded it and tossed it in the nearest fire.

She knew exactly why she hadn't. Because Thomas himself had written it. And even if it was meant for another person, it was the only thing of his she had. She had no hope of receiving word from him. None. She took some comfort from the fact that she wasn't dwelling on his lack of correspondence. Captain Appleby, the British sea captain who had brought the copies of *The Woman In White* from England, had

very graciously agreed to hand deliver Abiah's letter
to Miss Gwen the next time he shipped supplies to
New Bern. Abiah hoped that some contact with Miss
Gwen would make her feel less alone in the world.
Gertie's presence, lively though it was, hadn't reme-
died that awful, unprotected feeling of having no family to rely upon.

Which brought her to the *other* reason she'd come
downstairs. The judge had returned from his sudden
trip to Washington. It was amazing to Abiah the effect
the man's comings and goings had on the Winthrop
household. It was almost pleasant when he was away.
Mrs. Harrigan hummed as she went about her housekeeping duties. Bonnie and the rest of the servants
actually felt at ease enough to laugh out loud from
time to time. Abiah herself didn't have that feeling of
dread in the pit of her stomach anticipating having
another of their one-sided conversations. She had
come to understand Thomas's reluctance to be here. It
wasn't that the judge was violent or verbally abusive.
It was that he was never, ever satisfied. He was a mas-
ter at misinterpreting intentions and keeping everyone
perpetually off balance and in the wrong. She had
completely given up trying to please him.

First, he perceived her staying in her room, even
before she felt well enough to be up and about, as
overt rudeness on her part. It was her Rebel arrogance
and her disdain for the good people of Maryland—
what *must* they think of the Winthrops if she insisted
on behaving so? When Abiah sought to make some
small effort to appease him by sitting quietly in the

gallery and listening to the musical performers, she was then embarrassing him by provoking untoward comment and attention among the convalescent soldiers who attended. When she withdrew from that, she was deliberately trying to malign him in the eyes of his honored guests by making it seem as if *he* had refused her a simple pleasure. And while she might have liked to have devised all those ways to plague him, she had only just recently acquired strength and energy enough to do it—and *that* she had to save for their next encounter.

But today it was Gertie's turn. In the midst of the household preparations for yet another salon, he had commanded that Gertie bring herself to the library. Immediately. Gertie had gone along peacefully enough, but she was nothing if not irrepressible, and she did *not* suffer fools gladly. Abiah had no doubt that she would bite the hand that fed them—and bite it hard.

Abiah's second reason for coming down to the foyer had been to see if the meeting in the library was still in session. It was, and there was nothing for her to do but return upstairs. She left the door to her room ajar, anxiously hoping—praying—that she wouldn't hear any commotion from behind the library doors. She kept getting up and walking into the hallway to look over the gallery banister.

The third time she went, she caught a glimpse of Elizabeth Channing in the foyer, beautiful as always, walking into the drawing room with Mrs. Harrigan and chatting happily about her own recent jaunt to Washington. As far as Abiah knew this was the first time Elizabeth had been to the house since that rainy afternoon she'd made her so-called "visitation to the sick." Elizabeth certainly hadn't come to deliver any more baskets or books with surreptitious letters in them. Of course, tonight was the occasion of a particularly important salon. It would last the entire weekend, and according to Bonnie, half of Washington would make the ferry ride across Chesapeake Bay to be here.

The fourth time Abiah went to check on the meeting in the library, she saw Bonnie about to disappear down the back stairs.

"Wait," Abiah called after her as loudly as she dared. "Bonnie?"

"Yes, ma'am?"

"Is the judge still talking to Gertie?"

"No, ma'am. I think Gertie left."

Abiah frowned. "Left? For where?"

"Wherever the judge said to go, I guess."

Abiah stood there. "Bonnie…"

"I'm sorry, ma'am. That's all I know. Can I go see what Cook wants with me? She gets awful out of sorts if she has to wait."

"Yes, of course."

Abiah went back to her room, still frowning. Where could Gertie possibly go? Or more importantly, why would she leave without saying anything?

Abiah walked to the window and looked out. She immediately saw Gertie rapidly retreating down the gravel drive toward the main road. Abiah rapped sharply on the windowpane, but Gertie didn't hear her, so she grabbed up her shawl and hurried down the back stairs, nearly colliding with one of the kitchen maids on the bottom landing.

"So sorry," Abiah said, squeezing by her. She was already winded from the sudden exertion, but she kept going, through the kitchen and out the back door.

"Oh, ma'am, do take care," the girl called after her. "It's going to rain!"

There was, indeed, a thunderstorm coming. The sun was still shining in fits and starts, but there was a dark cloud to the west and the wind had picked up. Abiah grabbed up her skirts and hurried on, noting as she went that spring was almost here. The lawn was green now and the trees were beginning to bud. The roof of the Channing mansion was barely visible. How much better she would feel when she could look out the window and *not* see the place where Elizabeth Channing lived.

Abiah forced her thoughts back to the matter at hand.

"Gertie!" she called. "Gertie…!" Unless she was very mistaken, Gertie was deliberately ignoring her.

"Wait!" Abiah yelled, as loudly as she could. "Wait!"

This time Gertie stopped, but she didn't turn around. She stood ramrod straight in the middle of the gravel drive, waiting for Abiah to catch up with her. Even then, she didn't turn around. Abiah had to move in front of her to see her face.

"Where are you going?" she asked. "Didn't you hear me?"

Gertie didn't answer and wouldn't meet her eyes.

"All right, tell me," Abiah said. "What did the judge do?"

"The judge didn't do anything. I got to go. I got to take care of something. I don't know how long I'll be, so you can just go back to the house and mind your own business."

"No, thank you," Abiah said. "I think I'll go along with you."

"No, you can't."

"Then tell me what happened—"

"There ain't nothing to tell," Gertie said, walking again.

Abiah reached out and grabbed her by the arm, because she was too winded to keep running after her. She didn't even see the blow coming. Gertie whirled around and slapped her—hard.

Stunned, Abiah could only stare at her, her hand pressed to her cheek, her eyes watering.

"Nobody tells me what to do," Gertie said. "Nobody!"

Abiah had had many, *many* knockdown altercations with Guire in her time, and she still remembered how. "All right. If that's the way you want it." She returned the slap just as precipitously, making Gertie stagger.

"There's more where that came from," Abiah assured her. "If you think you're walking off from here without so much as a fare-you-well after what we've been through together, you are *very* mistaken!"

"Is that so!"

"It is!"

Gertie stepped around her and walked on.

"Gertie, please! Why can't you tell me?"

"Oh, I can tell you," she said over her shoulder. "It's simple. I'd rather have the money."

"What money? Do you mean you get money if you leave?"

"That's right!"

"What do you get if you stay?" Abiah called after her, again trying to keep up.

"I don't know what you mean."

"I mean I think there's more to this leaving business than you're saying. What did the judge threaten you with?"

"He didn't—"

"He did! I know you—and I know him. You wouldn't go without saying a word if he hadn't done something."

Gertie stopped walking. They both stood there, staring at each other. In the distance, beyond a row of budding, red maple trees, an impressive line of buggies and carriages rolled along the main road toward the front entrance of the Winthrop house. The ferry from Washington must have arrived early. The guests for the salon were already here.

The sun slid behind a dark cloud. Thunder rumbled in the distance.

"Tell me," Abiah said.

Gertie stubbornly shook her head.

"Tell me!"

"No!"

"Then I'll go ask the judge—"

"No, you won't. I'm not telling you anything! And I'm not letting *him* tell you, either! I'm going!" Gertie said. She wiped furtively at her eyes and started walking again.

"Maybe I already know," Abiah called after her.

"You don't know anything. What could somebody like you know about the way life really is? You're too damn delicate minded."

"I'm not as delicate minded as you think. I know about you. I know about your being with soldiers," Abiah said. "For money."

Gertie stopped walking.

"I heard things when I was so sick," Abiah continued. "Most of it's kind of vague, but I know what you *used* to be. I know why Zachariah Wilson thought he could just take you and you'd let him. And I remember what Sergeant La Broie said."

"What? You heard him come right out and say I was a army whore?"

"No," Abiah said pointedly. "I don't know where it was or when—I don't think he was even talking to me. But he said you were a good girl. And then, after the wedding, he asked me to take care of you—"

"He never!"

"He did! I asked him to take care of Thomas, and he said for me to look out for 'our Gertie.'"

"What did you have to go and tell me *that* for?" Gertie said, crying openly now.

"Well, it's the truth—"

"You don't understand what it's like! Letting all those men use me and never feeling nothing. That's how it was—until Pete. It wasn't that way with him, and now I...You want to hear something funny? I want to *marry* him—after what I been. Ain't that a joke? I want to live with him on a piece of land somewhere. I want to go to sleep with him right by me and wake up the same way. And it can't ever be. Not ever. I don't want to know he was thinking about me, you hear?"

"Gertie, I can't keep my word to Sergeant La Broie if you run off!"

"I ain't asking you for nothing! I ain't making no excuses for what I am! If I'm ashamed of it, it's my business!"

"Gertie—"

"I'm going," she said, mouth trembling. "I've got my bribe, and I'm going. And you can't keep me here now." She turned abruptly and began to walk away.

The rain began to fall. Abiah stood there, watching her go, not knowing what to do.

But there was nothing she could do. She couldn't hang on to people when they wanted to leave, and she'd better get used to that. She took a deep breath and tried not to cry.

The guests were still arriving for the salon. When Gertie had nearly reached the road, a soldier passing along the line of trees suddenly spurred his horse and galloped across the bowling green, intercepting her on the gravel drive. Abiah turned away. She had no wish to witness her friend's easy fall back into her old life, and there was no alternative but to return to the house. Unlike Gertie, she had no money with which to effect an escape.

She walked slowly, pacing herself. The emotional confrontation had taken more out of her than she'd realized. But the rain came down harder, and she tried to hurry. She didn't hear the horse and rider until they were almost abreast of her.

She looked around sharply—and directly into Thomas Harrigan's eyes. He reined in the horse. He was mud-splattered and wet and sorely in need of a good barbering. And he was angry.

"Give me your hand," he said, holding his out to her. He kicked his stirrup free. "Put your foot in the stirrup!"

"Thomas, what—?" she began.

"Give me your hand, damn it! I didn't come all this way to see you have a relapse."

She hesitated, then did as he asked—ordered—with a great deal of difficulty. She gave a soft cry when he none too gently hauled her up and set her on the saddle in front of him. The horse began to prance at the added weight. Thomas had to work hard to control the animal, then he unbuttoned his coat and pulled her closer to him, so that she had at least some protection from the rain. She was in real danger of falling, but she couldn't shift her position without upsetting the horse even more. Thomas's arms went around her to keep her steady, his one hand almost but not quite encircling her breast.

"Do you want to tell me what in the name of God

you're doing out here in the rain?'' he asked as the horse began a nervous sideways dance toward the house.

"No," she said.

"I suggest you do."

She tried to see him over her shoulder. "All right. I was brawling with Gertie," she said evenly.

"Yes, I saw that, and I can only suppose that the both of you have lost your minds. Are you trying to have a setback? Is that it?"

"No, of course not—I was trying to keep Gertie from leaving."

"She says you don't need her now. She thinks her going is for the best."

"I think it's not," Abiah said.

"You wouldn't be facing the kind of remarks she will if she stays."

"Wouldn't I?" she asked, because people here knew the scandal surrounding her marriage to Thomas. As she had grown stronger and had begun to meet some of Mrs. Harrigan's friends—albeit unwillingly— she realized by the questions she was asked that many of them were quite willing to think that a wedding had never really taken place. Abiah Calder was obviously not the Winthrops' "sort." Regardless of the surface politeness, she had the distinct feeling that they believed she was perpetuating some kind of subterfuge on the family.

She gave a quiet sigh. Thomas urged the horse forward instead of answering her. She tried to see past him down the drive. Gertie had disappeared.

"She'll be all right," Thomas said.

"Did she say where she was going?"

"Back to Falmouth. I think she wants to be where La Broie can find her."

Abiah could certainly understand that reasoning—and take comfort from it. "Thomas, what are you doing here?" she asked after a moment, because she'd never been one to simply let events unfold.

"I live here, Abiah. And my *wife* is here."

He reined in the horse at the back door of the house and slid off, lifting her unceremoniously down to the ground. "Stand!" he said to the horse, throwing the reins over its head and letting them drop. "You, too," he said to Abiah, catching her by the wrist when she would have escaped into the house.

"Thomas..." She stopped, because she realized suddenly how exhausted he was. She was more steady on her feet than he was.

She waited while he took his saddlebags down and slung them over his shoulder. Without saying anything, he pulled her after him through the kitchen door. One of the scullery maids cried out in alarm at the abrupt sight of them, and all the activity around the pots and sinks and tables abruptly stopped.

The elderly cook came bustling forward. "Tommy? Captain Thomas? Oh, it is you!"

"Hello, Vinnie, darling," he said, smiling.

"Now this is a surprise!" Vinnie said, still beaming. "There's not a one of us here knew you was coming home! Did you know, little missus?" she asked Abiah.

"No, I didn't," Abiah assured her.

"I didn't know myself until the last minute," Thomas said. "I would be very much obliged if you didn't mention my arrival to the judge. I'll let him know."

"Whatever you say, Captain Thomas. Is there anything you need? Would you be hungry, sir?"

"Vinnie, I'm starving. If you could send me up something to eat later—I don't care what, just make it a lot. And I need hot water for a bath." He smiled again. "But you can look at me and tell that—unless you happen to be downwind. Then you wouldn't have to look at me at all."

Everyone laughed heartily.

"Bless your heart, Captain Thomas!" Vinnie said. "You just leave it to me."

"Shall I stable your horse, sir?" one of the young men asked.

"Yes, thank you, Jack. Treat him well. He's had a hard ride."

Thomas glanced at Abiah. She made a feeble attempt to free her wrist. He wouldn't let go.

"If you will all excuse me now," he said. "I don't have much time."

He pulled Abiah along with him, not to the back stairs as she expected, but up the stairway that led directly into the main part of the house. He kept a firm hand on her elbow as they stepped into the hallway just off the main entrance foyer.

There were people milling about—guests waiting for the judge to call them to order. And Thomas's sudden appearance elicited much the same reaction among the judge's guests as it had among the kitchen staff—except that muted gasps replaced the squealing. He ignored the commotion, turning his back to them.

"I'm sorry," he said, apparently because of the look on Abiah's face. "I'm following Gertie's suggestion. She said you needed to be seen with me."

"No, I don't," she assured him. It was far too late for that.

She kept staring at him. His sudden homecoming had left her rattled to the point of giddiness—like everyone else in the household. She didn't know what to say to him. And she was very much afraid of what he had come to say to her. He was the same Thomas she'd always known, and yet he wasn't. She had never seen him this gruff and unkempt and determined. His very presence overwhelmed her. And she could still feel the exact place where his hand had rested near her breast, and that in itself was disconcerting.

"I have to go pacify the judge," he said. "When I'm done, you and I have to talk. Where will you be? Down here?"

"I don't know," she said, because she was ashamed suddenly. All she wanted to do was hide. Everyone must know why he was here. Elizabeth Channing must know.

"I'll find you," he said. He turned to go, then stopped. "It's good to see you well again, Abiah."

He rested his hand briefly on her shoulder and then left her there. She stood for a moment, feeling all the eyes on her. She nodded blindly in the direction of the people still standing in the foyer, wondering if Elizabeth was among them—and then picked up her skirts and escaped up the stairs.

He couldn't find Abiah. As soon as he'd finished humbling himself before the judge and seeing his mother, he went to the bedchamber in the west wing, where he thought she would be. She wasn't, and none of the servants seemed to be certain where she had gone. He had checked the library and the outer fringes of the salon, wading through clouds of cigar smoke and speaking briefly with the guests when he had to. He didn't see Abiah anywhere, and he was beginning to feel desperate. The fact that Elizabeth was supposed to be here tonight wasn't helping matters.

He gave a quiet sigh and kept looking. He was much more presentable now—not that he thought that would help. Robbins, the butler, must have had the devil's own time getting the mud off his uniform and getting it dried out enough to wear. Thomas couldn't remember the last time he'd had a decent bath, or real food, but he couldn't savor any of it. He had to leave in the morning. To his credit, the judge had pulled any number of strings to get him a short furlough. He'd made Thomas grovel for it, of course, and stand for a long time with his hat in his hand tonight, but it would be worth it if only he could talk to Abiah. Unfortunately, she seemed to always be one step ahead of him.

He finally saw her sitting in the gallery—alone— quietly listening to the chamber ensemble the judge had gone to great expense to bring in from New York City. She was wearing black, as befitted her mourning for Guire, and she looked so serene and above it all. He thought she looked absolutely beautiful, as well. So, obviously, did Charlie Mayron. So did half the room. He'd never seen so many lovesick soldiers in one place in his life. What a run there must have been to get a chair by the open doorway so that the gallery would be in plain view. And Thomas understood the dynamics at work here perfectly. There was nothing more challenging to a man than knowing a woman he admired had just cause to hate him.

There was so much he needed to say to Abiah. He wanted them to put the past behind them and begin again in the here and now. But he was very afraid that, whether she still loved him or not, for all intents and purposes she was done with him. She clearly had no desire to talk to him, regardless of how much trouble he'd gone to to get here. And how much that had to do with his former alliance with Elizabeth he could only guess. Who knew what Elizabeth might have said? He was reasonably sure she had been interfering with his correspondence. She might even have told Abiah of their encounter in the hotel—and how the hell could he explain that? He'd had a moment of weakness, but nothing happened? And if she wanted to know precisely *why* nothing had happened, could he in good conscience say anything but that the timely arrival of Sergeant La Broie and Bender had prevented it?

Elizabeth was used to having her own way. She was used to having her capricious notions instantly made real. He was sure now that was what he had been—a capricious notion. Some kind of whim. She must have thought it would be exciting to involve herself with Judge Winthrop's black sheep grandson. The trouble with black sheep, however, was that they couldn't be led. Sometimes they didn't even recognize the attempt.

He sighed again. He was dead on his feet. If Abiah knew he was down here among all her other admirers, she gave no indication of it. There was only one thing left to do. He began to climb the wide stairway to where she was. She didn't notice him at first, and when she finally did, she seemed every bit as startled as she had on the gravel drive this afternoon. He thought she would have actually bolted if only she'd had the room. He approached her with a good deal more confidence than he felt, bowing to her slightly and extending his hand.

She looked at it, but didn't take it.

"We're going now," he said.

She only looked at him, her beautiful dark eyes holding his.

"You know we have an audience," he said quietly. Indeed, he thought the chamber ensemble could stop playing and escape out the French doors and no one would even notice. "Perhaps you should also know I'm not above making a scene if that's what it takes."

When she still didn't respond, he took her by the hand anyway and pulled her to her feet.

"Thomas, people are going to think—"

"Yes, they are," he assured her. "They will think exactly that, and all the men here will envy me."

He tucked her hand under his arm and walked her

along the gallery in plain view of the overflow crowd in the foyer and the soldiers by the drawing room doors. And he did so to a spattering of quiet applause from the men who would have given anything to be in his shoes.

"Thomas—"

"We have to talk, Abiah. I'm leaving in the morning."

She didn't say anything else. She came quietly along with him, waiting in the hallway while he opened her bedchamber door. She went inside first and he followed, looking around. He must have seen it before—perhaps as a boy, exploring. Thomas vaguely remembered that there had been a room of some kind with red doors. Whatever this had once been, it was *hers* now. Her presence, the lavender-and-rosewater scent of her, permeated the room. She was tidy, but not tidy enough to please the judge, and by now she probably knew that. Her books lay scattered, about in various stages of being read, and she had been writing a letter at her desk. Of course, it wasn't addressed to him, but to a lady in New Bern.

It was raining still. He could hear it spattering against the windowpanes. Only the small lamp on the writing desk was lit. He moved to the fireplace and lit all the candles on the mantel as well, just for something to do. Then he took the coal shovel and stoked the fire, and immediatcly thought of that cold December day after Fredericksburg. He had built up the fire for her then, too, and tonight he was every bit as afraid of losing her.

Abiah stood in the middle of the room, waiting. She seemed composed enough outwardly, but he remained convinced that she would run away if she could.

"Will you sit down at least?" he asked.

"No," she said.

He drew a quiet breath and removed his uniform coat and tossed it aside. It landed on the fainting couch and slid to the floor. He made no attempt to retrieve it. He loosened his black cravat and tossed it aside as well.

"Why are you behaving like this?" she asked after a moment.

"Like what?"

"Like…a husband."

"I am a husband."

"Are you?"

"Abiah…"

"I can hardly bear look at you, Thomas. I can see it in your eyes."

"See what?"

"How much you *don't* want to hurt me."

"That's true. I never wanted to do that—"

"Do you remember what I said?" she interrupted. "Do you remember that I asked you about your engagement?"

"Yes."

"Well, now what?"

He looked at her. He had no idea what she meant. "I…don't understand."

"I'm not sophisticated enough to guess what is to be done," she said.

He tried to take her hands in his. "Abby, what are you talking about?"

She pulled her hands free. "What happens now? What do you want? If you made your plans thinking you'd be a widower, then—"

"For God's sake, Abby!"

She gave a quiet sigh. "Just tell me what you want."

What did he want?

An interesting question. He moved away from her and knelt down on the hearth to shovel more coal into the grate. He was so tired, too tired to think straight. He had to make her understand—somehow—without getting into his being with Elizabeth at that Falmouth hotel. He could truthfully say she had fooled him—in the beginning. But he had no excuse whatsoever for La Broie's catching him with his mouth on hers and his hand on her breast. How could he tell Abiah something like that? It was a stupid thing for him to have done. And if it cost him Abiah's love and respect...

He looked at her, then pushed the large, upholstered footstool in her direction. "Please sit," he said. "So I can."

She hesitated, then did so. He crossed the room and sat down in the only chair—the gilded Boston rocking chair that had once belonged to his grandmother Harrigan. It was practically the only thing he had from the black sheep side of the family, and he supposed that his mother had brought it in here for Abiah. He leaned back and closed his eyes. If he could just...

He must have dozed for a moment. He suddenly

leaned forward, expecting her to be gone again. But she wasn't. She was sitting on the footstool, waiting. And he had been asleep much longer than a moment. She had unbound her hair. It hung in a long braid over her shoulder. And she was no longer wearing the black dress. She was wearing a gray muslin one—light mourning, he supposed it was called. It was not the kind of dress he remembered from his visits to the Calder house, but she looked more like Abiah now. *His* Abiah.

"Shall I tell you what I want?" he asked, leaning back in the rocking chair again.

"Yes," she answered.

"I want you to come closer—so I can see your face."

"All right," she said after a moment. She stood and pushed the stool nearer with her foot. He could see her white stockings, ankle to knee, as she did so.

He looked abruptly away, lest she catch him at it.

She sat down again, and she lifted her eyes to his.

So beautiful, he thought. He had missed her. It was incredible to him how much. They had never been together for very long at a time, and yet he had felt their separation acutely. In these weeks since the marriage, her well-being had become imperative to him. She was all he thought about. Regardless of the way the marriage had come about or the fact that it had never been consummated, in his mind she was his wife.

"Did you mean it—when you said you loved me?" he asked abruptly.

She hesitated. He could recognize the very moment when she decided to tell him the truth. "Yes," she said.

"It wasn't because you were out of your head with fever?"

"I would like to pretend so, but no."

"I've lived a man's life. You know that. Guire told you. I've...been with women—different women—in...that way. Do you understand what I mean?"

"I understand," she said quietly.

He could see a question forming, and he waited.

"Have you been with...Elizabeth Channing?" she asked after a time. "In that way?"

"No," he said. "But I could have."

She looked at him, but she didn't ask anything else. He was glad of that, because he had come as close to the truth as he wanted to get. He should tell her about the incident at the Falmouth hotel. He knew he should. But when he looked into her eyes, he just couldn't do it.

"She must love you a great deal," she said. "To risk so much."

"No, it wasn't love. Not the way you mean. It was...more..." He sighed. "I think there must be a lot of the moth and the flame in Elizabeth. Her...willingness had nothing to do with an irresistible passion for me. It had to do with shocking her doting father—how outrageous could she be and still get away with it? It had to do with daring and competing with her friends. It had to do with...control."

"You loved her." It wasn't quite a question.

"I was flattered by her interest. I let that male certitude you always worked so hard to trample run wild for a time. I didn't understand the game."

Abiah was sitting close enough for him to touch her, but he didn't. He waited until her eyes met his.

"I'm so tired, Abby. And what I want—what I really want is…"

The music started up again downstairs. Not chamber music this time, but a fiddler playing a sad and lilting waltz.

He made an attempt to smile. "Shall I dance you around the room again, Abby? For old times' sake? Shall we pretend we're back at the Calder house and everything is just as it was…?"

She abruptly bowed her head, and he leaned forward.

"I've come a long way for you," he said quietly.

She looked up at him, her mouth trembling slightly. She reached for him then, and she held on to him tightly, her face pressed into his shoulder. His arms went around her. "This is what I want," he whispered against her ear. *"This…"*

Some part of him believed that their first kiss should be chaste, gentle, stolen in some dark corner at the end of a sad waltz. But he was leaving in a few hours and he might never see her again. Indeed, that they should have any time together at all was a miracle.

His mouth found hers. He pulled her upward. She fell against him, on him. He held her tighter, closer still. Her hands fluttered for a moment, tentative and unsure, before they slid into his hair, and he was lost.

He probed her lips with his tongue until they parted and he could taste—savor—the flavor of her mouth. Then he kissed her deeply. He couldn't get enough of her. His breathing grew harsh and shaky. He pressed her against him. He was hard now, aching with desire. His hands began to move in search of bare skin. He wanted to touch her—*her,* not layers of clothes.

"Abby, let me—"

He abruptly stopped and rested his forehead against hers, fighting hard for control, his arms wrapped tightly around her. His hands shook. He loved her—with all his heart. All this time he'd been afraid to admit it, even to himself. He didn't want to frighten her.

She lifted her head to look at him, her dark eyes staring into his. "Take me to bed, Thomas," she whispered.

"Abby, are you sure?"

"Take me to bed—"

His mouth found hers again. He managed to get out of the chair without letting her go. He half carried her across the floor and lifted her onto the bed. She lay there, watching as he frantically unbuttoned his shirt. He didn't remove it. He took off his boots and trousers instead, and he came to her half-dressed. He lay down next to her, and she reached up to touch his face. She was fearful of this—of him; he could tell that. When he reached for the buttons on her bodice, she caught his hand.

"I want to look at you," he said. "I want to touch you. Let me see you, Abby."

She lay there, her eyes half-closed, her chest rising and falling. He kissed her again. Then again. His hand cupped her breast. His thumb found her nipple and stroked it through the cloth. He could feel it contract into a tight bud; she made a soft "oh" sound. This time when he began to undo her buttons she didn't resist. He pulled the dress down over her shoulders, trapping her arms at her sides. He kissed her neck, the swell of her breasts, her nipples through her chemise.

He wanted to see her. He had to see her. He pulled her upright long enough to free her arms from the sleeves of the dress, then he tugged at her chemise until he had one breast bared. He nuzzled her gently there, kissed her gently, almost but not quite touching the erect nipple. She stiffened when he took it into his mouth. Her head arched back when he began to suckle her.

"Thomas—" she whispered urgently. "Is this—are you sure…?"

He understood immediately what she wanted to know. She was a virgin, and her fantasies about seducing him hadn't quite included this.

"I'm going to make you feel good, Abby. That's all. I'm going to look at you and…touch you…and taste you…"

His mouth found hers again. He ran his hand up under her skirt, untying the strings at the waists of her petticoat and drawers, searching for the tops of her stockings. He found them, and he pulled them down and off. She made no objection when he caressed her bare legs. He had wanted to hold her and touch her for so long. Her skin was soft and warm. Her eyes closed when he found the open inside seam on the leg of her drawers. He kissed her harder as he stroked the silky flesh of her inner thigh.

She caught his wrist when he would have done more.

He lifted his head to look at her. "Do you want me to stop?" he whispered, his breathing ragged. "I don't want to make you do anything you don't want to do."

He kissed her again before she could answer him. He wanted to give her time to decide, but he needed her. Now.

He broke away, still trying to hold back. "Abby— Abby, if you don't want this—"

She gave a wavering sigh and lifted her mouth to his, and she let go of his wrist. He didn't pursue his advantage. He sat up instead, working hard at getting rid of the rest of her clothes and his. He pulled down the covers on the bed and settled her against the pillows, then lay beside her, rolling her against him and covering them both with the sheet. He stroked her breasts, kissed them, made her catch her breath. He could run his hands over her body freely now, and he did so, appreciating every part of her he could reach. She felt so good!

This is the way it should be, he thought. Skin to skin. Heart to heart.

He kissed her eyes, her cheeks, her chin. "Say heart," he whispered, nibbling at her mouth, smiling into her eyes.

"What?" She was breathless and clinging to him. "What...?"

"Say 'heart' so I'll know it's you..."

She laughed then, and he thought she was no longer afraid. "Hea—" she began.

He abruptly kissed her, cutting off the word. The laughter bubbled from her mouth into his. He rolled her on top of him, then back again, just to make her laugh some more. His knee found its way in between her thighs. He moved over her, knelt there, grabbed her hips and brought her to him. He braced himself above her and pressed gently against that place he so desperately wanted to go. Her eyes widened, but she didn't resist. It took every ounce of strength he had to restrain himself, to enter her only slightly and then withdraw.

She squirmed against him, and it was nearly his undoing. He couldn't wait any longer, and he pushed into her. She was so tight around him. He pushed harder. She clutched at his shoulders, but she didn't cry out.

"Abby..." he whispered urgently. She turned her face away.

But then she looked at him, looked into his eyes, and she lifted her hips to give him better access. He began to move then, slowly at first, trying to give her time to grow accustomed to him. His arms trembled with the effort it took to hold back. He watched her face. When her eyes closed and her head arched back, he thrust deeper. A soft sound escaped her lips, and he stopped.

"I'm hurting you—"

"No!" she said, locking her legs around him, holding him close. "Thomas..."

He began moving again, more urgently now, seeking the rhythm that would give him release. Her body rose to meet his. He thrust hard and deep, so that she took all of him. The pleasure it gave him was unlike anything in his experience. He had known passion before, desire before, but never this joy.

Abiah—!

His pleasure peaked in a great rush of sensation. He cried out as his body grew taut and emptied into her. Then he sagged against her, knowing he was too heavy for her, his breath ragged against her neck. He lifted his head to kiss her again, her mouth, her eyes. With great effort, he tried to move aside, but she held on to him and would not let him go. He rested his head upon her shoulder, and he closed his eyes.

Chapter Ten

"I shot Zachariah Wilson."

"What...?" Thomas said sleepily. And then, "What!"

"I shot him."

She had been sitting beside him on the bed, watching him sleep for a long while. But she knew he was waking up again, and there was no point in waiting.

"Abiah, I don't understand—"

"It was that night—after the wedding. He was trying to force himself on Gertie. She was crying and begging him to stop, and he kept hitting her. I had Guire's revolver—it was in the hope chest. And I...shot him." She gave a small shrug. "I just thought you should know that."

"Well, yes, I guess I should. Abiah..."

"What, Thomas?" she asked, looking at him gravely. She felt somewhat better telling him exactly what he was getting in a wife. She didn't feel better knowing she'd trapped him into matrimony after all. The marriage was most definitely consummated now.

There couldn't be an annulment. There would have to be a divorce.

He reached up to touch her cheek, and she felt perfectly at ease pressing a kiss into his palm.

How strange, she thought. They were neither of them dressed. She was hiding behind a corner of the sheet. He was only barely covered, and yet they were having a conversation as if they were in a drawing room or standing on the church steps—if one discounted the topic, of course.

"He didn't hurt you, did he?"

"No. The gun finally went off."

"What do you mean, 'finally'?"

"It misfired."

"Misfired," he repeated, as if he were having a really difficult time following this.

"Yes. A few times. I guess the cartridges were damp."

"You were in a situation with this man that was serious enough for you to think you had to shoot him, and the gun misfired—a few times."

"Yes."

"My God, Abiah!"

She sighed. "It sounds so awful when you try to tell it, you know?"

"Yes," he assured her. "I do indeed."

"I didn't kill him, Thomas. I only nicked his earlobe. But I guess I would have if I'd had a better aim."

"And that's why you disappeared from his house—and he disappeared from Falmouth?"

"Yes."

"But where did you go?"

"I don't know. I was exhausted afterward. You know—the wedding and the…shooting, too. Gertie was afraid of what Zachariah Wilson would do, but she looked after me. I guess she got in touch with the lawyer you'd told her about—Staunton. He sent the telegram to your mother. And the next thing I knew I was here."

Thomas reached for her and drew her down beside him. He kissed her softly on the mouth and then held her tightly to him.

"My God," he said. "I put you in harm's way, and that's the last thing I meant to do."

She moved so that she could see his face. "You did the best you could. I know that. I just wanted you to hear about it from me. That's all."

"Abby…" His eyes searched hers.

"What, Thomas?" she said when he didn't go on, because she thought he really wanted to tell her something.

"Are you all right? Maybe we shouldn't have—"

She kissed him to keep him from saying anything more—and to show him how very all right she was. She was learning how to do this, how to kiss and how to touch, how to make his eyes grow hungry and dark with desire. No matter what happened tomorrow— even if he still told her he wanted to be with Elizabeth—Abiah would have this, now.

She rested her head on his chest, and she listened to his heart beating. He began to stroke her bare back. She closed her eyes for a moment, savoring the feel of his hands on her. She loved for him to do that. She loved having him inside her.

And she felt like crying.

She could feel the change in him, the return of desire, and need. She lifted her head, ready for him. This time she needed no coaxing. This time she understood, and she herself wanted. She wanted to wrap herself around him and take him into her body, into her soul. She thought of Gertie suddenly. How terrible it must be to do *this* with a man whose touch and scent and taste meant nothing.

"Thomas..." she whispered, lifting her mouth to his, opening for him like a blossoming flower. When he suckled her breasts, she thought she would faint from the pure pleasure of it.

But they had no time.

He entered her quickly, deeply. The dread of his leaving was so heavy in her heart. And all the while, he looked into her eyes. This time the pleasure was for her and she knew it. The feeling was so exquisite. Her desire for him began as a tiny ember, and he knew exactly what to do to make it flash and burn. She watched his face grow stormy with his own passion; she saw rather than heard him say her name.

She reached for him, drawing him closer still, holding on for dear life. She cried out when her release came, and she was not ashamed.

Thomas woke with a start, then realized that Abiah had called him.

"What?" he said sleepily, reaching for her. He opened his eyes, because she was now clothed.

"It's time," she said. Her eyes were red rimmed, and in spite of the fact that she forced a smile, he knew she had been crying.

"Don't," he said, reaching out to touch her.

She managed a wobbly smile. "I'm not going to weep all over you—truly, I'm not, I promise—"

Someone knocked quietly at the door.

"What is it?" Thomas called before Abiah could answer. She gave him such a scandalized look that he winked at her. He had spent the night with his wife—and he saw no reason the household couldn't know that.

"Sir!" Bonnie called through the door. "Jack has the horse waiting for you, sir. Judge Winthrop says he knows you'll miss the ferry!"

"I'll be right there."

He threw back the sheet and began looking for his clothes—not a difficult task because Abiah had already gathered them up for him. He dressed quickly, stopping to kiss her from time to time as he did so. It gave him great pleasure to let her tie his cravat, because he could enjoy studying her lovely face while she did so.

"Come downstairs with me," he said. "I want to look at you as long as I can."

She nodded. Then sighed. Then she was in his arms, clinging to him tightly.

"You will take care," she whispered.

"Yes," he said.

"You swear it."

"I swear it."

"And if you see Gertie in Falmouth, tell her if she needs a place to go, she's welcome to stay at the Calder house—if it's still there."

He nodded, and he kissed her hard. "God, how I want to take you back to bed."

She looked up at him and gave him a mischievous little grin. "And how I want to go."

"Abiah!" he said, to tease her. "Now I am scandalized."

"I sincerely doubt that, Captain Harrigan," she said primly.

"And why would that be, do you suppose?"

They both laughed, but their laughter quickly faded. They stood there, staring into each other's eyes. Hers began to well with tears, in spite of her promise, and she rested her head against his shoulder.

"Captain Harrigan!" Bonnie called from somewhere down the hall.

"You have my heart, Abby," he said. He kissed her one last time, and then opened the door. He had to reach deep now to steel himself against the ordeal of leaving. She took his arm and they walked together down the wide staircase.

He knew from his mother that someone would be bringing a packet of letters and personal items for him to take back to camp, even though he was in a Massachusetts regiment and not likely to encounter any of their loved ones firsthand. He would still do his best to see that everything got delivered. Save a wounding, there was nothing worse for a soldier away from home than not getting mail.

There were a number of houseguests up and about, regardless of the early hour. He—and they, apparently—could smell the heady aroma of one of the famed Winthrop breakfasts in the works. Vinnie and her crew would have had to have been at it since well before daylight to put together such a fine smelling meal for so many people. He would have liked to have had the time to partake of it himself, but when it had come down to a choice of eggs and bacon, crab cakes and oysters and fried potatoes, or making love to Abiah one more time, the breakfast had lost. Handily.

His mother was waiting anxiously in the foyer. And some woman he recognized from the Episcopal church, holding a letter pouch.

And the judge.

And Elizabeth.

He made no attempt to acknowledge her. She looked exquisite, as if she had dressed entirely with making an impression in mind. But it was wasted on him—even if he hadn't had Abiah on his arm. He turned his attention to his mother.

''Thomas, my dear,'' Clarissa said, coming forward to take him by the hand. ''Will you *please* prove to be a better correspondent in the future?''

''Mother, I have never been lax in that. I think perhaps you should make inquiries with the postmaster here as to the way my letters to you and Abby may have gone astray.'' He glanced at Elizabeth. She smiled.

He put his hand on Abiah's shoulder and walked with her to his grandfather.

"I ask you for a favor, sir," he said.

"Again? It seems to me you are making this a very bad habit."

"I ask that you continue to see to my wife's well-being while I'm gone," he said, knowing that everyone in the foyer could hear him. "I have the money put aside for whatever she may want or need, so you will not be inconvenienced on that account. You have only to notify my lawyer of the amount you require."

He had put the judge on the spot, and they both knew it. Thomas could feel Abiah stiffen in protest beside him, but she didn't interrupt. The judge was ever mindful of appearances, and after a moment he nodded.

"Very well," he said. "She will have my protection."

More people were entering the hallway. He kissed his mother's cheek. He could see the boy, Jack, waiting with his mount, and if he didn't leave right this minute, Thomas knew he was in real danger of not getting back to his company in time. Major Gibbons hadn't taken Thomas's manipulations to get to Maryland well. The man would likely be standing and waiting with a watch.

"Please, please take care of yourself," his mother said, trying not to cry.

"No tears," he admonished her. "I'll be back before you know it. And, Mother, thank you for bringing Abby here."

"Thomas, she was all alone. How could I not?"

He looked from her to Abiah. "I have to go," he said abruptly. "If you two will try to behave—and not vex the judge too much—it will make me very happy."

They both laughed, and he was about to offer each of them an arm to escort them outside, when someone called his name. He looked around.

"Captain Harrigan!" the woman cried again. "Oh, Captain Harrigan!"

"I beg your pardon—" he started to say, but then he recognized the woman. Mrs. Post—from the Falmouth hotel—bearing down on him. And there was absolutely no place for him to go.

"We meet again!" she said loudly. "Surprise, surprise! Oh, what a beautiful, beautiful home, Captain Harrigan. I am so fortunate to have been invited here! I fear my little hotel suffers mightily by contrast. Hardly more than a week ago—" she informed the assembly at large, "the captain and his lovely bride were my guests—and I told him then that I was coming to Maryland. You see? Here I am! It's just wonderful to encounter you and the beautiful Mrs. Harrigan again so soon. How are you, my dear?" she asked earnestly. "Your sweet husband was very much concerned that you were not well when you were in Falmouth." She was looking expectantly at Elizabeth, who was fighting a losing battle to ignore her.

"Dear Mrs. Harrigan!" Mrs. Post persisted. "You are well, yes?"

Thomas could literally feel the shock rippling

through the onlookers as they began to realize the significance of the woman's mistake.

''I'm afraid I really don't recall that we've ever met,'' Elizabeth said finally.

''But, of course, we've met! It was just a little over a week ago, in Falmouth—''

''No,'' Elizabeth said.

''—When you and the Captain stayed at my little hotel!'' the woman insisted.

''Mrs. Post...'' Thomas said, to take her attention away from Elizabeth. There was no way to get the woman out of the foyer. He glanced at Abiah. She looked so stricken that he reached out for her.

''Abby, this isn't what it seems. I swear to you—''

She backed away from him and turned toward the stairs. He followed after her, regardless of the scene it would make.

''Abby—I can explain this—''

''No, Thomas. Even if you did, I wouldn't believe you.''

''Wait! There are things I should have told you—I readily admit that. But you have to trust me now, Abby—''

She looked at him then.

''Trust? I have the letter, Thomas.''

''What letter?''

''I have the letter,'' she repeated. ''And I did trust you—in spite of it. I trusted you all of last night and right up until a few moments ago. Zachariah Wilson is an honorable man compared to you. I have *no* wish to stand between you and Elizabeth Channing. I have more pride than that—and believe me, it is a very uncomfortable place to be. Now, please! Meet her in whatever 'little hotels' you have to, but leave me some dignity and leave me alone!'' She picked up her skirts and began to ascend the stairs, her chin up, her back rigid.

But she had to get around the judge to make her escape.

"Did I not warn you you would rue the day you let yourself rely on a Harrigan?'' he said to her.

She didn't answer him. She didn't look at him. She continued up the stairs, and Thomas would have followed, but the old man stepped into his path.

"You have just asked me to protect this young woman, and by God, I will do it,'' he said.

"Stand aside, sir,'' Thomas said, his voice shaking with anger.

"I will not.''

"Stand aside!''

"Did you not see the look on her face? She wants nothing more to do with you! You have caused enough damage here. Captain Appleby—'' he said to a man nearby. "If my grandson persists, will you and your associates aid me in throwing him out of this house?''

"I...yes—yes, of course,'' the man said. "If that is your wish.''

"It is, indeed, my wish. I suggest you take your leave, Thomas—*now*,'' the judge said. "Unless we're to add trespass *and* military desertion to your sins.''

Thomas stared after Abiah. She never once looked back.

"I said take your leave!" the judge said. "By God, you are your father's son! Is my house to be filled with the women you Harrigans have ruined?"

Thomas clenched his fists. It was all he could do not to lay hands on the old man. Finally, he turned to go, meeting his mother's eyes as he did so.

But there was nothing he could say to her. There was nothing he wanted to say to anyone—except Abiah.

He took the letter pouch from the clearly distressed woman still holding it. He took a sack of food from Bonnie. And he took his time, calling on the self-control he'd learned as the judge's grandson and later polished as a captain of infantry who had lived through his baptism of fire. At Fredericksburg, he had lain all night among the frozen bodies of his dead comrades, pinned down by Burnside's stupidity and the murderous rifle and cannon fire from Marye's Heights. He could damn well manage this. He walked carefully toward the front door, sidestepping people as he went, looking them all in the eye. For once, Mrs. Post had absolutely nothing to say. Elizabeth was no longer in the foyer.

"Thomas..." his mother said, following along with him.

"I can't apologize for something I have not done, Mother. But I do apologize for the distress this situation has caused you. Tell Abiah I will write to her," he said. "I *can* explain."

"Thomas..." his mother said again, shaking her head sadly.

Jack was still standing by the door, and he handed over the horse's reins. Thomas mounted swiftly and rode away.

Abiah stood at the upstairs window at the end of the hallway, watching as Thomas galloped down the gravel drive and disappeared into the line of trees along the road. She felt completely numb. She could hear voices on the stairs, and knew that someone approached, but she didn't turn around.

"Mrs. Harrigan," Captain Appleby said behind her. "Forgive my intrusion. I...came for your letter. I said I would deliver it to New Bern. I'm sailing in a matter of hours. Do you still want me to take it?"

Abiah looked at him, thinking that here, at least, was a man of his word. But the urgency in his voice told her that he had expected to find her in hysterics—and still might if he didn't earnestly pretend that nothing was amiss and state his business quickly so he could go.

"Mrs. Harrigan," he said when she made no response. "Do you want me to take the letter?"

"No," she said quietly. "I want you to take *me*."

Chapter Eleven

No tears, Abiah kept thinking. She held on to the self-admonishment as if it had come directly from heaven itself. There were times when, all alone in the ship's dark cabin, she had been too frightened to cry. Though the voyage was short, the sea had been rough along the Outer Banks, and the North Carolina shoreline was notoriously treacherous. But Captain Appleby proved to be an able seaman. He sailed the little Baltimore clipper exactly where it needed to go, and Abiah was only just now letting herself consider the reality of her situation.

She had no money. She had nothing but the clothing on her back and the debt she owed for her passage. And there was the distinct possibility that she could find herself pregnant. But no matter how ill-conceived and precipitous this journey had been, she would always be grateful to Captain Appleby for not trying to talk her out of it. It was rare, she thought, for a man to understand a woman's desperation so acutely. Or perhaps he only understood what living humbled under the judge's roof would entail—because of the regard she thought he had for Clarissa Harrigan. At first, Abiah tried to tell herself that it didn't matter what these Maryland people thought. They were all supporters of the Union cause, and therefore her enemy—as Thomas himself was.

But it did matter. She loved Thomas Harrigan, and her love for him had become her shame. One way or another, she had to get away, and it had seemed easier to sail to New Bern than to get across the Rappahannock.

She had no idea what Miss Gwen would think or do about her unannounced arrival, or the fact that Abiah's first act would be to ask her for money to pay for her passage. Perhaps the woman wasn't even in New Bern anymore. Perhaps she'd gone inland to escape the Yankee army. Perhaps she, too, had died, and Abiah truly was the only member of the family left.

She sat in her cabin, waiting for someone to come and tell her when she could go ashore. She was not so tired from the journey as from the events preceding it. She hadn't regained her stamina yet, and she hadn't slept at all the night before the voyage. She had lain in Thomas Harrigan's arms instead, with no thought of anything so mundane as sleep.

She gave a quiet sigh. The truly shameless part was that she had no regrets about *that.* None, regardless of the obvious consequences. She loved Thomas, and in her ignorance of events to come, she had briefly thought he loved her, too. *You have my heart,* he had told her.

She knew Thomas well. He was never one for pretty speeches, and she had believed his simple declaration meant all, when, in truth, it meant nothing.

She realized now that she should have given him the letter he had written to Elizabeth. Instead of pretending that it didn't exist, she should have put it into his hand and asked him to explain it to her. The outcome of doing so couldn't have been any worse than this. Destitute *and* facing a possible pregnancy, she was well on her way to total ruination—and if she wasn't very careful, she would cry about it after all.

Someone knocked quietly on the cabin door and she moved to open it, holding on to the wall in order to stay on her feet. She could still feel the motion of the ship beneath her, regardless of the fact that it was now anchored and reasonably still. She had had no problem with seasickness. Her problem was walking.

She had to fumble a moment to get the door open. A member of the crew stood in the passageway, a noticeably older man she thought must be some kind of personal aide to Captain Appleby. Behind his spectacles, his eyes had the carefully cultivated indifference of a servant, and he was far too advanced in age to be swabbing the decks and climbing the rigging.

"If you please, ma'am," he said.

Abiah looked at him, a little unsettled by the term "ma'am." It was correct that he should use it—she was a married woman—but she could feel tears very close to the surface.

"The captain inquires if you're ready to go ashore."

She nodded, not trusting her voice. She needed to

make no preparations for her departure. She had brought nothing but herself—and, she was ashamed to admit, the infamous letter. She supposed it would be the salt she would rub into her open wounds from now on—a kind of glorified symbol of her own stupidity. She wasn't ashamed of her unabashed participation in her wedding night. No, indeed. She was ashamed that she could have gone into the marriage with her eyes wide-open and still have been fooled so completely. She would never ask herself again why women seemed to keep finding themselves in such bad situations. Women—herself included—clearly were masters at self-delusion.

"Could you tell me," she said, as she stepped out of the cabin, "what amount I owe for passage from St. Michaels?"

"I believe that has already been paid, ma'am," he said.

"Paid? By whom?"

"By a woman who was sympathetic to your...difficulty and wanted to give you aid, ma'am. I don't know her name."

"What did she look like? Did you see her?"

"I only saw her briefly when she spoke to the captain. A young lass, she was—a little older than you, maybe, but still a lass. I have seen her from time to time at the Winthrop house when the captain visited."

"Was she a guest or a servant?" Abiah asked, thinking that Gertie was the only person she knew with money who might do such a thing—if she'd forgiven their quarrel in the Winthrop driveway.

"Oh, a guest, ma'am. Quite beautiful she was, too. Golden hair. You wouldn't think a mere lass such as she would be having money so conveniently at hand like that—but then the rich ain't like the rest of us, I'm told."

Abiah faltered.

Not Gertie—Elizabeth. She owed her flawless and timely escape to Elizabeth Channing. She wanted to laugh—would have laughed, if she hadn't felt so incredibly foolish. Captain Appleby must have come to see her with Elizabeth's money already in his pocket. Perhaps it had been an outright bribe to get Abiah away from the Winthrop house and out of Thomas's reach. Or perhaps Elizabeth had presented her request as a sincere desire to help. And poor naive and unsuspecting soul that she was, Abiah had made it so easy for them both.

"Mind how you go, ma'am," the old man said, looking back at her.

She took a deep breath and followed after him. From now on, she would indeed mind how she went. It was her choice whether or not she wanted to play the helpless victim—Gertie had been right about that—and no one would know she had worth if she herself didn't behave as if she did. She had been very ignorant in this situation, and there were many things she still didn't understand. But she was a quick study, and as far as she was concerned, paying her passage to New Bern was the very least Elizabeth Channing could do.

Aabiah made her way carefully up on deck. There

was a stiff breeze coming off the water, and she didn't see Captain Appleby anywhere around. Apparently, his fee hadn't included token farewells.

"Do you need an escort, ma'am?" the old man asked her, and if he recognized that she expected to see the captain again, it didn't show.

"No," she lied. "It's very near here. Will you tell Captain Appleby that I thank him for his kindness. No, on second thought, perhaps not. It isn't a kindness at all, is it, if it's been bought."

The old man made no comment, but he did accompany her to the gangplank. "You be careful, ma'am," he said when she was about to disembark. "There's rough men on these docks and there's the soldiers about, too."

She nodded, then walked unsteadily down the gangplank, still feeling as if she couldn't quite keep her balance. She could immediately smell the fish and wet wood scents of the wharf. The place was noisy and crowded with people—men mostly, hastily unloading the supply ships. There were indeed soldiers standing around, apparently with nothing to do, and a few women plying their wares, which ranged from fried apple pies to themselves. Abiah thought briefly of Gertie as she passed them. At this point, she supposed that she herself was more in danger of having to take up harlotry than Gertie was.

"Pie, miss?" one of the women asked.

Abiah shook her head. She had no money for pie, or anything else. She could smell food cooking somewhere—fried onions and meat—and her stomach rumbled with hunger.

She kept walking. The afternoon was warm and sunny. Spring was much further along here than in Maryland. The town seemed quiet enough, but she immediately recognized the apparent peacefulness as the uneasy kind that came from having one's conquerors underfoot.

Now that she was here, she had no real plan other than to simply ask someone for directions to Miss Gwendolyn Pembroke's house. Thus far, as Abiah walked along the street leading away from the docks, there were no establishments she felt brave enough to enter. There were no signs to identify exactly what they were. Men loitered in the doorways, staring. As she passed one open door, she could hear someone playing a piano inside—very badly.

She turned the corner. She could see a church now, and residences with picket or iron or latticework fences, but no stores.

One of the brick, two-story houses on her right appeared to have been taken over by the occupation army. Three soldiers had apparently come out of an open upstairs window and were now sitting in a row on the flat roof of the porch. One of them called to her, while the other two laughed. Abiah put her head down and walked on.

The next house had a large sign nailed to the front-porch column: Sanitary Commission. She knew from her stay in Maryland that the organization was supposed to look after the health and spiritual needs of the Union soldiers, and she took its presence as an indication that the people of New Bern were considered to be firmly under control.

She neared a large church, and she could hear singing coming from inside—the kind of tightly harmonized renditions her mother had loved. This particular hymn, "North Port," was being beautifully done. She stood there, arms folded over her breasts, listening to the sweet a cappella female voices soar and then begin to intertwine with the deeper male ones, part by part and layer by layer, until the very air reverberated with the pure and joyous sounds.

The things she'd kept at bay so long suddenly threatened to overwhelm her. Her mind flooded with images of Thomas, and her mother and Guire. Dear God, how she wanted to go home! Maybe she could stand this, now, if she were back at the Calder house.

But even as the thought came to her, she knew that nothing would be the same there. Her mother was gone. Guire was gone. The house would be empty or looted and destroyed. The very essence of what "home" had meant to her was forever lost. And she understood suddenly, as she hadn't before, that she would never see Thomas again—

"Hey!" somebody yelled behind her. "Come here!"

She looked over her shoulder. The soldiers on the porch roof had seen fit to come down. One walked directly toward her on the sidewalk. The other two were cutting across the church cemetery.

"Hey!" the first soldier yelled again. "You!"

Afraid suddenly, Abiah didn't hesitate. She picked up her skirts and headed for the open church doors, walking faster and faster and then running because the two in the cemetery were going to cut her off. She made it all the way into the foyer before one of them grabbed her by the arm. She whirled around and struck him on the ear with her fist, wrenching free, leaving her shawl in his hand. She ran into the church, bursting in among the singers. The music abruptly stopped; several of the women screamed.

"Come here, damn you!" the soldier who had accosted her yelled into the sanctuary.

She kept going, looking back over her shoulder until she tripped and pitched headlong into the group. Hymnals dropped; hands reached out to save her from falling.

"Sergeant!" one of the singers—a Yankee officer—yelled. "What the devil are you doing? Pardon me, ladies," he hastily added.

"I'm following orders, sir! This—*woman*—won't stay down on the wharf where she belongs! We seen her come walking up from there all by herself as bold as you please. The general says he don't want them on the streets no more—"

"No—" Abiah said in a rush. "Please, I just…arrived on the *Anne Grey*—the captain can vouch for me. I'm looking for Miss Gwendolyn Pembroke…" She swayed on her feet.

"Here, sit," the officer said, taking her by her forearms and putting her in a pew. "Somebody go fetch Miss Gwen. I do believe she's got company."

* * *

It took Thomas a long time to write the letter. He understood perfectly that he needed to tell Abiah exactly what had happened at the Falmouth hotel; he just didn't know how to explain it without sounding like a weak and mindless fool. He couldn't in good conscience blame everything on Elizabeth and her machinations, and the only real excuse he could make was no excuse at all.

He *loved* Abiah. He wasn't sure when or how it had happened, exactly—perhaps it had always been there. He loved her, but he certainly hadn't behaved as if he did. He apparently would have taken advantage of Elizabeth's availability and willingness in that hotel room. That was the heart of it. In the end, he could only state the facts and take his chances. Once he'd put it all down in the letter and had let the mail carrier have it, there was nothing he could do but wait for Abiah to answer him.

And the waiting was agony, partly because he wasn't getting any mail from anyone else, either. He had no way of knowing how Abiah was. His mother would surely have told him, but he supposed that the judge must have declared him persona non grata and forbidden her to write to him. Sometimes he had visions of Elizabeth intercepting his letter to Abiah as she had likely done with the others—and Abiah never knowing the truth.

In desperation, he tried to put the entire business out of his mind and attend to his soldiering, which was no easy task, given the reproachful looks he got from La Broie *and* Bender. He could understand

Bender's disappointment. He was only a boy, and he had picked himself the wrong damn hero. La Broie's judgment was something else again. The sergeant was a man of the world, and for Thomas to have behaved in such a way as to shock that old soldier was very unsettling indeed.

But even without their tacit disapproval, there was still the ongoing problem of remembering. It took no effort at all on Thomas's part to relive that night. He could be anywhere, doing anything—asleep or awake, it didn't matter—and he was suddenly *there,* rolling in Abiah's arms, feeling her, tasting her, needing her. Unfortunately, it took no effort for him to remember the way she had looked at him after Mrs. Post's announcement, either.

In his lowest moments, he berated himself for not having defied the judge and ignored Abiah's wishes and followed after her until he could make her understand, regardless of the uproar it would have caused. His life was a damn, god-awful mess, and that was all there was to it.

Someone coughed discreetly behind him.

"What?" Thomas said.

"They're clearing out the hospitals, Cap," La Broie answered.

Thomas glanced at him. For the last few days there had been a great stir as the farriers got all the supply wagon and artillery horses reshod, and an exorbitant amount of ammunition and eight days' provisions had been issued. And now the walking wounded had suddenly been declared well again. It couldn't be more official. The war was about to reopen.

He looked out across the Virginia countryside. All along the edge of the woods, the dogwood and redbud trees were blooming. Once the hallowed harbingers of spring, they were now merely indicators that it was time to go forth and try to kill Johnny Miller and his kind. Thomas wanted to see his wife, damn it! He didn't want to go into battle with all this unfinished business hanging over him.

He realized that La Broie was still standing there. "What?" he asked.

"I seen Gertie, sir. She got back here without too much trouble."

"And?"

"And I gave her the message from Miss Abiah—about her going and staying at the Calder house if she needed to, if she can get across the river, of course. They ain't letting no civilians into Fredericksburg."

"And?" Thomas said again.

"And she bawled, Cap. She weren't expecting that. She wanted to know did I think Miss Abiah meant it. I said I don't reckon Miss Abiah goes around saying things she don't mean. Am I right about that, Cap?"

"Yes," Thomas said. Unlike the Elizabeths of this world, Abiah Calder Harrigan did *not* say things she didn't mean.

"I drew Gertie a map so's she could find it if she had to. She says if she hears anything from Miss Abiah, she'll try to send word to you."

Thomas nodded. It wasn't much, but it was something to hang on to.

There was a commotion suddenly at the far end of camp—riders coming in with dispatches for the senior commanding officers, the actual orders for what every soldier here already knew. The Army of the Potomac would be on the move before the sun was overhead.

"What do you hear, La Broie?" he suddenly asked. "What are they saying about Hooker?"

"Well, sir, you seen them mongrel dogs that go chasing wagons up and down the streets all the time. Joe Hooker has chased his damn wagon all the way to Washington and now he's done caught it, horses, driver and all—but he don't know what the hell he's going to do with it."

Thomas smiled slightly at the analogy. It fit the hard-drinking and feisty little general perfectly.

"Do you have any family, La Broie?" Thomas asked.

"No, sir. Just the army, sir. And Gertie. I reckon she'll be sorry if they kill me."

Thomas stood there, unmindful of the escalating activity around him. He ignored the drummers beating out the frantic cadence for the call to arms, and lit a cigar. La Broie was fortunate to have his conviction that Gertie would mind if he died. He, on the other hand, didn't know if he could say the same for Abiah or not.

"Rider coming, sir," La Broie said.

"Captain Harrigan!" the man called well before he got to them, and La Broie waved him over.

"Message for you, sir," he said, leaning down from the saddle. "Lieutenant Noah said to bring it straight to your hand."

Thomas took the sheet of blue paper, returning the man's salute. It was entirely the wrong color to be anything official.

"I reckon that's from Gertie," La Broie said, and Thomas glanced at him. "I give her some blue pages like that."

Thomas unfolded it and read the terse and somewhat obscure message: "Mrs. Post says she is in New Burn."

"New Bern?" he said out loud. "What the hell is Abby doing in New Bern?"

He walked away a few steps, then reread the note Gertie had sent. And swore. Of course, New Bern. He had seen the letter addressed to someone there. And of course, the ubiquitous Mrs. Post would be the one person hereabouts likely to know all about it.

"New Bern is occupied, for heaven's sake! You know what soldiers with nothing to do are like!"

"I do, indeed, sir," La Broie said helpfully, to keep Thomas from looking like a fool for talking to himself, if nothing else.

"She might as well be back at the Calder farm as New Bern.+... What?" he asked La Broie pointedly, because the sergeant was most definitely *not* "minding his face."

"Nothing, sir," La Broie assured him. "Of course, 'Peter, Peter, Pumpkin Eater' does come to mind."

Chapter Twelve

Miss Gwen wanted to know about everything—from the time word came that Guire had been wounded at Malvern Hill to Abiah's attempted arrest in front of the New Bern Methodist Church.

"I want to know *all*," she said, bringing Abiah a cup of hot tea. "So don't leave anything out. My dogs and I live a dull life these days, if you don't count the Yankees shooting up the place and then bringing their silly wives down here to take over everything—I can hardly even recognize the church service anymore! *You* are the only thing of interest I've had come my way in I don't even want to say how long. Besides that, I don't like guessing where I am in this play.

"All the world's a stage, my girl—Shakespeare said that. Now clearly I've got a part in this production and I want to know exactly what it is. So start at the beginning...no, wait. First, I have to let those traitorous dogs in before they break down the door. I ought to let them suffer, befriending Yankee soldiers the way they've done."

And so Abiah told her—or tried to. It was taking her a long time to do it, because Miss Gwen was forever asking her to elaborate on some fine point. She clearly didn't want to hear the sad tale all at once. She preferred it piecemeal. It was as if the old lady enjoyed pondering over it revelation by revelation.

"Tell me again what Thomas looks like," she said once.

"He's tall," Abiah answered after some resistance. "His hair is dark and his eyes…"

"Like yours—yes, I remember now. I remember seeing the two of you with your heads together over a book. You were like two halves of a matching pair."

Were we? Abiah thought, feeling the sudden urge to cry. If she wasn't very careful, she would lose herself in the remembering.

It became an almost daily ritual for them to sit down together after they had finished the household chores. They would drink their tea in Miss Gwen's small parlor, and Abiah would relate yet another episode of her recent and painful history. She supposed that the two of them must be the very picture of genteel domesticity, seated in front of the fire every evening with the dogs sleeping at their feet—if one discounted the Yankee soldiers who were forever coming in and out of the house.

Miss Gwen had boarders, whether she wanted them or not—officers from the Forty-fourth Massachusetts. Her large two-story house was not far from their brigade headquarters, and at the time of the Union army's unwelcome arrival last March, Miss Gwen had been the only person living in it. The fact that she vigorously protected what the looters had left of her home and her belongings by trying to drive the occupation soldiers away from her door with a riding crop apparently made them decide that this location suited them perfectly. They paid her nothing for "renting" most of the second floor, but they did offer her a few luxuries like coffee, tea or cocoa from time to time. And they had enough sense not to try to give anything to her outright lest they had to deal with that riding crop again. Instead, they left the various items around the house for her to "find."

"Look at this," she'd say, loudly enough for them to hear. "Look what some careless Yankee scalawag left unattended on the fence post! Too bad! Finders keepers!"

It was a game Abiah thought Miss Gwen and the soldiers both enjoyed, and it was no wonder the officer at the church had known immediately who Miss Gwendolyn Pembroke was and that he should send for her.

At first the boarders made some effort to engage Abiah in conversation, she thought because they had apparently found out what she had had to reveal to their commanding general to keep from being arrested—that her husband was also in a Massachusetts regiment. Now, in lieu of conversation, they eyed her curiously—sometimes appreciatively—whenever she encountered any of them on the stairs or in the front hallway. But they no longer took the liberty of trying to speak to her, and she was glad of that.

Their presence was extremely difficult for her, not just because they were the enemy, but because some of them had Thomas's same Boston accent. She didn't know how many times she'd looked up at the sound of one of their voices, half expecting him to be there, no matter how much she knew it to be an impossibility.

Abiah had been in New Bern nearly two months before Miss Gwen pressed her to explain the details of her marriage to Thomas Harrigan. As always, the old lady listened carefully, but for once she didn't ask for any more than Abiah was willing to tell.

"Well, your mother saw that alliance coming—if not the circumstance, then the possibility," Miss Gwen said at one point, and Abiah looked at her in surprise.

"She couldn't have—"

"Could and did," Miss Gwen said. "I know that for a fact, because I'm the one who pointed out your interest in young Mr. Harrigan."

Abiah's surprise progressed to absolute incredulity.

"It stuck out all over you, my girl. It wasn't that you were all silly and moonstruck over him. It was that you worked so hard to show everybody you weren't. Especially him. Now am I right or not?"

Abiah sighed instead of answering.

"So what reason have you given yourself for leaving this very precipitous marriage?" Miss Gwen asked bluntly.

"I didn't have to give myself a reason," Abiah said.

"You didn't have to come here, either. You could have stayed with his mother in Maryland."

"I've told you her situation."

"Yes, but you haven't quite told me yours. And *her* situation didn't keep her from having you brought to her when you were so ill and alone there in Falmouth. She's got more of a hand on the reins than she wants people to think—or the judge to think, either. But never mind. Whatever the reason, you obviously found it intolerable. I surmise that because you've made no attempt to send Thomas word of your whereabouts— or the other thing."

"What other thing?"

"He's in harm's way, Abby. You've heard all the war news even if the Yankees won't let the truth be posted on the signboard in front of Mr. Beers's book-shop. The Union army got whipped again at Chancellorsville. More than likely Thomas was there. Assuming that he survived, shouldn't you tell him he has left you with child?"

Abiah looked at her, speechless. Even she had only just come to suspect—admit—that she was carrying.

"You needn't look so astounded, Abby. It's very simple. You had an embarrassingly hearty appetite for breakfast when you first arrived here. It is now suddenly gone and the smell of cooking turnips sends you bolting from the room. I was with your mother when she first discovered she was going to have Guire," Miss Gwen said. "You are like her. Morning sickness and food aversions *very* early on. And you should tell your husband."

"I don't think he'll care," she said quietly.

"Nonsense! He's a decent man or he wouldn't have gone to such trouble to save your life. And he certainly didn't have to marry you."

"He thought I was going to die, Miss Gwen."

"So what if he did? What reasonable person wouldn't, given the state you were in? It doesn't matter what he was thinking *then,* silly girl. It's what he's thinking *now* that matters. I believe it would give him comfort to know that whatever happens, something of him—and you—will live on."

"You don't understand—"

"I understand regret. It is a bitter pill, let me tell you. And if you don't tell him, and he gets himself killed like Guire, you will regret it for the rest of your life."

"I don't want to talk about this anymore," Abiah said, getting up and unsettling the beagle that had been sleeping soundly on her feet. He gave her a reproachful look and rolled over onto his back.

"Neither do I," Miss Gwen said. "I have made my feelings on the matter very plain. I have given you the benefit of my wisdom and my experience, but I'm *not* one to harp—no matter how much harping may be indicated. I would say that you know best, but I don't happen to think you do. I think your feelings are hurt—for whatever reason—and that's all you can think about. *Your* hurt feelings. I don't believe in condemning a person out of hand—the way you seem to have done with the man you willingly married. I believe in telling people the facts, thereby giving them at least the chance to behave honorably. And if they don't, then you have all the proof you need that they are not worth your time and consideration. Do you see what I mean?''

"I see that you're harping," Abiah said, and Miss Gwen laughed.

"Why, Abiah, you're not nearly so dense as you sometimes seem," she said with the tartness Abiah had come to appreciate regardless of how hard she tried now to be offended.

"If you don't want anything to do with him, then you should at least tell his people in Maryland where you are."

"I expect they know where I am," Abiah said. What they wouldn't know was who had financed her trip.

"But they don't know *how* you are. Given your recent illness, I should think they would wonder—or are they as indifferent as you think Thomas is?"

"I don't know."

"Well, even if they are, you were brought up to know how to behave. Whatever happened between you and her son, Mrs. Harrigan took you in when it counted, and that is likely the reason you're still in this world today. You might at least want to find some gratitude for that, my girl, minuscule though it may be. Now. I think I'll go annoy my boarders."

Abiah sat for a while after Miss Gwen had left. Of course Thomas had the right to know that she was carrying his child, but she just couldn't bring herself to tell him. First her illness, and now a baby. It would

surely seem like just another trap to him. He wanted
to be with Elizabeth—Abiah had the letter to prove it.
And regardless of how well she had been brought up,
she wouldn't write to Clarissa Harrigan. It was true
that the woman had been kind to her. It was true Abiah
had left without even a word of thanks or farewell. It
had hurt too much to behave well then—or now. And
given the situation surrounding Abiah's departure, the
last thing Clarissa Harrigan would expect from her
was a bread-and-butter note.

The only thing Abiah could do was try to stay busy.
She couldn't very well volunteer to knit socks for the
Sanitary Commission. Instead, she worked hard to fill
every day with a relentless round of household activ-
ities so that she wouldn't think about Thomas. She
wasn't afraid to go out now. She went to the post
office for Miss Gwen and to the dry goods shop. She
even sang sometimes in the same church choir she'd
disrupted the day she'd arrived in New Bern. She had
no idea whether Miss Gwen's friends knew that
Thomas was in the Union army or not. She suspected
that Miss Gwen had advised them all that *he* was not
an appropriate topic of conversation.

One afternoon during the first week in June, Miss
Gwen met her at the door when she returned home
from doing their meager shopping at the dry goods
store.

"You've got a visitor, my girl," she whispered. "A
doctor—"

"Miss Gwen, you didn't tell anyone about
my…condition," Abiah said in alarm.

"No, of course not. This man came from Maryland—on behalf of the mother-in-law you think is so disinterested."

"I don't want to see him."

"That is too bad. He's in the parlor and he saw you coming up the walk. Surely, you don't expect *me* to hand deliver your rudeness."

Abiah gave a sharp sigh. "Miss Gwen, *you* used a riding crop on his kind. I hardly think you're one to worry about rudeness."

"And I can still find that riding crop if I have to," Miss Gwen said pointedly. "Were you not listening when I made my speech about regrets?"

"I was listening."

"Then go and see what the man wants!"

Abiah went, mentally dragging her feet if not literally doing so. Dr. Nethen was standing in the small parlor, clearly more anxious than she had ever seen him.

"Abiah," he said without prelude. "I have come with some news—my God, you look well!"

"Please," Abiah said, ignoring the remark. "What is it?"

"Thomas was wounded at Chancellorsville—"

She gasped, because she hadn't expected that announcement at all. She'd expected to hear that the marriage had ended, not that Thomas had been hurt. When Guire had been killed, she'd been overwhelmed by a sudden, inexplicable feeling of dread. She loved Thomas more than life itself, and incredibly, this time, she had sensed nothing at all.

''We're assured it isn't serious,'' Dr. Nethen said. ''But Clarissa was very anxious that you should know. She was also anxious to know how *you* are. So here I am. On a little intelligence-gathering excursion with the very accommodating Captain Appleby.''

He smiled. Abiah didn't.

''You've seen Thomas?'' she asked. ''After Malvern Hill they sent word to us that my brother was all right—but it wasn't the truth.''

''No, I haven't seen him. But he is not in a hospital and he hasn't been sent home. I would say that in this instance we can trust the reports we were given—particularly since it was Gertie who gave them.''

''Gertie?''

''You trust her, don't you?''

''I...yes. If she says she saw him, talked to him.''

''She sent word that she did. She thought we might know how to reach you.''

Abiah took a deep breath to try to stay ahead of the whirlwind of emotions Dr. Nethen's announcement had just unleashed. ''Who told you I was here?'' she asked abruptly.

''Appleby, of course. Clarissa was so distressed after you left, he could not keep your confidence.''

Abiah looked at her visitor, wondering what kind of crimp that put in Elizabeth's plans. Abiah never for a moment thought that the lovely Miss Channing would herself inform anyone of her whereabouts.

''Mrs. Harrigan was good to me,'' Abiah said. ''It wasn't my intention to ever cause her any difficulty. I am sorry for that.''

''The difficulty wasn't your doing, Abiah.''

''Wasn't it?''

"Of course not. And Clarissa has weathered scandal before. It hasn't been nearly as upsetting for her as for Elizabeth Channing. That young woman actually thought she could behave the way she has and still be received in polite society. I dare say it has been quite a shock for her not only to have been disinvited to every major social event for the rest of the year, but to find herself in a situation that her father cannot fix."

Abiah didn't say anything—but it was all she could do not to ask if Elizabeth had mentioned Thomas.

"I have one other reason for coming," Dr. Nethen said, reaching into his coat pocket. "This arrived for you a short time after you left. Clarissa wanted to make certain that you received it. She thought the judge might interfere if she tried to forward it to you through the mail—or that it might not reach you."

He held an envelope out to Abiah a long time before she finally took it. It was addressed to "Mrs. Abiah C. Harrigan." She recognized the handwriting immediately.

"Now, I have some other business to attend to. Shall I see about that, and then return—in case you want to send Thomas a reply back with me?"

"That won't be necessary," she said. "I have nothing I want to say to him."

"But surely—"

"No," she interrupted. "I thank you for your offer—and for the trouble you've gone to on my behalf. But no."

"How will this ever be resolved it you don't at least—"

"No," she said again, forcing herself to meet his eyes. How could she explain to him that this letter, as long as it was unread, gave her a small glimmer of hope? And she needed hope desperately.

"Dr. Nethen," she said when he reached the door. "Thank Mrs. Harrigan. I wish..."

She didn't go on. There was nothing more to be said. She stood there with the letter clutched tightly in her hand.

The mail carrier came at the end of the week—not that it mattered. There was no reply from Abiah.

And it was clear to Thomas now that there wasn't likely to be one, just as it was clear to him that it was his military lot in life to be led by a succession of lunatics. Joseph Hooker had been more inept than he could ever have imagined. In the fiasco at Chancellorsville the son of a bitch had blatantly misinterpreted the obvious at every turn. He had stubbornly insisted that what could only be a flanking movement was a Confederate retreat. His staff, his pickets tried to tell him otherwise, and he simply refused to listen. Even when the deer and rabbits came bounding out of the woods straight toward them, terrified by the advancing Rebel army, Hooker remained unconvinced. The Union line had been cut to pieces, and all for nothing.

Thomas himself was lucky to have only been slightly wounded—a spent mine ball that cut a short but deep gash into his scalp. The bleeding had been markedly disproportionate to the injury itself. His head still ached, but he wasn't dead, and he supposed that was something.

And if he and the entire army weren't demoralized enough, by the third week of June, a new problem presented itself. Robert E. Lee was clearly no longer concerned about the Grand Army of the Potomac coming after Richmond or anything else, for that matter. He dismissed the threat entirely by marching his army northward into Maryland, leaving hysterical citizens in his wake and nothing to be done but to chase after him.

Which was exactly what Thomas did *not* need. How would he ever get to see Abiah if he was forever going entirely in the wrong damn direction? He had never felt so down in his life. He had nothing of her to carry with him. No photograph, no ribbon or lock of hair, and for damn sure, no letter. All he had were the memories it hurt too much to think about. And he and La Broie both knew the gravity of this military situation, if no one else did. The mongrel dog was chasing conveyances again. And if Joseph Hooker caught up with *this* damn wagon, there would be hell to pay.

On June 28, Hooker was replaced by George Meade, and Thomas wrote two letters he could not mail, one to Abiah and one to his mother. On July 2, he waited with his regiment in a Pennsylvania peach orchard, his mind strangely calm but his heart aching with what might have been. His men were lying on their bellies in the dirt in front of him, out of sight of the Confederates, who were rapidly massing on the other side of an open meadow. Thomas walked up and down in the blazing hot sun, trying to keep everyone's courage up—and his. At one point, he thought he saw a particular regimental banner in the line of trees— Johnny Miller's, if he still lived.

Bender returned with all the canteens he could fill with water and still carry.

"Keep your head down, Bender," Thomas admonished as the boy began to distribute them down the line.

"Aw, Cap, they ain't going to shoot *me* when they got you to aim at," he said, causing a ripple of laughter along the line.

"Cap," La Broie said at his elbow. "I got something to say, sir."

"Then say it," Thomas said, watching the Rebel line swell and swell as more men got into position.

"If you see Gertie again—and I don't—would you say to her that I wish I'd married her, and that's the God's truth."

Thomas glanced at him and nodded.

"And, sir—well, there's one other thing, sir."

"Hurry it up, La Broie, they're bringing the artillery around."

"I want you to tell Miss Abiah she and Gertie don't have to worry about Zachariah Wilson no more."

"What do you mean?" Thomas said, looking around sharply.

But the cannonade began in a great, sequential booming that drowned out the question.

"La Broie!" Thomas said, trying to be heard over the cannons' roar.

"It's been a pleasure serving with you, sir," Thomas saw him say more than heard. La Broie gave him a smart salute and moved away.

Chapter Thirteen

Abiah could hear someone whispering in the hall-way. That in itself was enough to get her attention, because the Yankee boarders heretofore had never minded how much noise they made, regardless of the hour. She opened the parlor door. Miss Gwen was standing toe-to-toe with Dr. Nethen, and if Abiah had thought he looked worried at their previous meeting, she had been wrong.

"What's happened?" she asked.

"Abby…" Miss Gwen began. She gave a heavy sigh. "Dr. Nethen," she said, giving over to him.

"Abiah, Thomas was at Gettysburg," Dr. Nethen said. "You understand that the lists are often wrong. The confusion is…"

Abiah waited for him to go on, but whatever he was about to say, she was determined not to believe it, and she supposed that her face must have shown it. He abruptly handed her the folded newspaper he had in his hand. She looked down at it, but she couldn't read it, not with Miss Gwen and Dr. Nethen watching her so closely. She turned abruptly and walked out of the house, taking the newspaper with her. There were a few people out, promenading Yankee wives who had come down from Massachusetts to ease the tediousness of the occupation for their husbands. They looked at her curiously as she passed, one of them holding her child closer to her skirts as if she thought Abiah might be a source of harm.

She kept walking until she reached the Methodist church, but she didn't go inside. She went into the cemetery instead, and she didn't stop until she reached the low stone wall at the far end. There, in the dappled shade of an oak tree, amid birdsong and bees and cicadas incited by the intense July heat, she began to read. The wind rustled the canopy of oak leaves overhead. Her hands trembled.

She finally found Thomas's regiment on the list. The names under it went on and on, and they weren't in alphabetical order.

She kept reading.

"Oh, dear God," she whispered, seeing a name she recognized.

La Broie, Peter, Sgt., killed.

And then,

Harrigan, Thomas, Capt., killed.

She made a small anguished sound. He couldn't be dead. Even seeing it in print, she believed that she would have known if he was. How many days since the battle? Twenty? Twenty-one? Every day since the news of the terrible losses at Gettysburg came, she had grown increasingly certain that Thomas was all right.

"Abiah."

She looked around. Dr. Nethen had come after her.

"How old is this?" she asked, unfolding the newspaper even as she asked so she could see the date, her voice accusing and filled with unshed tears. It was over a week old. "Has there been any news since?"

"No. Or at least when I left, this was all we knew. The judge is trying to verify it—for Clarissa's sake. He has people searching the hospitals, and the houses in and around the town. I understand there were so many wounded, the citizens of Gettysburg had to take them into their homes. Apparently Thomas was in a very...bad place during the second day of the battle. But thus far, they can't find anyone from the regiment to ask."

"Anyone alive, you mean."

"Yes. Anyone alive."

"He's not dead."

"Abiah—"

"He is not dead!"

Dr. Nethen was looking at her with such pity that she abruptly turned away from him. She could not allow him to make her doubt her conviction.

"Abiah, Miss Pembroke told me about your...condition."

She looked at him. "She had no right to do that."

"Perhaps not. But she has the good sense to want what is best for you. This pregnancy could be very hard on you. You've only just come through a life-threatening illness. Your body may not yet be strong enough, particularly now with the shock of Thomas being—'' He broke off. ''I think you should come back with me to Maryland—where you can be looked after properly,'' he said after a moment.

''No.''

''It would mean a lot to Clarissa to know Thomas left a child.''

''Thomas is *not* dead!'' she said vehemently. ''I would know if he were. I knew about my brother, Guire. Everyone said he was fine—but I knew better. I knew he was dead and I know Thomas is alive.''

The doctor sighed and sat on the stone wall. ''Did you read the letter I gave you?''

''No,'' she said, looking across the cemetery so she wouldn't have to meet his eyes. The grave diggers were at work in the far corner. She hadn't noticed them earlier. One of the women from the church had gone to Pennsylvania to bring her son's body home, and the undertaker was making ready.

''Abiah, for God's sake! He may have explained this thing with Elizabeth—''

''I don't want it explained. I don't want to know about it. I don't want to think about it. I have a child coming. I have to save all my strength for that. I can't let myself be distracted by Elizabeth Channing.''

''Abiah —''

''Dr. Nethen, you realize, I hope, that this is none of your business.''

He gave a slight smile. ''I can't help it. I had truly hoped things would work out between you and Thomas. How have you been feeling—physically, I mean?''

She looked at him. Her first inclination was not to answer him.

"I feel...all right," she said after a moment.

"Can you get enough to eat here?"

"We manage. We have a garden, and Miss Gwen has some...very charitable friends."

"How charitable will they be if they find out your husband was a soldier in the Union army?"

"They are *her* friends, not mine. I don't believe they would hold the actions of her relatives against her. And please. Stop referring to Thomas in the past tense."

"Abiah—"

"Please! He may be wounded. He may be injured very badly, but he's alive. I believe it. I *feel* it...."

He didn't say anything else. After a moment he offered her his arm. She took it and walked with him back to the house. Miss Gwen was waiting anxiously on the veranda.

"Abiah, are you—" she began.

"I think I'll lie down for a while," Abiah interrupted.

"Yes, my girl," Miss Gwen said. "You are so very pale. Doctor...?"

"I don't need anything," Abiah insisted. "I just want to lie down."

She left them standing, and hurried up the stairs to her room. She stretched out on the bed, her eyes closed, the newspaper still in her hand.

He's not dead! I would know if he were dead.

She rested her hands protectively over her belly.

We would know.

The afternoon breeze had finally risen, and the lace curtains Miss Gwen had managed to save from the looters billowed outward from time to time. It was still so hot. Abiah could smell the heat, smell the dust in the curtains each time they stirred. Somewhere nearby a dog barked. Somewhere nearby children laughed and played.

She closed her eyes. She was not ill. She was filled with regrets.

Chapter Fourteen

"Abby!" he said aloud, startling himself with the sound of his own voice.

"Ah, no, sir. It's me."

Thomas took a quiet breath. He had to stop doing that. He had to stop thinking every sound, no matter how insignificant, was her. Sometimes he thought he heard her singing—the same sad ballad he remembered from that summer night at the Calder house so long ago.

How did that go? *I can't remember. I can't—*

"What was your name again?" he abruptly asked the orderly, because he couldn't remember that, either.

"Private Murphy, sir."

"Yes. Murphy. How…long have I been here?"

From the look on the man's face, Thomas immediately realized that he must have asked that question before as well.

"It's now the last day of August, sir. You've been here since the fifth of July."

"In Washington."

"Yes, sir! That's right, sir!" the man said enthusiastically—as if Thomas were a small boy and he'd just managed to count to ten. "Would you be remembering your name now as well, sir?"

"My name?"

"Yes, sir. We've kind of had to be guessing about that, you see."

"Harrigan. Thomas...W. Harrigan."

"And your rank?"

"Captain ... Twenty-second ... Massachusetts... Infantry. Company...B."

"I see. Let me write that down. We have folks asking after soldiers all the time, you know. It's good you can remember. Now we can let your family know."

Thomas reached up to touch the side of his face. It was heavily bandaged. In spite of the pain, he abruptly lifted his head, trying to see his arms and legs.

"No, now don't be worrying about that, sir. You're all there—every bit of you. You've got a few holes in you you didn't have before, but they're healing. You've lost nothing important at all—except time. From the looks of you when they brought you in—all the dirt and rocks stuck in your hide—I'd say you were close to a shell when it landed. But not too close, or you'd be dead now for sure. It'll take a while to get you back to your former loveliness, but your Abby will be knowing you at first glance. I promise you that."

"Who did you say?" Thomas asked, because for one brief moment he thought that perhaps she'd been here, after all.

"I said 'your Abby,' sir. You've been calling for her since they brought you in. Even in the delirium."

"Delirium," Thomas repeated, trying to take in everything the sergeant was telling him.

"Yes, sir. That's like having a terrible nightmare, only you're not asleep. There's been many a soldier here these last few weeks suffering that—ones that came from the same hell you were in there in Gettysburg mostly. But we whipped the Rebel sons of bitches and that's the truth. You're going to be getting well now, sir. You'll see. The ladies of Washington will be arriving this afternoon—I'll be sending one of them 'round to write a letter for you. You rest now. What a fine day this is, when a brave soldier comes back to his own."

But Thomas didn't want to send a letter. He felt a pang of guilt that his mother would be worried about him—if she hadn't given up on him already and assumed that he was dead—but he wanted to be stronger first. He didn't want to be pounced upon and dragged off to Maryland, as Abby had been. That may have saved her life, but he had no notion that it would do anything to further his. He would not be indebted to his grandfather any more than he already was.

He did have "holes" he hadn't had before the battle—three of them—and by God's grace they all seemed to have passed through spots he didn't particularly require. The worst was in his right thigh just above the knee. Somehow a ball had traversed the muscle without hitting the bone. It hurt like hell when he tried to stand. And when he finally looked into a mirror with the bandage off, he thought that Private Murphy had been a bit generous in his assertion that Abby would still recognize him. How could she when he hardly recognized himself?

But he was lucky to be alive, and he was lucky to have encountered a surgeon who apparently sometimes tried measures other than radical amputations. He was still feverish at times, but he was in his right mind. Every day he pushed himself to his physical limit—sitting, then standing, then hobbling the length of the hospital ward, and for no other purpose than to be able to go look for his wife. When he wasn't sleeping in total exhaustion from his efforts, he passed the time talking to the other men.

Everyone he spoke with had come from Gettysburg. He didn't remember much about the battle himself— how he had happened to be wounded in three places— and he didn't want to. He knew that his corps commander had disobeyed orders and moved them to an exposed position in a peach orchard and a wheatfield too far out from the Union lines. And he knew that not many of the men who were there with him had survived. But those events were too recent and too raw for examination. He was here and he was more or less on his feet, and that was enough for now.

He made inquiries about the men in his company— La Broie and Bender in particular. No one could tell him anything. And absolutely no one would provide him with a casualty list. It was as if they thought learning a comrade was dead would come as a surprise. Some days he walked through the wards himself, thinking that some of his men could be in the same condition he had been—senseless and therefore unidentified—but he never recognized a single one.

The middle of September he had a visitor—a weary-looking colonel from the War Department who advised him that he had been promoted to the rank of major.

"Why?" Thomas asked the man in all sincerity.

"The reports say for gallantry and extreme bravery—at the peach orchard salient. You were mentioned by name in several accounts by commanding officers who were on the field that day. It seems the federal line would have broken many times if not for you."

"I don't want it," Thomas said bluntly. If he'd forced men to stand and be murdered on account of a commanding officer's stupidity, he couldn't see being decorated for it.

"I'm afraid what you want doesn't enter into it. You have been declared a hero and you have been made a major. And that, as they say, is that."

Thomas looked at him, wondering if his grandfather had anything to do with this recognition. If so, then he must know that Thomas had survived. He could easily see the old man's reasoning—a wounded and decorated war-hero grandson did much to cancel out the scandal-making, seemingly adulterous one.

"Are your injuries such that you will petition to be mustered out, Major Harrigan?" the man asked.

"No, sir."

"If you intend to stay, I have been authorized by

the secretary of war to tell you that you may ask for reassignment—wherever you choose. Given your leg injury, if you'd prefer a cavalry unit this time—''

''No, sir. If there are still occupation forces in New Bern, I would like to be assigned there.''

The colonel stared at him. ''There is a Massachusetts regiment there. The Forty-fourth. It's a plum posting,'' he said.

''Is it?'' Thomas asked, because he didn't know anything about that. He only knew that the last he'd heard, Abiah had gone there.

''But I dare say you deserve it.''

One of the men a few beds down began to weep loudly. It had a visible effect on the colonel.

''I understand there isn't much of your brigade—or the Third Corps—left,'' he continued, when the soldier had grown quieter.

''I don't really know, sir,'' Thomas said, but a fleeting memory of the peach orchard came into his mind in spite of all he could do. He realized that his hands were beginning to tremble. He clenched his fists and cleared his throat and tried to concentrate. ''The surgeon hasn't said when I may leave here,'' he offered after a moment.

''I will have the orders for your new posting sent to him. He can authorize them when he sees fit. Now, if you would be so kind, Major. Thus far, I have spent the war safely here in Washington. The sacrifices you and your regiment have made are not unappreciated. You would do me a great honor if you would allow me to shake your hand.''

Thomas shook the hand the man offered. The colonel's grasp was firm, and Thomas thought, sincere. If he noticed Thomas's trembling, he gave no sign.

"Good luck, Major Harrigan," he said. "But perhaps in New Bern you won't need it."

Chapter Fifteen

Abiah walked to church in spite of the rain and the cold, leaving Miss Gwen at home in front of the warm fire, applying hot flannel to her rheumatism. Church was the only place Abiah could go where she could find some solace. There had been no word from Maryland about whether Thomas's death had been confirmed or not and no more visits from Dr. Nethen, and she had retreated into a place where nothing existed for her but her coming baby. She felt well enough. The baby moved often and vigorously enough to reassure her.

The church wasn't far from the house, but it was on the other side of the street, and the steady downpour had made crossing a matter of wading into a smelly quagmire of mud and horse and pig manure. If one was on foot, the only way to safely cross was a line of stepping-stones some distance from the church. Unfortunately, it was a favorite loitering place for off-duty soldiers because the granite pillars were at least a foot above the street itself and widely spaced to allow for the passage of wagons and buggies. The soldiers obviously hoped to catch a glimpse of a well-turned ankle—or more—as the ladies struggled with their voluminous skirts to reach the other side.

Abiah had hoped that the inclement weather would have thinned the crowd this morning. It hadn't. She waited her turn among the group of other women churchgoers and the one elderly man who was their token escort. She kept her eyes averted from the enthusiastic military audience, her demeanor as indifferent as she could make it. Finally, there was nothing left for her to do but go. She was the last one of the group to cross, and she was on the third step well out into the muddy street when the loud comments began.

The wind was blowing, driving rain into her face. She couldn't see. Her bonnet blew off and hung down her back by the ribbon ties. She stood there, in spite of vigorous coaxing from the men on the sidelines to hike up her skirts and carry on. When she was about to step to the next granite pillar, they began to whistle loudly.

"Come on, darlin'," one of them yelled. "Come to Billy! Come—"

There was a loud thud, and Abiah looked around. An officer had ridden his mount into the group and was now scattering soldiers left and right with the well-aimed toe of his boot.

"Sons of bitches!" he berated them. "Is this all you have to do?"

Abiah took the opportunity to continue to the next stepping-stone. When she looked up, the officer was riding in her direction. She glanced away from him, and then immediately back again. And the breath went out of her.

"Thomas..." she whispered. Her knees grew weak. It was all she could do to stay on the stepping-stone. He was so...changed. He was thin to the point of gauntness, and there was a livid scar on his right cheek.

Thomas!

He said nothing. He simply rode toward her, his eyes on her all the while. The effrontery of his staring caused a murmur of protest from the women waiting on the other side of the street. He paid them no mind. Abiah kept expecting him to say something, but he didn't, not until he was riding slowly past.

"Don't worry," he said. "I've ruined your reputation once. I won't do it again."

She stood there, not knowing what to do, trying not to cry. She had believed with all her heart that he was alive, but the reality of seeing him again—*here*—was nearly more than she could bear. And if he'd made even the slightest gesture toward her, if he'd given any indication at all that he wanted her to come with him the way he had that rainy afternoon in the Winthrop driveway, she would have gone. Anywhere. It wouldn't have mattered.

She felt so light-headed suddenly. The baby fluttered in her womb. She turned carefully and began to make her way back the way she had come.

"Abiah?" one of the women called. "Are you all right?"

"I—yes," she said. "But I need to go home."

"…Uncalled for!" she heard the woman say to the others in the group. "Abiah, are you sure you can—"

But Abiah didn't wait to hear the question. She kept going, her bonnet still tied around her neck and bouncing along behind her, until she reached the house. Two of the boarders were in the front hall, and she pushed past them, bursting into Miss Gwen's small parlor so suddenly that the dogs leaped to their feet and began to bark.

"What?" Miss Gwen cried, apparently startled from a sound sleep in her chair.

But now that Abiah was here, she didn't know what to do with herself. She stood, then began to pace. Miss Gwen grabbed her by the arm.

"Abiah, look at you! What's happened? You're soaked—sit down, for heaven's sake!"

Miss Gwen all but forced her into a rocking chair. The dogs were still unsettled.

"What is it? Is it the baby?"

Abiah shook her head. "Thomas," she said. "He's here."

"Thomas," Miss Gwen repeated. "*The* Thomas, husband of one Abiah Calder, active participant in that army we generally despise?"

Abiah nodded.

"And he's *here*—alive—in New Bern?"

"Yes."

"Well!" Miss Gwen said. "I'm beginning to like that boy better and better all the time!"

* * *

Thomas waited in the cold damp foyer. He kept drawing covert looks from the general's staff—because his face was scarred, for one thing, and the scar in itself was a blatant symbol to these soldiers of exactly what their "plum" posting in New Bern really meant. He noted that their facial expressions almost always fell into the same two categories: shame at not having done their duty at Fredericksburg or Chancellorsville or Gettysburg, or profound relief at having escaped the trial by fire.

Commanding officers ordinarily didn't come down to brigade headquarters on a Sunday at all. They passed the day quietly at home with their wives and children and a big chicken dinner instead. But the general himself was here now, and they—and Thomas—knew he was not happy.

"Major Harrigan, the general is ready to see you," a young lieutenant finally came out of the inner sanctum to say, his eyes focused somewhere above Thomas's head.

Thomas got up with some difficulty; he had long since discovered that cold, rainy weather made his right thigh sing. He could feel the young lieutenant watching him as he limped past.

"Damn you, Harrigan," the general said before he had even closed the door. "What have you got to say for yourself?"

The remark was so like his many audiences with the judge that Thomas very nearly laughed. And he could only give his same standard answer.

"I'm...sorry, sir. I don't know what you mean—"

"The devil you don't! I have had hysterical church-women in my parlor all afternoon!"

The general was glaring at him, expecting...damned if Thomas knew what.

"You haven't even been here three days! What the devil were you thinking? The young woman you insulted on the street this morning has connections. She belongs to one of New Bern's oldest families. Are you out of your mind?"

"Sir, I intended no insult—"

"Whores are one thing, respectable women on their way to church are something else again! You can't blatantly show your carnal inclinations like that! It will *not* be tolerated, do you understand?"

Thomas did, finally, but he had the good sense not to interrupt.

"I'm not going to have the townspeople up in arms over this incident," the general continued. "We are getting along fine with these people, and I'll be damned if you're going to upset the applecart with your uncouth behavior. If you can't control yourself, I suggest you go visit one of the women down on the docks—or better yet, send for your wife to join you here!"

"Sir, the lady in question *is* my wife," Thomas said.

The revelation didn't impress the general in the least.

"Well, if she is, it is obvious from the reports delivered in my parlor today that she wants nothing whatsoever to do with you. I understand her distress is such that she has even taken to her bed. *Her* bed, not yours."

"Sir, is she all right?"

"It's a bit late to worry about that now, Major. What I said before stands. You *will* stay away from her. I'm not having those Rebel Amazons stirring up the whole town over this thing. You stay away from her, or you'll find yourself back in a fighting unit—wounded or not, hero or not, influential relatives or not. Do you understand me?"

"Yes, sir," Thomas said. "Perfectly."

He stood outside the general's door after he had been dismissed, looking out the front windows. The rain still fell steadily, but his leg didn't ache nearly so much now. Or perhaps that pain had been usurped by the pain in his heart.

Now what?

There was no question in his mind that he would make another attempt to speak to her—without the onlookers and without the general's permission—if he could just find her. He gave a quiet sigh. New Bern wasn't all that big. He'd just have to do what he'd been doing and keep watch for her. Sooner or later he was bound to run into her again—hopefully without the churchwomen. She must be staying someplace near those stepping-stones.

He realized that the lieutenant had said something to him.

"I beg your pardon?"

"I said that I didn't make the connection, sir—the name, Mrs. Harrigan."

"You...know Mrs. Harrigan?"

"Not exactly, sir. I board at Miss Pembroke's house. Neither of the ladies invite familiarity from the officers staying there."

"I see," Thomas said after a moment. He had a thousand questions pertaining to that remark, but he didn't ask any of them. He didn't want the general to come out of his hole and find him interrogating the lieutenant as to Abiah's whereabouts.

"We all knew Mrs. Harrigan's husband was in a Massachusetts regiment, but I didn't realize you were he."

Thomas couldn't keep from asking one question.

"Mrs. Harrigan is...well?"

If Thomas's ignorance surprised the lieutenant, it didn't show.

"I have not seen her today, sir, but I believe she is. I have seen Miss Pembroke, and she gave no indication that there was anything amiss. I believe she would have been after us not to make so much noise coming and going if Mrs. Harrigan were not well. I always thought—"

"Thought what?" Thomas, asked when he didn't go on.

"It wouldn't be appropriate for me to make the observation, sir," the lieutenant said, flushing slightly.

"Make it," Thomas said.

The lieutenant looked at him, clearly trying to decide if he wanted to take that liberty or disobey what was obviously an order.

"Well, sir," he said after a moment, "she seemed

sad to me. Not weepy or anything like that. Just…sad.''

"I see," Thomas said, but he didn't see at all.

"Sir, could I ask you a question?"

"As you please," Thomas said, expecting some inquiry about his personal life he would have to reject.

"I have heard that you were at Gettysburg, sir." The lieutenant looked at him, this time scar and all. "I was wondering…what it was like."

Thomas stared at him. It wasn't a question he had anticipated, and he couldn't find the words to either answer it or dismiss it. What words were there to describe hell on earth?

"Sorry, sir," the lieutenant said as the silence lengthened into a painful awkwardness. "I shouldn't have asked. It's just that well, there's no one else here who—"

"Lieutenant Howell!" the general yelled through his closed door, and the young officer was off and running, Thomas supposed, in order not to find out "what it's like" firsthand.

There was no point in hanging around here any longer. Thomas wasn't quite sure yet what his duties were, but he did know this was not the time to ask.

He stepped outside into the rain. There had been a heavy downpour at Gettysburg after the battle—or so he'd been told. He didn't remember it all, but he felt as if he did. A day like this left him no defenses against the heavy melancholy that constantly threatened to overwhelm him. He didn't remember the rain, but he was beginning to remember everything else.

Sometimes his hands shook so badly he couldn't hold on to things. He jumped at sudden noises. He couldn't sleep; he hardly remembered to eat. He had had two setbacks with the wound in his thigh, and here it was December. The army surgeon at the hospital in Washington had been reluctant to declare him fit for duty, but Thomas had insisted. He simply couldn't bear the waiting any longer.

Abby.

Seeing her stranded in the middle of the street being insulted by his own men, he had wanted only to rescue her one more time. Would she have come with him? He didn't know. She hadn't looked away in horror at the sight of him, at least, and that was something. If he could just talk to her. If he could just put his head in her lap and tell her what had happened to him and to La Broie and Bender.

But even as the thought came to him, he knew that he couldn't speak of those things to her. He was in the wrong army, the same army that had killed her brother. How could he say anything to her of the hatred he'd felt for those people—her people—that hot July day?

He mounted his horse and set out toward his quarters. The house where he'd been assigned to stay had been completely taken over by the military. There was no token "boarding," and no New Bern resident he could ask about Miss Pembroke.

"Major Harrigan!" one of the orderlies called when he was about to ride around to the back of the house to stable his horse. "There's a matter that needs your attention, sir!"

Thomas dismounted painfully and made his way slowly up the front steps, expecting some petty military matter that needed some kind of disposition.

"She's waiting in the parlor, sir," the orderly said.

She?

Thomas opened the door. A little old lady sat on a straight chair near the stove, both feet propped up on the rail. The bottom of her skirt and her shoes were wet and muddy. She seemed not in the least surprised to see him.

"Well, don't just stand there," she said.

He looked at her. "I beg your pardon?"

"Get in here," she said pointedly.

"Ah, yes, ma'am," he replied after a moment. If this was another dressing-down for his behavior at the stepping-stones today, he supposed that he might as well get it over with.

"Thomas," she continued. "It is Thomas, is it not?"

"I...yes. I'm afraid you have me at a disadvantage—"

"Sit down," she interrupted. "It hurts me to look at you. Well, come on!" she insisted, when he continued to stand. "I won't bite you. At least I don't think I will. Actually, when it comes to damn Yankees like yourself, I prefer riding crops."

"Riding crops?"

She dismissed that topic with a wave of her hand.

"We don't want to talk about that. We want to talk about your wife. Yes or no?"

"Forgive me, but who *are* you?"

"Miss Gwendolyn Pembroke," she said primly. "Now which is it? Yes or no?"

"Yes," he said, pulling another straight chair close to the stove.

"Abby was very upset by seeing you today."

"I'm sorry," he said. "It was…unexpected."

"So I gathered. You realize that our only information here was that you were dead. You were on the casualty list Dr. Nethen brought—the one printed in the *New York Times.* 'Harrigan, Thomas, Captain, killed.' And we've never heard otherwise. Abby didn't believe it, of course. *No one* could make her believe it.

"I see," he said.

"Do you?" she asked pointedly.

He sighed. "No."

"Well, that's where I come in. What do you want to know?"

"I want to know if Abiah is all right," he said without hesitation.

"She's…tolerable. The fever she had hasn't come back, but she's still not the Abiah she was the last time I saw her in Virginia. I saw you then, too. You liked my hounds."

"Miss Gwen," he said, suddenly remembering. "You're Miss Gwen."

"I am. And you are the scalawag Yankee who has broken my Abby's heart."

"She told you that?"

"No, she did not. I don't know the cause of her present mental state. I can only make my conclusions after seeing the result. My question is what are we going to do now? Are you her husband or aren't you?"

"I am."

"You know there were rumors to the contrary—people who said the marriage was not bona fide, that it was only done so that she might die happy."

"Who said that?"

"People in Falmouth who repeated the rumors they heard and then wrote them down and mailed them to their relatives here."

"Does Abby know that?"

"I can't say. If she does, it would account for some of her melancholy."

"There were *three* chaplains at the ceremony, Miss Gwen."

"Three!"

"I can assure you I am her husband."

She looked at him for a moment. "Good," she said finally. "Of course, it doesn't matter what people think. It's what Abby thinks."

"What does she think?"

"You know, Thomas, I am not sure *she* knows—which is why I'm here. I think you need to talk to her."

"Then let's go—"

"Not *now*. She's too upset by your resurrection, even if she didn't think you were dead. Wait a day or two. I don't see why you can't come to the house one evening. I don't see any reason why you can't just walk right in—half your sorry army does that whenever they feel like it, anyway. I would suggest after supper—when she won't have any excuse to go skittering off someplace if she thinks she doesn't want to talk to you. If fact, I would suggest some time *well* after supper. Her room is at the top of the stairs, the first one on the right. The window faces the street. You will be able to tell she's awake if her lamp is still lit. Perhaps it would go more smoothly if she weren't.''

He looked at her. What was she telling him to do— break into the house, into Abby's bedchamber? At this point he had no idea whether Miss Gwen was an ally or not.

''You'll be able to find your way,'' she said. ''The officers leave a lamp burning in the foyer at all hours. It's a terrible waste of oil—but then, your army has it to waste, doesn't it? Do you understand me or don't you?''

''I understand,'' he said.

''Good. Now help me up—or should I help you? Neither of us are very accomplished at walking these days, are we?''

He assisted her out of her chair and offered her his arm. ''I dare say we could use some improvement,'' he said as they both limped to the door. ''How will you get home?''

''I have my buggy. Here,'' she said, giving him a sheet of paper from her pocket. ''These are the directions to the house. I expect *not* to see you arrive there.''

He abruptly smiled, and so did she.

''You should smile more often, Tommy,'' she said. ''It helps a body understand what Abiah sees in you.''

He stood for a moment after she had gone. The only thing he knew for certain was that he would *not* be waiting a day or two.

Chapter Sixteen

Abby woke suddenly not quite knowing where she was. It was still raining—she could hear it beating against the windowpanes, and for a brief moment it was as if she were in Zachariah Wilson's house again. The room was cold. She fumbled in the dark to light the lamp, and she would have gotten out of bed to stoke the fire, but Thomas was sitting in the chair by the bed. She breathed in sharply, recognizing him only a split second before she would have cried out.

"I'm sorry," he said. "I didn't mean to scarc you."

"Well, you did. What are you doing here?" she asked, pulling the bedcovers tightly around her, as if that would be some protection against the onslaught of emotions his presence caused. She had expected to encounter him again, but not so soon and not here, not when she'd had no time to prepare herself, not when she could hardly look at him without weeping.

"You're here," he said quietly. "Where else would I be?"

She looked at him for a moment. "I don't think we want to get into that."

He ignored the remark.

"If you won't write to me, if I don't know whether or not I have to pretend we're strangers whenever we meet, then I have no choice but to come to you like this."

Their eyes met and held; he was the first to look away. She could see the scar on his face, and she could see the effort he was putting into not letting her see it. She had thought him changed before, but now—still—she barely recognized him. And it wasn't just the scar. It was the terrible haunted and forsaken look in his eyes.

"Are you all right?" she asked.

"Well, I'm a hell of a lot better than I was." He tried to smile and didn't quite make it.

She shivered suddenly, more from nerves than from the cold.

He got up from the chair, slowly, painfully and walked—limped—to the fireplace to put on another log. "I would have done this sooner," he said, "but I didn't want to wake you."

"How—how long have you been here?"

"Awhile," he said.

"You just...walked in, just like that?"

"Just like that," he said.

"Thomas..."

"What, Abby? You don't want me here? I know that. But I..." He gave a quiet sigh.

She could see his weariness, so much so that when

he returned, she didn't protest when he sat down on the side of the bed instead of in the chair.

He looked at her and gave an offhand shrug. "Can't sleep," he said.

"Why not? Are you in pain?"

He didn't answer either question. "I thought maybe I could just sit here for a while," he said after a moment. "With you. Maybe we could talk a little—like we used to when I came to your mother's house. If you and I can talk, then I won't have to think about...anything."

He was looking at her so gravely.

"I'm not making sense, am I?"

"About as much as you ever do, Thomas," she said, and he actually gave a soft laugh. She moved over. "Come lie down."

He hesitated, to decide if she meant it, she supposed. She had no wish to be coy, and she was not hypocritical enough to pretend that they had not once been as intimate as it was possible to be.

He took off his boots, a procedure that clearly caused him a great deal of pain. She had to fight down her inclination to help him, because if she did, if he saw her, he would know. She could hide her condition under petticoats and jackets and shawls in the daytime. She couldn't hide it under a nightdress.

Finally, he stretched out beside her on top of the covers.

"God, I am so...tired...." he said, sighing heavily and lying back on the pillow, his arm thrown over his eyes.

"Can't you take something?" she asked. "So you can sleep?"

"Yes."

"Then why don't you?"

"Because it makes the nightmares worse..." He looked at her. "Could we just skip this and go straight to the serious discussion?"

"No," she said. She made no move to lie down beside him, as much as she wanted to. "We have nothing to discuss."

"Don't we?"

"What's done is done."

"Ah," he said. "I see. We're to approach this with a pragmatist's point of view."

"One of us has to be practical."

"Meaning I am not?"

"You're the one who came up with the idea of us marrying."

"So I am," he admitted.

"There was nothing practical about that."

"That's a matter of opinion, Abby. Given the circumstances—even given the consequences—I would do it again."

But you don't know the consequences, she thought.

He closed his eyes, and she could look at him openly now. He had shaved before he came. She could see the razor nick on his chin, smell the soap. She wanted to touch him. She was so glad to see him, so glad he was safe.

"I thought you'd throw something at me when we met face-to-face again," he said after a moment.

"So did I," she said, and he smiled. She had to look away so that he wouldn't see the effect it had on her.

"I wrote to you."

"I know."

"You got my letter?"

"Yes and no."

"I don't know what that means, Abby."

"It means I didn't read it."

"Why not?"

She didn't answer him. There was no answer she wanted to reveal to him. Her heart was broken, she was afraid of what it said—and she just...hadn't.

"Where is it?" he asked.

"Why?"

"Because I want you to read it now—with me here."

"It won't change anything."

"Abby—"

"It won't change anything," she repeated.

"I want the chance to explain."

"You don't have to. I understand." She understood perfectly that she had been an unexpected inconvenience when he found her so ill. And she understood that she was even more of an inconvenience when she recovered. But she would not continue down that same path with her most inconvenient pregnancy, and what a great surprise it was to her to realize that she was not so willing to "trap" him after all.

"I should have told you about Elizabeth and the hotel—"

"It doesn't matter!"

"It *does* matter, damn it!" He reached out as if he were going to touch her, but at the last moment he didn't.

She made no attempt to move away from him. She lay down beside him instead. "I never should have married you," she said, turning her head so that she could look into his eyes. "Never. It's not *your* fault I keep getting the two things mixed up."

"What two things?"

"The real man and the schoolgirl's idea of him."

"Abby…"

She reached out to lightly touch his lips with her fingertips, because she didn't want to talk about this anymore. He took her hand, his fingers gently caressing hers.

"Are *you* well?" he asked.

"I'm very well, thank you," she answered, as if they were in the parlor at the Calder house instead of lying in bed together.

There was sudden commotion in the hall—drunken singing that accompanied a noisy stumbling past the door.

"Way down South in the land of traitors! Whoresons! Tarts! And instigators! Look away! Look away! Look away, Dixie's land!"

"No!" she said, when Thomas was about to get up. "It's just the Forty-fourth Massachusetts Quartet Club."

He looked at her, she thought because it must be obvious to him that she could tolerate the singing much more easily than she could tolerate having the "quartet" know he was in here.

"La Broie is dead," he said, lying back on the pillow. "And Bender."

"Bender?"

"Private Theodore S. Bender. I wrote to you about him."

"I didn't get the letter."

"Didn't get it or didn't read it?" he said.

"Tell me about him," she said, ignoring the remark.

He gave a quiet sigh. "He was just a boy. Old enough, though, to go to war and to be in love with a confectioner's daughter. He was the first one to congratulate me on my marriage. I don't know how he died. I don't know how La Broie died."

"Are you certain they were both killed?"

"Their names were on the casualty list."

"So was yours," she said, looking into his eyes. He seemed about to say something, but he didn't.

"Maybe Gertie will know about La Broie," she said. "I have heard from her—about her. One of Miss Gwen's Virginia acquaintances wrote that there was a woman living in the Calder house. I suppose it's her. I hope it's her."

"Right before the battle, La Broie asked me to tell her something if he couldn't. He wanted her to know that he wished he'd married her." Thomas looked at Abiah. "At least I was spared that regret—" He broke off and closed his eyes. It was a long time before he said anything else. He still held her hand. She thought he had gone to sleep.

"Do you ever think about the way it was before the war?" he suddenly asked.

"Yes."

"I think about it all the time. I think about Guire and Miss Emma…and you. There was this one picnic I remember—somebody's little boy called it the 'fried chicken picnic.' My God, the food! We all went by buggy—half the county went by buggy—down by that shallow place in the river. There was an old man who played the fiddle, and you and the rest of the girls kept singing rounds. There was a kind of echo from the rocks and it sounded so fine. Do you remember?"

"I remember how annoyed you got when we started singing that one song—'Tommy, he is oh, so sweet. Tommy, he's a dandy…'"

"You girls were shamelessly trying to discompose me."

"You were always so serious, Thomas."

"I was not," he said.

"Actually, you flatter yourself. The song had nothing to do with you."

"Oh, and the fact that it was sung to the tune of 'Yankee Doodle' was just a mere a coincidence."

"Most certainly," she assured him.

They both laughed.

"And I remember that Guire got drunk and challenged Johnny Miller to a duel over the Dearing girl— both Dearing girls. You broke it up," she said.

"I wouldn't have if I'd known Johnny wanted you."

"Oh, but he didn't then."

"I think he was at Gettysburg. I saw his regimental banner across the meadow on the other side of the battlefield—just before they came at us. It was so...strange. Knowing every man over there had a reason to want to kill me—and Johnny Miller had two."

She didn't say anything to that. She didn't quite understand the remark, and she didn't want to get into it.

He was quiet again, lying with his eyes closed. The house had become very still. No drunken soldiers stumbling about. No singing. She could hear the rain, the popping and cracking of the fire. She tried to memorize the exact line of his profile so that she could remember always. Once again, she wasn't sure whether or not he was asleep.

Not, she thought, because she suddenly realized that he was looking at her. He didn't say anything, and neither did she, not when he moved closer and not when his mouth gently, tentatively touched hers.

He leaned back to see her face, waiting, staring into her eyes.

I want him, she thought. *I want him!*

She ached with it, trembled with it. All this time she had been without him, thinking she would never see him again. He was everything to her. He'd been hurt and he needed her. She could feel how much he needed her.

I love you, she thought.

But she couldn't say it. Perhaps she could make him feel it instead. She reached up to touch his face and then to kiss the corner of his mouth and finally his scarred cheek.

He stopped her when she would have kissed his lips.

"You'd better send me away, Abby. Now—because I can't—" His mouth found hers, and there was nothing tentative about it this time. The kiss was hard and hungry and welcome.

She made a small sound, one of desire and longing; her arms slid around him and her lips parted under his. His hands pulled at the quilt so that he could touch her. She tried to hold on to it.

"Thomas..."

He wasn't listening.

And a moment later she didn't want him to listen—

Someone knocked sharply on the door. Thomas stiffened and raised his head, his breathing warm and quick against her cheek.

"Who is it?" she asked a after a moment.

"Ah, it's Lieutenant Howell, ma'am. I'm trying to find your—Major Harrigan."

Thomas gave a sharp sigh. "What is it, Howell?"

"The general's got people out looking for you, sir. Begging your pardon, sir, but I think they'd better not find you here."

"What time is it?" Thomas said.

"Quarter past midnight, sir," the lieutenant said through the door.

"All right. I'm on my way—say that if the general asks."

"Yes, sir!"

"Good man, Howell," Thomas said, putting on his

boots as hurriedly as he could manage. "In some ways at least. Abby, I'll come back—"

"Take care of yourself, Thomas," she interrupted.

"Abby, I will come back—"

"Please don't," she said quietly. "For just a little while we were able to be Thomas and Abby again. No war. No…anything. For my sake, let's just leave it at that. You are very dear to me and I am so happy that you are safe. I owe you my life, but don't ask more from me than I can give. I have too much pride to pretend."

"Abby—"

"Please!" she cried, and she was very near tears.

He looked at her for a long moment. "Very well. If you need me, I expect you know where I am." He seemed about to say something else, but he didn't. He turned and left the room, looking back at her once before he went out the door.

Abiah lay in bed for a long time after he had gone, trying not to cry, her mind in turmoil.

I should have told him, she kept thinking. *He's here—sooner or later he's going to know.*

She finally gave up trying to sleep and got up, dressing quickly and going down to the kitchen. It was still dark outside and still raining. She made biscuits for Miss Gwen's breakfast with the little bit of flour they had remaining, just to have something to do. When she took them out of the oven and turned around to set them on the table, she found Lieutenant Howell standing there.

"Excuse me, ma'am," he said. "I realize I'm intruding, but I thought you might be worried—about the major, I mean. I thought you'd want to know that he hasn't been sent into harm's way or anything. It's nothing like that at all. Some people came in on one of the supply ships tonight. They were very anxious to see him as soon as possible, and the general felt he should oblige them.''

''I see,'' she said.

''I think they must be the major's family.''

''His family? His mother and grandfather?''

''I'm not certain about that,'' he said. ''I saw two gentlemen—one older. And a very lovely young lady.''

This time Thomas didn't walk into the situation as blindly as he had that night at Sumner's headquarters in Falmouth. Howell had advised him as to what had impressed the general enough to have Thomas hunted down. A Judge Winthrop of Maryland had arrived by ship from St. Michaels.

Consequently, Lieutenant Howell was made privy to even more of the peculiarities of Thomas's personal life. Thomas managed to delay seeing the judge for a few days by having the lieutenant hand deliver a perfunctory note to the old man saying that Thomas was currently attending to some pressing military duties. Then Thomas more or less disappeared into the ordnance yard on Craven Street. It was not imperative that he inspect the huge stockpile of artillery there—God knows there was no threat at the moment of having to use any of it. But it was an acceptable excuse for a newly arrived officer who supposedly wanted to improve his commander's bad first impression.

Thomas now had *no* hope of seeing Abiah except by accident on some street corner. And he couldn't chance forcing the issue for fear of being sent elsewhere. So he trusted Howell with yet another task. He had no expectations that Abiah would read anything he wrote to her, so he sent verbal messages via the lieutenant instead, to be delivered when he went to his quarters at Miss Gwen's in the evening—with no embellishments.

"Say to my wife that I trust she is feeling well today."

"Say to my wife that I hope today was pleasant for her."

But there were only so many cannons and caissons to be accounted for, and it was clear that the judge had come to New Bern with something to say. Thomas finally sent word to meet him at New Bern's only restaurant. The old man was already waiting when Thomas arrived, and it was obvious that he was startled by Thomas's appearance.

The place was noisy and crowded with soldiers, and it smelled of the only fare on the menu—coffee, biscuits and some kind of onion-more-than-meat stew. Thomas made his way among the tightly packed tables, stepping carefully on the sawdust-covered floor and trying not to favor his bad leg. It was important somehow that he not seem weak or vulnerable. The judge acknowledged him by gesturing curtly to an empty chair, and Thomas sat down.

Despite the crowd, an indifferent waitress almost immediately brought two tin cups and began to pour hot coffee from a large pot. He had heard from Howell that the general's wife refused to let their children eat here, because she was afraid the Rebel staff would poison them. Given the obvious contempt in the coffee bearer's facial expression, Thomas could understand her concern.

But threat of poison or not, his only wish was to get this ordeal over with.

"Sir, our parting in April was hardly cordial," Thomas said bluntly. "Surely you realize that I didn't expect to see you here and can't imagine why you've come."

"No one knew for certain how you were—" the judge began.

"My mother did. Perhaps you could have asked her and saved yourself so dangerous a journey."

The old man stared at him. "Perhaps," he said finally. "But I can assure you I have a reason and I will now get to it. I'm here on Elizabeth Channing's behalf."

Thomas was completely taken aback, but he didn't say anything because the stew and biscuits arrived, plunked down with a good deal more force than was necessary. For once, the judge let the lack of proper servility in an underling pass.

"At the behest of her father," the judge continued. "As you know, he and I are longtime friends. It has been very painful and embarrassing for me that my grandson has ruined his only daughter's life."

Thomas looked at him. If the judge expected some kind of confession of guilt or an apology, he was going to have a long wait.

"Elizabeth's ruination came about by her own hand, not mine."

"You brought her to that hotel in Falmouth—"

"And how do you suppose I could have done that? No civilian was allowed into Falmouth without a pass, and I certainly didn't have the authority to arrange one for her."

"Then I can only assume that you enticed *her* to make the arrangements herself by trading on her father's influence. But be that as it may. There has always been some question as to whether or not you and the Calder girl are legally married. The assertions of the Falmouth lawyer who stood to gain financially and the camp follower you saw fit to hire as a sickroom nurse are hardly significant. I only acquiesced to the situation for your mother's sake, but I could not locate any witnesses to the event in Falmouth and I can assure you I am far from convinced."

"I don't give a damn whether you're convinced or not! The public at large was not invited to the ceremony and my best man is dead. That aside, you could have asked *me*."

"You are too besotted by the Calder girl to tell the truth—"

Thomas made a move to stand up and the old man caught his arm. Several of the officers at the nearest table turned to look.

"I'm not finished! If she is a dalliance and nothing

more, then it is time for you to give her up and do the
right thing for Elizabeth. People will forgive certain…indiscretions in wartime—*if* they see that both
parties are making a concerted effort to set them
right.''

''I am married to Abiah!''

''If that is so, there are legal means to rectify that.
If a misguided loyalty to the Calder girl's dead brother
is the reason you behaved so foolishly, then you have
no real reason to maintain the union. No one would
expect it, given the traitorous actions of her family—''

''My God, is this the same kind of meddling you
used to ruin my parents' marriage?'' Thomas asked.

The old man ignored the question. ''Once you are
wed to Elizabeth, I can assure you you will have no
money worries of any kind. It is important to both
Pearson Channing and myself that she continue to live
in the manner she deserves—''

''You can't buy me, Grandfather.''

''No? Not even if I have already bought your so-
called wife? Fortunately *she* understands the practi-
calities here. I have spoken to her—''

''When?''

''When you were so busy accounting for your cannons. Given the very generous financial arrangement
I am prepared to make her, she has no objections to
your doing your duty by Elizabeth—''

''You're a liar!''

''No, indeed. She accepted my offer of money with
just as much enthusiasm as that camp follower did—''

Thomas abruptly lunged at the old man, grabbing

him by his lapels and upending everything on the table.

"Damn you!" he yelled, unmindful of where he was or the consequences. The old man paled, and a dozen hands must have pulled Thomas away and thrust him bodily out the door.

"Easy, son!" a colonel said as Thomas struggled to get free.

"You stay away from her, you son of a bitch!" he yelled over his shoulder at the judge, while the men who had removed him from the premises kept him from going back inside.

"All right!" somebody yelled from a carriage in the street.

"That's enough! Harrigan! By God, now what are you into?"

Thomas looked around to see the general hanging out of the carriage window. The man was livid—not surprising, given their last meeting.

"I'm all right," Thomas said to the men still restraining him. "Let me go, damn it—"

"He's got his wife with him, son," the colonel said. "You watch your language. You're in enough trouble as it is."

Thomas stood there for a moment before he stepped forward.

"It's nothing, sir," the colonel called. "All is well."

"Not as well as it's going to be. Colonel, you are patrolling upriver today, are you not?"

"Yes, sir, that I am. Today and all week."

"Well, take Major Harrigan with you. And if he misbehaves, by God, shoot him!"

"Sir—" Thomas started to say.

"Yes, sir!" the colonel said loudly, to drown him out. "Salute, damn you!" he said under his breath to Thomas.

Thomas saluted. The general's carriage moved on.

"All right," the colonel said. "Let's go."

"I...need to get my gear, sir."

"The hell you do. Anybody who can get in that much trouble sitting in front of a plate of biscuits and stew isn't going anywhere except where the general authorized. I have direct orders to get your sorry carcass on a river scow and that's what I'm going to do. *You* might want to spend a couple months in the prison at Fort Macon, but I don't..." Thomas stopped listening. He ignored the crowd that had gathered on the sidewalk and at the restaurant windows. He ignored the judge who had just stepped into the doorway.

I have to see Abiah. I have to....

Surely to God she wouldn't think he had sent the judge to get him out of the marriage.

But Thomas had no choice but to follow orders. If he got any further on the general's wrong side, Fort Macon would be the least of his worries.

He rode in an army wagon down to the wharf, the colonel riding along beside it on horseback.

"Sir," Thomas said at one point. "I'm afraid I don't know your name."

"Bingham," he said, stopping long enough to light

a cigar. He spurred his mount to catch up. "Colonel Fitzhugh Bingham, at your service."

"Major Thomas Harrigan—"

"Oh, I know who you are, son. Let's just say, that since the churchwomen descended upon us, your reputation has preceded you."

One of these days, Thomas thought, when he had the time, he was going to sit down and try to understand just how he'd become a man with a "reputation" in the first place. Guire Calder had labeled him "wild" in his discussions with Abiah—and it had been all downhill ever since.

"The old man in the restaurant—" the colonel said after a time. "He insulted your wife."

It wasn't a question, and Thomas made no attempt to answer it. He had no idea how much the colonel had overheard. All of it, he supposed.

"That's what I thought," the colonel said.

They arrived at the river, and Thomas had already boarded the scow when he heard somebody on the dock calling him. It was Lieutenant Howell.

"Sir! What shall I tell Mrs. Harrigan?" he yelled, and every man on the deck and on shore stopped and turned to listen.

The hell with it, Thomas thought. The scow was beginning to move out into the river. This was the only chance he would have.

"Tell her I had nothing to do with my grandfather coming to see her! Nothing! Understand?"

"Yes, sir!"

"And tell her—tell her I love her!"

The men within earshot began to whistle loudly.

"And make her believe it!" Thomas yelled over the din.

"Yes, sir!" Howell yelled back.

Thomas looked around to find Colonel Bingham grinning from ear to ear.

"Harrigan," he said, still puffing his cigar. "They ought to post your name on the signboard outside Beers's Book shop—right up there with 'Gipsy Bess' and the rest of the weekly entertainment."

Chapter Seventeen

"Abby, Lieutenant Howell is asking to speak to you. He's very…insistent. I believe you should see what he wants."

"Miss Gwen, I don't care—"

But the lieutenant was indeed insistent. He came walking into the kitchen anyway, unannounced, without waiting to see if he would be summoned or dismissed.

"Mrs. Harrigan? Ma'am, I'm sorry, but I was given an order and you see, I have to carry it out."

Abiah gave a quiet sigh. Her back ached. Her head ached. She couldn't eat. She hadn't slept. How could she when all she did was cry? She was exhausted, and she was trying so *hard* not to let Miss Gwen see how unhappy she was. It wasn't good for the baby. Abiah knew that—and she couldn't help it.

But right now she only wanted a little peace. It was obvious from the look on Lieutenant Howell's face that she wasn't about to get it.

"What is it?" she asked, because she had no choice.

"Forgive me, ma'am, but I think he would want me to tell you this in private." He glanced at Miss Gwen, who sniffed and, surprisingly, withdrew into the other room, pointedly leaving the door slightly ajar.

"Abiah," she called. "If you need me, you have only to say so."

The lieutenant stared after her for a moment, trying to decide if she'd actually gone, Abiah supposed. "Ma'am," he said, slightly louder than a whisper. "Major Harrigan has been sent on a river patrol for now, and he has instructed me to tell you that he had nothing to do with his grandfather's coming to visit. Nothing."

He waited, apparently to see if she wanted to make some kind of response. She didn't.

"He also said that I should tell you that he—" the lieutenant cleared his throat "—he loves you, ma'am. And he has specifically ordered me to make you believe it."

Abiah looked at him, and in spite of all she could do, her face crumpled and she began to cry.

"Oh, no, ma'am," the lieutenant said in alarm. "Don't do that! Please, the major will have my hide if I've upset you—oh, Lord, you are crying. What can I do—can I get you some water? Will you sit down? Shall I get Miss Gwen…?"

Abiah heard the barrage of questions, but somehow each seemed farther away than the previous one. There was a kind of roaring in her head, and…was he calling her name?

Oh, yes, she thought at the last moment. This was

like what had happened after she'd shot Zachariah Wilson....

Thomas had learned a great deal from La Broie, more than he had ever realized. He would have been hard-pressed to say when exactly he had become a soldier, but he undeniably had. Command came easily to him now. It was second nature to him to look at a situation and know what to do and who should do it.

The jaunt up the Neuse River was uneventful enough. They located what had probably once been a Rebel encampment, but there were no signs of any kind of recent military activity. In Thomas's opinion the Confederate army was spread too thin now, and the losses at Gettysburg had only worsened the situation. Still, there was no accounting for the tenacity of Southerners, and he couldn't begin to guess when or if the war here might start up again.

It was cold on the river; his leg ached all the time. But the scenery was noteworthy, and he might even have enjoyed himself, if not for the ache in his heart. He had no idea exactly what the judge had said or done, and he had no way to find out. He kept thinking about the way Abiah had kissed him before Lieutenant Howell's untimely knock on the door, and he had come to realize that even then, before the judge's meddling, she had been telling him goodbye.

He returned to New Bern after six days. He was "dog tired and pig dirty," as La Broie might have said.

"You go report to the general, Major," Colonel

Bingham said. "Tell him exactly what we've been up to."

"Sir—"

The colonel held up his hand. "The man never forgets anything. He's going to want to know where you are first thing, so I might as well kill two birds with one stone and let you make the report. You know all the particulars. You can answer his questions better than I can—which means I get to go find myself a big whiskey and a hot bath. Rank has its privileges, son. Dismissed!"

Thomas went straight to headquarters, intending to get the session with the general over as fast as he possibly could. And then...

He didn't know what he would do then.

There was nobody around when he went inside. While he stood waiting for someone to wander through, he examined the details of the actual house. It had obviously been someone's residence, and a fine one at that. But it had been stripped bare, and it was hard to imagine people—a family—ever living in it.

He heard footsteps coming up the hallway, and he turned to see one of the aides-de-camp approaching, but he didn't get the chance to make any inquiries. The general's door opened, and the general himself came out.

"Major Harrigan," he said when he saw him, and he was clearly startled to find him there.

"Sir, the river patrol—"

"Never mind that. You need to go see your wife."

"My...wife?"

"You do know where she's staying."

"Yes, sir."

"Then go. Now. Tell Private Yardley out front you're to take my mount."

"Sir—"

"Now, Major."

Thomas didn't hesitate any longer, and luckily for the private, he didn't give Thomas any trouble about taking the general's horse. None. Which was odd.

But he had no time to worry about that. He rode hard down the street until he came to Miss Gwen's house, and he left the animal wandering inside her picket fence. Miss Gwen opened the front door before Thomas got to it.

"What's wrong?" he asked, trying to get by her.

She wouldn't let him pass. "You're not welcome here," she said. "I have never been so mistaken about another human being in my life. Abby is well rid of you."

"Miss Gwen, what has happened?"

"You mean besides the bribe you sent your grandfather to make?"

"I didn't have anything to do—"

"Could you not have just *asked* her to set you free without adding that insult? She would have done it, you know. No matter how much it broke her heart..." The old lady began to weep.

"Miss Gwen, please! Is it the fever again? Tell me, damn it!"

When she didn't answer him, he took her by her forearms and moved her bodily out of the way. He bounded up the stairs to Abiah's bedchamber and pushed open the door. Another woman stood near the fireplace, and to his left, the brigade surgeon who had examined Thomas's wounds when he first arrived in New Bern.

He sidestepped them both and went immediately to the bedside.

"Abby," he said.

She was so pale.

"Abby!"

"She doesn't hear you, Major," the surgeon said. "Come away. Let her—"

"What's wrong with her? Tell me!"

"Her constitution has been very taxed by the ordeal of childbirth. The labor was unduly prolonged—"

"Childbirth?"

"Major, did you not know your wife was with child?"

"No, I—no. Is she going to be all right?"

"I don't know. We'll just have to wait and see. She is very weak. And the baby has come early."

"The baby?"

"You have a son. He was born shortly after midnight. We have him down in the kitchen where we can keep him warm, and every effort has been made to find him a wet nurse."

"I see," Thomas said, his eyes never leaving Abiah's face. He sat down on the edge of the bed and took her hand. Seeing her like this was so much a repeat of that day he'd found her in the Calder house that it was almost a physical pain.

"Abby..." he whispered. This time she opened her eyes.

He leaned forward to press a kiss on her forehead. "Why didn't you tell me?" he asked, still whispering because he didn't want anyone to hear.

She closed her eyes again without answering. He wasn't even sure she recognized him.

"She's been given laudanum, Major. She will sleep now. It's the best thing for her. Her body must be given the opportunity to restore itself. Do you plan to...stay?"

"Yes, of course, I plan to stay!" Thomas said, knowing even as he said it that from the doctor's point of view, the question was perfectly appropriate.

"Very well. Try not to disturb her. There is nothing else for me to do here. You can send for me if you need me. And, Major," he said as he opened the door. "Perhaps you should see your son."

Thomas looked at him, hearing plainly what the man didn't say.

Before it's too late.

He nodded and stood, touching Abiah's face gently before he followed the doctor out. There seemed to be a lot of people in the house—Thomas caught a glimpse of Lieutenant Howell standing anxiously in the foyer. But he spoke to no one.

He followed the doctor into the kitchen. It was full of women—the churchwomen, he supposed, who had tried to protect Abiah from his inappropriate and unwelcome attention. Perhaps they had been right to do so. They stared at him as he passed among them, all conversation stopped. He didn't see the baby, but he said nothing.

Finally, one of the women spoke up. "Your son is here, Major."

They had placed him in a well-padded wooden crate near the cookstove. The oven door was open to allow the heat to radiate outward. Several pieces of flannel lay stacked and warming on a nearby chair.

Thomas stood there, staring down at the baby. He was so little! He had dark hair like Abiah's, like his own. The fingers of one tiny hand lay spread against his cheek. Thomas reached into the box to touch him.

"We have found a wet nurse," the woman said. "She is on her way."

Thomas looked at her. "Good. Whatever fee she requires—"

"She won't require a fee, Major. She—all of us— knew Abiah's dear mother. It's for *her* that we're here."

He nodded. He understood loyalty to Miss Emma perfectly well. He looked around the room and then at his son.

"I will be upstairs with my wife," he said to no one in particular. "I ask that you call me if...if I'm needed."

He didn't wait for a response. He turned and went back upstairs. And he did the only thing he could do. He kept vigil, sometimes sitting in a chair, sometimes lying beside Abiah on the bed. He lost all track of time. Women came and went. Someone brought him food and coffee—and a basket of apples courtesy of the general's lady. Twice he left Abiah's side to go see his child.

And he prayed. He had never been one for praying; God had always seemed too much like the celestial version of Judge Winthrop to him. Thomas had made no entreaties before Fredericksburg or Chancellorsville. He had made none in that Pennsylvania peach orchard.

But he did now.

Please. Please....

The doctor returned. He seemed satisfied that Abiah still slept, and Thomas tried to take what comfort he could from that. He sat dozing in the chair by the bed after the doctor had gone, close enough to reach out and touch her if he wanted—needed—to.

"Thomas..."

He opened his eyes. The judge stood just inside the door. Thomas got out of the chair and walked to him.

"What do you want?" he asked, and he had to fight hard to keep his voice down.

"I have come to speak to you—"

"You and I have nothing to speak about," Thomas said. "Nothing."

"I can assure you it is important."

"Not to me."

"I beg your indulgence," the judge said.

"You *beg?* Why? What have you and the Channings decided now? I can *not* believe that the three of you are being so incredibly dense about this. I can't take away Elizabeth's notoriety. I wouldn't if I could.

I understand that you think her the victim here. Believe me, she is not."

"Did you or did you not ask her to marry you?"

"I did. She accepted and she insisted that it be kept a secret. Then *she* broke the supposed engagement last fall. She dismissed me quite handily in a letter. The problem for her was that I took the dismissal seriously—I had no reason not to believe whatever she said then. But it was all some kind of 'test' she was giving me in order to show off for her Washington friends. She thought I could just leave a war and come plead with her to change her mind. As far as I was concerned, that was the end of it. I never heard from her again—until she showed up in Falmouth and sent me word that my 'wife' was waiting for me.

"I realize that you—all of you—think my marriage to Abby is something that can just be thrown away because *you* wish it. But I can assure you that is not the case. I stole Abiah Calder out of her mother's house with the Rebel cavalry at my heels. I brought her at great risk across an enemy-held river—and I didn't care how many orders I had to disregard to do it. I had to threaten a ferryman's life to get him to take us across—and, trust me, my sergeant or I would have killed the son of a bitch where he stood if he had refused.

"I lived through weeks of anxiety about Abby because she was so ill and I didn't know what had happened to her, because Elizabeth was intercepting my letters to her *and* my mother. Then I had to come begging to you to get me a furlough so that I could come to Maryland to see her. You thought it was a great show of weakness on my part, but I can assure you it was the hardest thing I've ever done in my life to have to humble myself like that and have you think that your harsh judgment of me was finally justified.

"But don't worry, Grandfather. I'm not altogether above reproach. I came very close to giving in to temptation at that hotel and for that moment of weakness I am most heartily ashamed. Even so, it was Elizabeth's machinations, not mine, that the ubiquitous Mrs. Post revealed in your foyer that morning.

"Last July I managed to live through the closest thing to hell on this earth it is possible for men to create. You couldn't even begin to imagine what it was like—and my only thought was to see Abby again. I have since rearranged my entire military career in order to follow her here, because I love her with all my heart. My son has just been born. Do you actually think you can undo all that?

"There was a time when I thought I wanted to marry Elizabeth Channing—that was when I still hoped to somehow gain your approval. But that time is long gone. If you want to think me some kind of blackguard and seducer of women, then do so! But I know the truth and so does Elizabeth. Go home. Take the Channings with you. And have the decency to leave me and my family alone."

Thomas opened the door, giving the judge no choice but to go through it. The old man stared at him for a long moment before he complied.

"I think you will regret this," he said. "Or *she* will."

"I think not," Thomas said. "And the sad thing is that it will be *your* loss, not ours."

The old man pushed past him, and Thomas stood for a moment, watching him go down the stairs. The break was final now. He knew that, and so did the judge. What he didn't know was that he would feel such regret. There was still left in him some of that boy who had believed there must be some way he could make his grandfather proud.

The judge hesitated once when he reached the foyer, but he gave no backward glance before he went out the front door.

Thomas walked back into the room and sat down. He was so tired suddenly. After a moment, he got up again to put a log on the fire. When he returned, he pulled the chair closer to the bed and rested his arms and head on the edge. He must have slept, but he had no idea how long. He awoke with a start when someone put a hand on his arm.

"Thomas…" she said, her voice barely a whisper.

He lifted his head. Abiah was awake and looking at him. "Oh, God," he said, reaching for her, holding her close, feeling her warmth, loving her. "Abby!"

"Is he all right, Thomas? Our boy—where is he?"

Thomas moved so that he could see her face because she sounded so afraid. "He's down in the kitchen, where they can keep him warm. He's all right. He's eating and crying—ah, Abby, why didn't you tell me we had a baby coming? Why?"

Her mouth trembled and tears slid out of the corners of her eyes. "Thomas, I—"

"You should have told me!"

"I know—"

"Then why didn't you?"

"Because I didn't want to trap you, after all. Not knowing the way you feel…about Elizabeth."

"The way I feel? I told you the day we married that she had no part in any of this."

"Please, Thomas. I read the letter."

"You keep saying that! What letter? Tell me. What letter?"

She gave a wavering sigh. "It's in the Bible. There on the table."

He leaned away from her to reach it. There were two loose sheets of paper inside the front cover. He recognized them immediately. They were part of a letter he had once written to Elizabeth.

"I don't understand," he said, quickly reading over the pages. "Where did you get this?"

"I…found it."

"Where is the rest of it?" He looked at her when she didn't answer. "I don't understand. Why is this important—?"

"Thomas, it says you want out of the marriage."

"No, it doesn't. It says I want the war to be over…. Wait. When did you think I wrote this? Did Elizabeth give you this?"

She didn't answer him.

"Abby, I wrote this letter after I joined a Massachusetts regiment, over two years ago. Elizabeth was upset with me because she wanted me to ask the judge or her father to get me some kind of political appointment in Washington—something with a little more cachet than that of a lowly infantry captain. This letter has nothing to do with my wanting to be free of my obligation to *you*. It has to do with my obligation to the Grand Republic. It has to do with trying to pacify Elizabeth.''

''You never wrote to me, Thomas.''

''Yes, I did! But Elizabeth got my letters somehow. I told my mother to check with the postmaster at St. Michaels, to see if he knew what had happened to them. That's probably why Dr. Nethen hand delivered the last one—and *that* letter you wouldn't read.''

''And the hotel?''

''I thought I was coming to see you. The message I received was that my 'wife' was in Falmouth. I didn't know it was Elizabeth.'' He gave a quiet sigh. ''And I didn't…leave…when I should have.''

''I see,'' she said quietly.

''No, you don't. I didn't take her to bed, Abby.''

''But you wanted to.''

It wasn't a question, and he didn't know what to say. She had seen what he had written to Elizabeth. She had read his professions of love for her. How could he explain that he had done what Guire had warned *her* about? He had taken no time to know the real woman; he had been far too busy chasing his idea of her.

''I love you, Abby. Don't you know that?''

''How can you? I threw myself at you. You never

thought of me in that way. How can you care about someone you could have so easily?''

''Easily! Abby, do you have any idea how hard it's been to keep up with you *and* Robert E. Lee? Don't you understand? There is the woman some men need to adorn their houses and their arms. And there is the woman a man comes to in the middle of the night when the pain and the nightmares are too bad—because he needs *her*. Because she is the one he loves—''

She reached for him then, clinging to him hard. He kissed her mouth and her eyes and her mouth again.

''It's going to be all right,'' he whispered.

''Is it?''

''Yes!''

''I'm afraid, Thomas—''

''Do you love me?''

''I—yes, I love you. I have *always* loved you.''

''Well, then, we're going to start over again. Right now. You and me and our boy downstairs.''

''I want to see him, Thomas. I want to hold him...''

He nodded and went to the door. Lieutenant Howell was at what had become his more or less permanent post in the foyer.

''Howell!'' Thomas called. ''Ask one of the women to bring my son.''

''Yes, sir!''

A woman came almost immediately, carrying the baby close to her ample bosom. Thomas held out his hands, and she hesitated so long that he thought for a moment she wasn't going to give him up. But she did finally, and Thomas held him gently, looking down into the small wrinkled face.

How tiny he is!

"All right, young sir," he said. "It's time to meet your mother."

"Put him right next to her, Major," the woman said. "So she can keep him warm."

Thomas pulled down the quilts enough to place the baby against Abby's breast. The woman brought a piece of the flannel that was always kept heating in front of the fire and placed it carefully around them both.

When the woman had gone, he sat on the side of the bed.

"He's...beautiful, isn't he?" Abby asked after a moment.

"Yes," Thomas agreed, his voice sounding husky and strange to him.

"I wish Mother and Guire—" She broke off to gently lay her cheek against the baby's head. "Would you...mind if he's called after Guire?"

"Guire Calder Harrigan. It suits him. One day we can tell him about his rascal of an uncle—" Thomas abruptly stopped in turn, and his eyes held hers.

"Abby," he said. "Can we start over? Will you take the chance? Will you stay with me?"

She looked at him, trying not to cry. "Yes," she whispered.

He kissed her then. She made room for him on the bed, and he stretched out beside her, putting his arms around her and the baby both.

He held them close. He didn't know what the future would bring—what events or what persons might still conspire against them. He only knew that he loved her and young Guire with all his heart. He had come a long way to get to this point in his life. The journey had been arduous and full of peril. It might not be over yet.

But at long last, he, Thomas Harrigan, most willing husband of Abiah Calder Harrigan, had found home.

Epilogue

June 1865

Abiah went out on the porch to look down the long muddy road that eventually led into Fredericksburg. The spring rains had left it nearly impassable, but she still kept watch, hoping, praying to see a certain horse and rider coming from the crossroads, just as she had when she was all of fourteen.

Little Guire was intent on helping her keep vigil even if he didn't quite understand, walking back and forth with her, hand in hand, solemn and watchful and so like his father.

"See?" he would say from time to time, pointing into the distance.

"Yes," she would answer with a smile. "Mama sees." But there was nothing, no one on the lonely road.

She walked closer to the edge of the porch, careful of the missing boards she hadn't been able to replace.

The house had been occupied for a time, and the porch banisters and much of the flooring had been taken up for firewood. Gertie hadn't said by which army, and Abiah hadn't asked. With a husband in one army and a brother in the other, it hardly mattered.

There had been a yellow fever outbreak in New Bern last fall, and a very real chance that the warm weather would bring another. Thomas had wanted her out of there before the town was quarantined again, but she still hadn't thought she would be able to come back to the Calder house. The war was over in mid-April, but thanks to General Sherman and General Grant, the railroads from New Bern inland and from Richmond northward were torn up and apt to stay that way. There was no reasonable means to travel anywhere with Miss Gwen and her dogs *and* a baby.

It was her old friend Captain Appleby who made the homecoming possible. After much soul searching, Thomas accepted an offer from the captain to transport his family by ship to Norfolk and then on to the railhead north of Fredericksburg at Aquia Creek. Gertie met them there. She had indeed been the woman Abiah heard was living in the house. Gertie, and what was left of Sergeant Peter La Broie.

Gertie had gone all the way to Pennsylvania to get him, finding him nearly dead and unattended in a barn near the battlefield. She'd stayed with him there and when they moved him finally to one of the tent hospitals in Washington. And when he was able, she brought him back to Virginia.

He had lost his left leg below the knee and the use

of his left arm. And he had lost his iron will. Nothing interested him—until young Guire took him over. The boy simply didn't see the wall the sergeant had put up around himself. He climbed into his lap without coaxing—missing or useless limbs meant nothing to a child used to seeing men who were not whole. Sometimes he sat on the arm of La Broie's chair and fed him bits of his honey bread whether he wanted it or not, chatting happily in baby talk that only he understood.

Abiah could hear La Broie approaching now, his heavy, peg-leg gait uneven as he came down the wide hallway. Knowing how self-conscious he was about his ability to get around, she waited until he was nearby before she looked toward him.

"Peep," Guire said immediately, letting go of her hand and holding up his arms.

"Well, let Pete take you, then," La Broie said. He leaned against the porch column so that he could lift Guire up with his good hand. And if he minded being called "Peep," he hadn't said so. Guire immediately lay his head on La Broie's shoulder.

"Any sign of him?" La Broie asked.

"No," Abiah said. "He should be here by now. His letter said he was leaving New Bern three weeks ago."

La Broie didn't say anything. He stood there, working to keep his balance and still hold on to Guire, who was already half-asleep.

"I'll put the boy to bed," he said finally.

"Sergeant La Broie," she said as he turned to go.

"Ma'am?"

"When are you going to make an honest woman of Gertie?"

"Ma'am?" he said again.

"You heard me. When?"

"Gertie isn't going to want to marry the likes of me."

"How do you know? Have you asked her?"

"No, I ain't asked her—"

"Well, why don't you? She loves you, Sergeant La Broie. Or did you think she was hanging around here for your home cooking?"

He actually smiled. It was the first time she'd seen him do that since she had arrived.

"Thomas says you are a bold and fearless man," she said as he was about to go inside. "You don't want to be afraid of a woman's love."

He looked at her a moment, but said nothing. Abiah gave a quiet sigh. She could hear Miss Gwen through the open window in what used to be the parlor.

"There was a piano there," she was saying, apparently trying to make the empty, pillaged room come to life. "And the refreshment table was over there. Oh, such fine things were offered."

"Like what, Miss Gwen?" Gertie asked, clearly interested. The truth of the matter was they were all interested in food these days—particularly the things no one could get at any price.

"Oh, coffee and tea and lemonade—and a huge silver platter of little ham biscuits. Miss Emma and Abiah and I worked for *days* getting everything ready. We had angel food cake and cocoa pound cakes—eight of them! And not a one of them 'sad.' And vanilla wafers. And blackberry preserves. And cracker bonbons. I do love a good cracker bonbon. That rascal Guire—Abby's dear late brother?—he brought *champagne* all the way from Boston—and what a bother *that* caused. Miss Emma was temperance, you know,'' she added in a very audible whisper.

"And Thomas Harrigan led the cotillion. Everybody was surprised by that, him being a Yankee boy. But he did it so he could open the dance with the oldest unmarried daughter of the house—as was the custom. That was Abby, of course. He wanted the evening to be special for her, because she was coming out, you see. He brought Abby in through there,'' she said. "There were flowers and candles everywhere. He was so handsome and she was so beautiful, with her hair put up and woven through with a pale pink ribbon. And they were playing a waltz—how did that go, Abby?'' Miss Gwen called.

"I can't remember, Miss Gwen,'' Abiah called back, because the reminiscences had brought the worry she'd been trying to keep at bay these last few days dangerously close to the surface. She couldn't trust herself to recreate the melody of that particular waltz without crying.

She kept staring down the road. There were a thousand things that could have delayed him, all of them bad—from yellow fever to bushwhackers to some renewed effort by Elizabeth Channing. Thunder rumbled in the distance. There was another spring storm on the way.

"Oh, I know. It went like this,'' Miss Gwen called, beginning to hum.

Abiah listened for a moment. It was quite an adequate rendition of the song.

She glanced toward the road, then immediately back again. After a moment, she came down the steps, a few at a time, until she was finally standing in the yard. And then she began to walk, to run. Behind her, Miss Gwen's beagles began to bark.

"Thomas," she whispered. *"Thomas!"*

She didn't even remember getting to him. He kicked his stirrups free and reached down for her, lifting her up just as he had that day in the Winthrop drive. And this time she did exactly as she had wanted to do then. She kissed him, hugged him, again and again.

"Oh, Thomas! You're here—"

"Don't cry," he said, trying to hold on to her and keep the horse steady. "Kiss me hard and don't cry...."

She leaned back to look at his face. "You're all right?"

"I'm fine."

"Then where *were* you!" she demanded, and he laughed.

"A few last-minute duties I hadn't counted on. My God, you look so good, feel so good!" He kissed her soundly. He was still kissing her when someone gave a discreet cough.

They both looked around to see La Broie standing there with little Guire in his good arm.

"Evening, Cap—Major," he said. "Stealing Miss Abiah away on your horse again, I see."

* * * * *